WE JOINED THE NAVY

'An intelligent man,' the President of the Admiralty Interview Board tells the other members, 'never makes a good naval officer. He embarrasses everyone.' They nod and eighty cadets in brand new uniform are plunged into a strange and uncomfortable world inhabited by such characters as the destroyer captain, Poggles, who anchors his ship with the aid of brewers' signs, and dislikes cadets; Captain Sir Douglas Mainwaring Gregson, Bart., who breeds red setters and ignores cadets; and Able Seaman Froggins, who lives a malevolent, hermit-like life in the darkness of his locker and thinks all cadets are as wet as scrubbers.

Their training is more comprehensive than they expect. They scrub decks in the early morning and repel the advances of amorous Spanish barmaids by night. They paint the ship's side and play cricket against a West Indian team, the ground, the crowd and a calypso steel band. They sail boats and quell a revolution in Central America. All who love the sea and all who enjoy laughter will revel in John Winton's first book. We predict for it an outstanding and enduring popularity.

We Joined The Navy

JOHN WINTON

London

MICHAEL JOSEPH

First published by
MICHAEL JOSEPH LTD
26 *Bloomsbury Street*
*London, W.C.*1
MARCH 1959
SECOND IMPRESSION APRIL 1959
THIRD IMPRESSION MAY 1960
FOURTH IMPRESSION DECEMBER 1961

Set and printed in Great Britain by Tonbridge Printers Ltd,
Peach Hall Works, Tonbridge, Kent, in Baskerville ten on
twelve point, on paper made by John Dickinson at Croxley,
Herts., and bound by James Burn at Esher, Surrey

1

THE President of the Admiralty Interview Board had been a naval officer for a very long time. He had started as a scrubby-faced boy at the Admiralty Interview and he had served as a Midshipman in a battle-cruiser at Jutland, as a Sub-Lieutenant in a Yangtse gunboat, as a Lieutenant in a cruiser on the South Atlantic station, as a Commander in a battleship of the Home Fleet, and as a destroyer Captain in the North Atlantic. He had served in every sea from the Timor to the Adriatic, in every strait from the Bering to the Magellan, and had suffered every wind from the sirocco to the trades. Now, by hard work, attention to detail, and marrying late, he had become an admiral and was once more at the Admiralty Interview, interviewing another generation of scrubby-faced striplings, one of whom would grow up to be an admiral and interview a further generation of scrubby-faced striplings and so on and so on. Never had he had so clear a vision of the slow process of evolution in the Royal Navy. Never had he seen that evolution entrusted to poorer hands. In the Admiral's opinion, the mighty tree of the Navy, which had produced such magnificent branches in the past, was now dying at the roots. He and his colleagues were gathering the last diseased twigs before the final crash. The Admiral leant his forehead in the palm of his hand and sighed.

The remainder of the Board, the Headmaster, the Civil Servant, the Psychiatrist, the Commanders (E) and (S), and the Lieutenant-Colonel, Royal Marines, marked their President's sigh and hunched their shoulders. They dropped their heads and waited expectantly, like Victorian children waiting for Papa to say grace.

The Admiral sighed again.

'Well, gentlemen,' he said at last, 'here we are again. I hope I see you refreshed and ready for one more battle with the latest products of our present day and age? Frankly, I don't know what the schools *do* to them these days. I can't believe that the basic stock has changed. It must be the environment. By the time we get them at eighteen years of age it takes us five whole years or more to make them any damn use to man or beast. Here we have a country bleeding itself white to provide education for all and what happens? We spend half our time interviewing cretins and morons and the other half interviewing communists and embryo politicians. It takes us all our time to find enough boys in one year who are not clearly destined for the Old Bailey to keep the service going.'

The Admiral shook his head and sighed a third time. The Board listened with pleasant approving smiles on their faces. One or two of them nodded. These were the very phrases with which the Admiral opened each fresh series of interviews. The Board sat like contented members of an audience who hear again the well-loved curtain-raising words of a familiar play. Not that the Board did not entirely agree with the Admiral. It was Monday morning, the first morning of a new Interview Board, and each member of the Board knew that several weeks of trying work lay ahead.

The Admiral passed a hand wearily over his forehead.

'As this is the first day,' he said, 'I may as well refresh your memories on one or two items of policy.'

The Board slumped in their seats.

'Remember we are not looking for normal boys. We are looking for boys who will make naval officers. There's a difference. We are looking for half-wits. The service will add the other half in its own way and in its own time.'

The Board nodded.

'None of these boys will be very intelligent. If they had any

6

intelligence they wouldn't be here. They'd be applying for jobs outside which carry more pay and less work, like most of their contemporaries. But lack of intelligence need not concern us. An intelligent man never makes a good naval officer. He embarrasses everybody.'

The Board glanced briefly at their President and nodded again. After all, he had been a naval officer for nearly forty years. He should know.

'I need not tell you not to be surprised at anything you hear in this room. I myself have long since lost the capacity for amazement.'

The Board pursed their lips. They remembered the candidate who had tried, with a pin, to convince the Admiral that Christian Science worked for the common man.

'Keep off religion and politics. They know more about that sort of thing than we do.'

The Board began to rouse themselves. The Admiral was approaching his peroration.

'One last point. Make sure, I *implore* you, gentlemen, make *sure* you know what the boy's father does for a living. If the man's an admiral then of course you can be as facetious as you wish, but if he's a plumber or a boilermaker or anything which remotely sounds as though it has a trade union then I must beseech you to be careful. We just cannot afford any more questions in the House. It upsets the First Lord and I get it all back from him later.'

The Admiral wound up his watch, shot his cuffs, gathered some papers together, and looked round the Board.

'Well,' he said. 'Who have we first?'

The Civil Servant consulted a list.

'John Paul Henry Marchant Vincent, sir.'

The Admiral frowned.

'What nationality's his father?'

'American, sir.'

'What does he do?'

'Not recorded, sir. His people appear to be divorced.'

'Never mind. Let him in. Nerve yourselves, gentlemen.'

*   *   *

'John Paul Henry Marchant Vincent.'

Vincent was a tall dark boy with thick black hair and brown eyes. He looked less American than French. His rangy build and slightly hooked nose reminded the Admiral vaguely of pictures he had seen of young men in berets who pedalled furiously across France with bicycle tyres wound across their chests. The boy looked clever, perhaps too clever, as though he might be more than a match even for the Admiralty Interview Board. The Admiral wondered what had prompted a boy like this to try for the Navy.

'Sit down, Vincent,' said the Admiral hospitably.

The tables in the board-room were arranged in the form of a capital T. The Board sat along the cross-piece and the candidate sat at the bottom of the tail, confronted with a long expanse of bare table which ended in the formidable array of the Board's faces. It was an intimidating prospect, and the Board were accustomed to seeing candidates sit down as though they expected the seat to burn them. They had seen candidates miss the chair altogether and sprawl upon the floor. One candidate had sat down and immediately slid off the chair in a dead faint. The Board had seen many candidates, but Vincent was the first in their experience to take his seat and wait for their questions as calmly as though he were waiting for his mid-morning aperitif.

The Admiral placed his elbows on the table, clasped his fingers together and stared at Vincent from under his bushy eyebrows.

'Now, Vincent. Why do you want to join the Navy?'

It was a crucial question. It was asked of every candidate and although it seemed an obvious question to ask of a prospective naval officer, the Board were no longer surprised at the number of candidates who were nonplussed by it. It was the jackpot question.

But Vincent appeared to be ready for it. His might almost have been called the jackpot answer.

'Well, sir,' he said, 'that is a very fundamental question for me to answer in a short time. Briefly, I have always felt that everyone should make an attempt fairly early in life to choose the way in which he can best serve the community. You may then say, and

8

rightly, sir, how can one be sure which is the best way? Some people are lucky. They don't have to make a choice. They know. They have a vocation. I'm not quite so lucky as that, but I do think one can choose something and persevere at it. I chose the Navy, sir.'

Vincent leaned back and shrugged his shoulders. He appeared to be waiting now for the Admiral to counter with the reason why he joined the Navy.

'Is that why you have chosen to be an engineer officer, Vincent?' asked the Headmaster.

'Yes, sir. I realise that the Navy offers many spheres of opportunity and I think that offers the most. For me at any rate, sir.'

'Quite,' said the Headmaster. Vincent seemed to have left none of the usual loopholes in his answer. The Headmaster decided to change the subject. He asked his favourite question, one which he asked of every candidate whose Christian names permitted it.

'Vincent, your name is John. Can you tell me any famous Johns in history?'

Vincent considered. He was marshalling his facts.

'Off hand, sir, I would say the Apostle John, John Bull, Don John of Austria, John of Gaunt, John Knox, John Gay, John Paul Jones, John Masefield, John Milton, John Keats, John Nash, John Jacob Astor, John Barbirolli, Augustus John perhaps, and if you take the foreign equivalents there's Johannes Brahms, Jan Masaryk, Ivan the Terrible, Ian Hay, Jacques Fath—'

'Thank you, Vincent. You have answered that reasonably well, I think. There are a few notable omissions, of course. Jack the Ripper might have been worth a place. You might have mentioned the distaff side. Joan of Arc, for instance. And the animal kingdom you have left completely untouched. Brown Jack springs to mind. . . .'

'Thank you, Headmaster,' interrupted the Admiral sharply. He had noticed the Headmaster's tendency to dwell on this question. 'I see you played cricket at school, Vincent. Were you in the Eleven?'

'I was captain of it, sir. But I'm afraid cricket was my only sport.'

'I see. Did you bat or bowl?'

'Bat, sir.'

'What was your highest score?'

'A hundred and sixty-four, sir.'

'I *see*. Who was that against?'

'Incogniti, sir.'

'Are you the Vincent who opened for the Public Schools, Vincent?' put in the Headmaster.

'Yes, sir.'

The Board beamed at each other. A wave of approval passed amongst them like a Pentecostal wind. A boy may look like a Parisian apache but there cannot be much wrong with any lad who can knock up a hundred against respectable club bowling.

'You say you play no other games? None at all?'

'I play a bit of tennis occasionally, sir.'

'Don't you ever play golf?' asked the Lieutenant-Colonel of Royal Marines. A lad with a natural eye like this could probably get down to scratch, given a few years in the right hands.

'No, sir. I have always thought golf a game for revoltingly healthy young spinsters, and revoltingly senile old men, sir. One of the few things I can remember my father saying was that he thought golf was a good walk spoilt and I agree with him, sir.'

There comes a time in the stage run by an Olympic torch-bearer when the torch becomes almost too heavy to bear and the distance too far to run. At such a time he is only too glad to hand over the torch to his successor. The Admiral looked round his Board for support.

The Commander (E), a thin angular man with a profile of a Caesar, caught the eye of his stricken chief and hurriedly made up a question which had been debated in that morning's *Times*.

'Vincent, how far would you say that young men entering the engineering profession today should be engineers? What I mean to say is, do you think that engineers need a broad education? Or just one in engineering subjects?'

'I would say the broader the better, sir.'

'Why?'

'It's obvious, sir.'

10

'Why is it obvious?'

'You wouldn't go to a doctor who only knew how to doctor and who couldn't have a round of golf with you occasionally, would you, sir?'

'A hit, a palpable hit,' murmured the Headmaster under his breath.

'You're trying for the wrong profession, young man,' remarked the Admiral viciously. 'The House of Commons would welcome you. Now, I want you to look at that picture on the wall and tell us what you can deduce from it.'

The picture was of a sailing boat leaving a narrow wooded harbour. On the nearest hill was a church. Various posts, buoys and anchored boats lay in the channel. It was an ordinary water-colour which could have been bought at any seaside resort. Vincent could see nothing remarkable in it, but the picture plainly had some significance for the Board. He studied it carefully.

'The boat is a ketch, sir.'

'How do you know?'

'The rig, sir.'

'What do you mean?'

'Two masts, the after one smaller than the for'd but placed before the rudder post, sir.'

'Good. What else can you see?'

'Tide is ebbing, sir.'

'Why?'

'You can see by the buoys and the other boats, sir.'

'Good. Go on.'

'I can see a weather vane on the top of the church. I think the harbour is on the south coast. It's evening.'

'How do you know that?'

'The shadows of the trees are very long, sir. And one side of the harbour is lit up by the sun and the other is in shadow.'

'Very good, Vincent. That's not at all bad.'

'Thank you, sir.'

The Commander (S) was a portly man who greatly resembled

11

Mr Pickwick. He realised that he had not yet asked Vincent a single question and heaved himself up in his chair.

'Vincent, what's the difference between a planet and a star?'

Vincent paused. He did not answer for some time. The Admiral was jubilant.

'Come, come, Vincent, there *is* a difference, you know.'

'I know there is, sir, but I can't think of it for the moment. I'm afraid I'm no watcher of the skies and the question is a new planet in my ken.'

The Headmaster applauded.

'Very neatly turned, Vincent.'

The Psychiatrist wrote on his little pad : 'Vincent—shifty.'

'All right then,' said the Admiral. 'That will be all, Vincent.'

'Thank you, sir.'

As soon as the door had closed behind Vincent, the Admiral breathed a great sigh of relief.

'That boy should have been a politician,' he said. 'Living in a wardroom with him would be like living at the feet of Plato. Crafty question of yours that about the planets, Scratch.'

It was significant that the Admiral had used the word 'wardroom.' The Board adjusted their assessments accordingly.

Outside in the corridor, Vincent was speaking to the next candidate.

'All yours, old man. Watch out for the Headmaster. He's a bastard.'

'Thanks,' said the next candidate.

'What's your christian name, by the way?'

'Horace George.'

Vincent went off down the corridor, chuckling.

'Horace George Dewberry.'

Dewberry could not have provided a greater contrast to Vincent. He was small and rather tubby with bristly brown hair cropped close to his head. His expression was secretive, though not furtive, as though he was constantly on his guard against aggressors. He gave the Admiral the impression that he had been bullied at his preparatory school. He was plainly suffering under

12

a severe strain to keep his nervousness from gaining complete control of him and reducing him to fluttering silence. He perched on the edge of his chair, twisting his fingers and looking anxiously at the Board as though he were wondering which of them would first lean out and assault him. The Admiral regarded Dewberry sardonically; the nation which had produced Horatio Nelson had also produced Horace George Dewberry.

'All right, Dewberry,' said the Admiral in his most reassuring manner. 'We're not going to eat you. We're only going to ask you some questions.'

Dewberry jerked in his chair.

'Tell us first of all, why do you want to join the Navy?'

'Oh dear,' said Dewberry. 'I knew you were going to ask me that, sir. It's rather difficult to say exactly. My mother has always told the family and friends that I was going in the Navy. There's never been any thought of anything else, sir.'

'And how do you feel about it?'

'Well sir, my mother has always—'

'We don't want to know what your mother thinks, Dewberry. We want to know what *you* think.'

'I'm quite keen, sir. I *think* I might do quite well at it.'

'Splendid.'

'I hope so anyway, sir.'

'Good.'

'I'll *try*, anyway, sir.'

'All right.'

'I *think* I might do quite well, sir.'

'All right, Dewberry, all right. Now why do you think we have a Navy at all?'

Dewberry could not at first call to mind a single reason why there should be a Navy. Only that morning he had read a leader in the *Daily Disaster* proving that the country did not need a Navy. Then a memory came to him of a remark made long ago by one of his old-fashioned uncles, who never read the *Daily Disaster*.

'Horace boy, when you grow up and take over yer father's seat always remember this. Never footle with treaties and agree-

13

ments. Just send the Navy or the Army. Show the flag. That's the only way to deal with wogs. Show the flag, Horace.'

'Show the flag, sir,' said Dewberry.

'We can't live merely by showing the flag.'

That was true, Dewberry reflected. Another memory came to him, of one of his aunts showing him a map of the world. Most of the map had been coloured red and the red patches had been connected by blue lines across the sea.

'The red parts are the British Empire, Horace dear. The blue lines are the trade routes. Without the trade routes you and all the family, even your uncle, would starve.'

'Protect trade routes, sir,' said Dewberry.

'Good. Quite right.'

Dewberry had another memory of his uncle.

'And to provide an education for the male members of the Royal Family and husbands for the females, sir,' said Dewberry.

The Board came to life. They looked searchingly at Dewberry. For the first time they began to wonder whether the boy was as harmless as he looked. The Civil Servant thought it time to change the subject again.

'Do you have any hobbies, Dewberry?' he asked.

'Not hobbies exactly, sir.'

'What do you do in your spare time then?'

'I play the french horn, sir.'

'Ah. Don't you find it rather monotonous going oomphah, oomphah all the time?'

'You're thinking of the tuba, sir. There's some lovely music for the french horn. Mozart wrote some beautiful concertos for it and you've only got to examine some of Beethoven's scores to see how highly he thought of it. It can be a fascinating instrument, sir.'

The Civil Servant had struck fire from Dewberry. He was startled by the effect of his question.

'Do you think you'll get much chance to play the french horn in the Navy, Dewberry?'

'I don't see why not, sir. I think music and the Navy might

14

possibly go together. After all, Rimsky-Korsakov was a serving naval officer at one time, wasn't he, sir?'

'Ah *yes*. Quite right. So he was.'

Part of the President's duty was to keep the interview on a plane where the Board, as well as the candidate, could follow it.

'Drop it, Pills,' he said. 'Now, Dewberry, I want you to look at that picture on the wall and tell us what you make of it.'

'What I make of it, sir?'

'Yes. Tell us anything you notice about it.'

Dewberry swallowed nervously. Soon it was plain that the picture meant nothing at all to him.

'Come on, Dewberry. What's the picture of?'

'A boat, sir.'

'What kind of boat?'

'A sailing boat, sir.'

'Any particular kind?'

Dewberry had an inspiration.

'A *yacht,* sir.'

'Right. What's it doing?'

Dewberry's inspiration failed him.

'I'm afraid I don't know, sir.'

'Never mind, Dewberry.'

The Board asked Dewberry some more desultory questions but they were unable to rekindle the fire aroused by the french horn. The Board began to picture Dewberry in the Royal Philharmonic; they could not imagine him in the Royal Navy. The Admiral thought otherwise.

'I may be mistaken,' he said, 'but I think there's the right stuff in that boy. Provided he gets away from his mother and marries the right girl he'll do well. The service will do the first part and I expect the girl will do the rest.'

The next candidate wore a tweed hacking jacket and grey flannel trousers which caught the Board's attention immediately. He was the biggest young man the Board had ever seen, yet he gave the impression that he was still only half-grown. His bones were like scaffoldings, solid struts and bars, which supported his clothes. He was plainly a rugger player. His fair hair was tousled

15

and fluffy from innumerable shower-baths after the game. His lips were purposefully pursed, as though he were just on the point of exhorting his forwards to use their feet and stop mucking about. The corners of his eyes were puckered, as though from long hours of chasing enemy fly-halves through driving rain. He was a plain, solid young man with a plain, solid name.

'Thomas Bowles.'

Thomas Bowles. The Board were surprised to find how refreshing the name sounded in their ears after the exotic John Paul Henry Marchant Vincent and the enigmatic Horace George Dewberry. The Admiral warmed to Bowles.

'Sit down now, Bowles,' he said heartily.

Bowles sat down carefully, as though he had known chairs collapse under him.

'Now Bowles, tell me why you want to become a naval officer.'

'I just want to, sir.'

'Just want to? But don't you feel that sometime early in life you must choose the way in which you can best serve the community and though you're not sure at first you choose something and persevere at it?'

'That's a very involved way of putting it, if you'll pardon me saying so, sir. I hadn't really thought about serving the community. It's just what I want to do, that's all.'

The Admiral was delighted. He felt like a man who, after floundering in quicksands, finds himself once more upon solid, dependable ground.

'What do you particularly want to do in the Navy, Bowles?'

'I want to be a pilot, sir.'

'A *pilot*? Why?'

'There again, sir, I'm afraid I can't give you a definite plausible reason for it. It's just what I want to do, sir.'

'Do you think you'll be able to get into a cockpit?'

'Oh yes, sir. I've tried it.'

'Where did you try it?'

'Navy Days, sir.'

'Do you go to many Navy Days?'

16

'I go to a lot, sir. I find them very interesting. I usually go with my father. He knows a lot of people in the Navy.'

'Was your father a naval officer?'

'Yes, sir. He's retired now.'

'Oh yes, I remember now.'

The Admiral seemed disconcerted and embarrassed. The Board wondered why.

'Bowles,' said the Civil Servant, 'since you want to be a pilot, can you tell us why we have a Fleet Air Arm?'

'We need aircraft to extend the offensive and defensive range of the fleet, sir. If we'd had a lot more fleet carriers earlier in the war a lot of things might have been different. There might have been no Dunkirk, at least not in the way it turned out, we might have held Singapore longer, we most certainly would not have lost the *Prince of Wales* and the *Repulse* in one day like that if they'd had air support, and the Atlantic convoy losses would have been lighter. A lot of things would have been different, sir.'

'That's a good answer, Bowles,' said the Admiral. 'You've obviously studied the question.'

'I have, sir. It's one of my father's pet hobby horses.'

'Did your father have any influence on your decision to join the Navy?'

'Well, I suppose he must have done, sir. But only indirectly. He left the choice to me. Naturally he's very pleased that I'm doing it.'

'Of course.'

The Lieutenant-Colonel, Royal Marines, asked two leading questions at each interview board. One was to ask the candidate if he had ever heard of Florence Nightingale, and the other was one about which the Lieutenant-Colonel of Royal Marines had often wondered himself. He decided that Bowles was the most likely candidate he had seen for some time to be able to give him the answer.

'If I said to you, Bowles, "the proper study of mankind is man," what do I mean?'

'It almost defines and describes what I imagine a naval officer does, sir.'

17

'I think that's as good an answer as any,' said the Admiral. He was anxious to change the subject.

'Will you look at that picture on the wall, Bowles, and tell us anything you notice about it?'

Bowles looked at the picture. The Board could almost see him absorbing the details, arranging them in his mind, and forming a conclusion.

'It's a picture of a ketch, coming out on the evening ebb tide. Two men on deck, which means two girls below cooking supper. The harbour is on the south coast, probably by the shape of the hills and the red soil, Devon or possibly Dorset. Racing pennant, dinghy lashed on deck, spinnaker boom lying up for'd, they've probably just finished a day's racing and are on their way home to the next place round the point before closing time. They're just passing a starboard hand buoy with what looks like a wreck buoy close inshore. Leading mark on the hill.'

The Board looked at Bowles with respect, almost with reverence. The Civil Servant examined the picture carefully. He had been looking absently at it for a number of years and had never realised what a lot was taking place in it. He had always thought it a peculiarly dull picture but Bowles had shown it to be a veritable hive of industry.

'Do you do much sailing, Bowles?' asked the Commander (E).

'Not as much as I'd like to, sir. We don't live anywhere near the sea.'

The Admiral's mind was already made up.

'Well, Bowles,' he said. 'I think that will be enough. You can go now. Thank you very much.'

'Thank you, sir.'

When Bowles had gone, the Admiral looked triumphantly round the Board.

'Well, gentlemen, I don't think there are any arguments about that. I think we're all agreed, are we not?'

The Board nodded. The Psychiatrist wrote: 'Bowles—recommended for aircrew. Hussar-type.'

*　　　*　　　*

'Only one more before lunch,' said the Commander (S). The Commander (S) found interviews fatiguing. The mental exertions of the candidates tried him almost as much as though he underwent them himself. He often sighed for his last appointment where he had signed papers between ten and eleven, lunched at one, and golfed in the afternoon. He had run the wardroom football pool syndicate once a week, dined with the Admiral's secretary once a month, audited the wardroom wine fund once a quarter and advised the Captain on his income tax rebates once a year. It had been a gentlemanly existence. Now, he was condemned to watch future naval officers, some of them possibly future Commanders (S), writhing on the hook for eight hours a day. To a civilised man, it smacked of sadism. Even now, the next candidate was waiting.

He was a brown-haired boy of medium height with the type of frank, honest, untroubled features which suggest that their owner had been a beautiful baby, as middle-class babies go.

'Michael John Hobbes.'

The Admiral was impressed. The boy looked normal enough.

'Have you read a life of Nelson, Hobbes?' asked the Headmaster.

'I started one, sir, but I'm afraid I didn't finish it.'

'What sort of books do you read?'

'Oh, novels and things. I read my mother's library books occasionally, sir.'

'Did you ever take part in any school plays?'

'Only very small parts. When we did Shakespeare I used to be a courtier or a friend of the hero and stand around for a long time and then say "Here comes Northumberland, sire" or "Ha! God save you!" or something like that, sir.'

'That didn't give you much scope, did it?'

'No, sir.'

'What else did you take part in?' asked the Psychiatrist.

'I sang in the choir once a year when we performed the "Messiah." I was there for quantity rather than quality. I was a member of the debating society. And I was . . . well, that's about all, sir.'

19

'Did you play any games?'

'Oh yes. I was in the second rugger fifteen and the second cricket eleven, sir. I used to play in the first if anyone got crocked.'

'Were those your only games?'

'Oh no, sir. I used to play almost everything we had at school at odd times. I was fairly good at them all but not very good at any one of them.'

'Do you play golf?'

'I've never actually tried it, sir. I'm willing to give it a shot.'

The Board beamed. Here was a broad-minded lad, free of prejudice, who was willing to try anything once.

'Hobbes,' said the Admiral, 'why do you want to become a naval officer?'

'I've always had it in mind, sir. I've never really thought about doing anything else.'

'Do you come from a naval family?'

'No, sir, this is all my idea.'

The Psychiatrist wrote: 'Hobbes—no sense of humour.'

The Board were not getting any satisfaction from Hobbes. The Admiral tried a new tack.

'If you were walking down a street, Hobbes, and you saw a taxi-driver knocked down and left lying by another man who ran off, what would you do? Would you leave the man where he was and drive the taxi to a hospital for an ambulance? Or put the man in the taxi and drive to a hospital? Or take the money from the meter and get another taxi to the hospital? Or leave the money . . .'

The Admiral was suddenly conscious that somewhere the problem had gone astray. He wondered where he had made a mistake. Hobbes, however, solved the problem.

'There's no money in a taxi-meter, sir,' he said.

'Quite so. All right, Hobbes. That's all. You can go now.'

'Thank you very much, sir.'

'A very diffident young man,' said the Admiral. 'Obviously has no idea of his own capabilities.'

The Board looked significantly at each other and wrote.

*　　*　　*

20

Another candidate followed Hobbes after lunch, and after him, still another. The next day another batch arrived and the Board began again. One by one, the faces sat down in the chair, answered questions, and left again. Day after day, the Board questioned, probed, selected, and discarded, until they had interviewed over 200 boys. Their only method was by patient and never-ending questioning and by careful appraisal of the candidate as he answered.

'Edward Maconochie.'

'Why do you want to join the Navy, Maconochie?'

'It's not me who's all that keen, sir. I thought it was *you*. They told me you were short of recruits, sort of like the Salvation Army. . . .'

'Peter Eric Cleghorn.'

'Why do you want to join the Navy, Cleghorn?'

'They told me at Pangbourne I hadn't a snowball's chance in hell of getting in the P. & O. and I'd better try the R.N. . . .'

'Colin Timothy Stacforth.'

'No need to ask you why you want to join the Navy, eh Stacforth? How's your father keeping? . . .'

'Isaiah Nine Smith.'

'Why do you want to join the Navy, Smith?'

'It was either that or being a parson, sir.'

'Frederick Augustus Spink.'

'Why do you want to join the Navy, Spink?'

'Do you know, sir, when I see you all up there and me down here, do you know it reminds me of that picture "When Did You Last See Your Father?" '

'Raymond Ball.'

'Why do you want to join the Navy, Ball?'

'Got a bit fed up with the girls round our way. Thought I'd try pastures new, so to speak. Dad says blokes that drink rum live to a great age.'

When the last candidate had been interviewed, the Board checked and rechecked their opinions. When they had finally passed their verdict they sent the list to the Admiralty. Their job was now finished until the next entry but sometimes, when they thought over the events of the last weeks, they likened themselves to men who have made a huge snowball on a hilltop and who now set the snowball on its unpredictable path downwards. Where the snowball would land, and what the consequences of that landing would be, the Board had no means of knowing, but they believed that it was more blessed to give than to receive and were thankful for it.

The end of an Interview Board normally found the Admiral in a state of acute melancholia. When he thought of the personalities he had seen across the table and considered that he was launching some of them, of his own free will and while in his right mind, into the service he loved, he sometimes prayed for guidance other than that given by the Admiralty.

'*Must* be something wrong with the recruiting these days. Or else there just isn't any better material to be had. I've been in the game a long time now and never have I seen such a bloody awful shower as that last lot. I think I'd better write to Dartmouth and warn them or I'll never be able to look Reggie in the face again.'

The Board nodded. The end of the Interview Board was proceeding as much according to precedent as the beginning. This was the Admiral's usual verdict on every new term of Special Entry cadets.

2

IT was not until Vincent, Dewberry, Bowles, Hobbes and the rest of the new term saw the uniforms on the platform at Paddington that they believed that they had really joined the Navy, with seniority in their rank of that day. The sight of each other convinced them far more than the arrival of the Admiralty letter announcing their success (which had convinced and delighted their fathers) or the arrival of their uniforms (which had convinced and delighted their mothers and sisters). Neither of these two previous events, sensational though they had been, compared with this present sense of pride when they saw each other, this feeling that they were about to become part of a great fighting service with a mighty tradition. It was a feeling which would not wear off until they had been in the great fighting service with a mighty tradition for at least another twenty-four hours.

Paul Vincent was accompanied by his mother and Cedric. Mrs Vincent wore a close-fitting dark blue wool suit and a tiny black hat with a veil. She had the type of features most often seen at fashionable weddings—their natural habitat—and her poise and grooming suggested that she might be at that moment waiting for the photographers. But that was only a surface illusion. Mrs Vincent was afraid that she might break down at any minute and present an appearance which would have shocked her friends in Lowndes Square, and for that reason she had asked Cedric to come with her.

Cedric was a tall, pale man in morning dress. He wore a carnation in his buttonhole and looked like an usher at a fashionable wedding. He was Mrs Vincent's stockbroker but his attendance on the platform was not in a financial capacity but as moral support when Mrs Vincent's composure showed signs of breaking down, as it did.

Mrs Vincent took out a small lace handkerchief and dabbed behind her veil. Cedric put his arm round her shoulders.

'Steady, Louise, my dear,' he said. 'You mustn't make an exhibition of yourself in front of these young devils.'

'Oh Paul, darling, do look after yourself,' sobbed Mrs Vincent.

'Mother, don't be so *lachrymose*,' said Paul. 'Anyone would think you had to commit suttee after I've gone. It's me who's joining the Navy. *I* should be in tears. I will look after myself and I'll write every week and tell you how I'm getting on. Does that make you feel any better?'

'Oh Paul, darling.' Mrs Vincent sniffed and dabbed again.

George Dewberry was also accompanied by his mother. Dewberry's mother was a large woman, deep-chested like the hunters she rode, with a voice which could start a fox from its sleep a mile away. She wore a tweed suit with a W.V.S. badge in the lapel and a beret with a ptarmigan feather in front. She also carried a shooting stick.

'Pity your father couldn't see you now, George,' boomed George's mother. 'He'd have had a stroke.'

'Why, mater?'

'He told me a thousand times before he died that any son of his would join the Navy over his dead body. You have, so buck up and look cheerful about it, my lad.'

'I'll try, mater.'

'Looking at some of these little tykes you shouldn't do too badly.'

'Yes, mater.'

George Dewberry put a finger in the rim of his cap and lifted it from the position of equilibrium it had assumed over his ears. The naval outfitters had given him a cap many sizes too large.

George Dewberry was philosophical about it; it was only one and a minor one of the inconveniences of joining the Navy.

Tom Bowles was alone and walked up the platform and straight into a carriage.

Michael Hobbes was seen off by his mother and father and his eldest sister Susan. Michael was the first of his family to join the Navy and the news that he was about to do so had sent an electric tremor along the family grapevine only equalled by a birth or a marriage. His immediate family were delighted and particularly Susan who was captivated by the uniform. When Susan had first seen Michael in his uniform she had been struck dumb by his transformation from the chrysalis of a rather odious elder brother into the glorious butterfly of a Cadet, Royal Navy. She had regarded him with almost worshipping eyes but now that she saw so many other young men, all in the same magical dress, she was more critical of her brother.

'They're quite a lot of them taller than you, aren't there?' she said to Michael when they arrived on the platform.

'Oh shut up. You're supposed to be seeing me off, not making funny remarks.'

Michael tried to conceal his nervousness.

'It's almost like going back to school again isn't it Michael?' said his mother.

His mother knew more certainly than any other person in the family that they were about to lose him. She sensed that the break which was just approaching would be far more permanent than a return to school. She also sensed her son's fear of the future.

'Don't you think it's like going back to school, Michael?'

'Almost.'

'Remember to write now, won't you, and let us know if you're doing all right.'

'Yes, mum.'

'Got your ticket?'

'Yes, mum.'

'Handkerchief?'

'Yes, mum.'

'Michael, don't be such a drip,' said Susan. 'You'll be back in three months. Which are the boys who are going to be captains?'

'How on earth should I know? I've never seen them before in my life.'

As the time of departure came nearer, each cadet and his attendant circle tended to draw away from the rest. The families' reactions varied from the stoical to the wildly tearful. Some families regarded their sons coldly and unemotionally, like Red Indian families sending their young braves out to fight against the white man. Others nearby wept and embraced each other, as though they were saying farewell to their boys before they disappeared into the gas-chamber.

A whistle blew. Mrs Vincent was almost extinguished behind her lace handkerchief and her veil. She could find no words to say to her son at this moment but hugged him tight.

'Here,' said Cedric, taking a five pound note from his wallet. 'Don't spend it all on one woman.'

The whistle blew twice.

George Dewberry's mother opened her handbag, which appeared to have been hacked from the carcass of an otter.

'Here is your ticket, George,' she said. 'I've kept it as long as I can. You'll have to look after it yourself now.'

George and his mother kissed briefly, like horses recognising each other.

A third time the whistle blew. Michael Hobbes hurriedly kissed his mother and his sister. He shook hands with his father.

'I suppose I really ought to have given you some advice,' said Mr Hobbes. He held out a pound note. 'Don't take up smoking too early.'

The whistle blew again, in exasperation. There was a rush to the carriage doors. Michael Hobbes got in with Paul Vincent and George Dewberry. There was another cadet already sitting in the fourth corner.

The train began to move out of the platform. Michael Hobbes

leant out and waved and afterwards remembered nothing more of the final parting from his old life than faces sliding by, handkerchiefs waving and a shrouding blast of steam and smoke as they left the platform behind.

The four cadets, in their four corners, surveyed each other.

The fourth cadet in the compartment was a red-faced, belligerent-looking boy with sandy hair and pouting lips. His tie drooped down his collar, exposing his front stud, as though it had been tied by hands unaccustomed to stiff collars. A copy of *Life's Snags,* by Baden-Powell, lay on the seat beside him. Paul looked the red-faced cadet up and down and addressed himself to Michael.

'Michael Hobbes, isn't it?' he asked. 'Weren't we at the interview together?'

'That's right,' said Michael. 'You're Paul Vincent.'

'How right,' said Paul. He turned to George Dewberry. 'You're Horace, aren't you?'

George Dewberry winced.

'That's one of my names, but everybody calls me George,' he said.

'My name is Edward Maconochie,' announced the red-faced cadet, suddenly.

'Splendid fellow,' murmured Paul. He took up a copy of *The Connoisseur* and began to read it. He had summed Maconochie up already and his manner clearly showed that his conversation with Maconochie had been an ideal one. It had been short, concise, to the point, and was now closed. But Edward Maconochie was not so easily put off.

'The Troop called me Ted,' he said.

'You mustn't believe everything people say,' remarked Paul. He turned back to *The Connoisseur* again. But still Maconochie was not discouraged.

'Oh, they didn't mean anything by it! It's a *compliment*!'

Paul raised an eyebrow.

'Of course, not everybody called me Ted. The Tenderfeet didn't *dare*!'

'I should think not!' replied Paul, righteously. 'Whatever next?'

'Though naturally I didn't want to be too hard on them, I was a Tenderfoot once myself, you know.'

'Never mind, Ted, I'm sure they'll overlook it at Dartmouth.'

'Oh everybody's got to start at the bottom! Not that I was a Tenderfoot long. It didn't take me long to get to know who were the important people in the Troop. . . .'

'Look Ted, old boy, I can think of nothing which interests me less at the moment than Boy Scout politics.'

'. . . You see, you start as a Tenderfoot and after you've passed your test you become a . . .'

Maconochie continued and Paul, Michael and George Dewberry were compelled by his persistence to listen. Maconochie described for them the primrose path of promotion in the Boy Scout Movement, from obscure and timid Tenderfoot to that glorious and omnipotent being, only a little short of Jove, a County Commissioner. Maconochie himself had done well. At the time of speaking, a Scout First Class and a Troop Leader eke was he.

Paul listened to Maconochie as he might have listened to the dripping of a tap which he thought he had repaired.

'My!' he said, at last. 'Isn't it strange how history repeats itself? Here we are, like Xenophon's Ten Thousand on our way to the sea, and we are harried and set about by Babylonians! How many miles to Babylon? Ye gods, only Reading?'

Paul took out his cigarette case.

'Cigarette, *Ted*?'

Maconochie recoiled, as though he had come upon two Tenderfeet chalking up rhymes in the Peewit Patrol Corner. He had opened his mouth to speak when his attention was distracted by something outside the carriage window.

'Look!'

Paul, Michael and George gazed out of the window at the peaceful Berkshire countryside speeding past. They searched for a runaway horse, or a fire, or even a Boy Scout.

28

'What's the matter?'

'Just fancy that! We're just coming to the place where we had our summer camp last year. Yes, look! There it is over by that white house. I passed my axemanship test there, you know.'

'Drop dead, *Ted*,' said Paul.

Maconochie stopped short, his mouth hanging open. Then he picked up *Life's Snags* and thumbed through it, almost as though he were looking for a mention of Paul. Michael opened *Two Years Before the Mast*, which had been given to him by a well-meaning uncle, and pretended to read the first chapter. He wondered what the brave new world of the Navy would be like, that had such people as Paul Vincent and Ted Maconochie in it.

After a time Maconochie tired of *Life's Snags* and stood up. He preened himself in front of the mirror. He combed his hair and examined his fingernails. He tried on his cap. It was too small and perched on the top of his head. George Dewberry watched him and then made his first contribution to the conversation.

'I say,' he said, 'would you mind changing caps with me?'

Tom Bowles was in the next compartment. Opposite him sat an old man balancing a pork pie on a cloth on his knees. The old man was preparing to have the pork pie for lunch.

First the old man took out a small penknife and carefully cut the pie into halves. Then he cut the pie into quarters, measuring the quadrants meticulously by eye. Then he took the quarters one by one and neatly bisected them into eighths. But when he attempted to cut one of the pieces of eight in half it crumpled into an asymmetrical mass. The old man grunted.

'Going to join the Navy, son?' he asked.

'Yes, sir,' said Tom.

'It's a great life, they tell me.'

The old man wiped his nose meditatively on his sleeve.

'If you don't weaken, that is.'

He gazed ruminatively out of the window, as though he were recalling sailors he had known.

'Met with some 'orrible deaths, sailors 'ave.'

'They didn't tell me that, sir.'

'Oh no. I don't suppose they would. Not until you're *in*, they wouldn't. 'Ave you signed anything yet?'

'No, sir.'

'Don't.'

The Royal Naval College, Dartmouth, looked exactly as a tourist or a real estate salesman would imagine a Naval College ought to look. The College looked as though it had been designed by men who planned it so that archaeologists of the future discovering the ruins would immediately drop their spades and exclaim 'Ah, yes! This must have been where they trained their naval officers!'

The College stood on a hill overlooking the town of Dartmouth. It could not be said to dominate the town because nothing constructed by or for the Royal Navy would commit so flagrant a breach of good manners as to presume to dominate anything; rather was it just there, above the town, so that the locals could look up at it and say 'Yer, the College.'

The main block of College buildings faced out to the harbour of Dartmouth and the English Channel. Wings jutted out at the ends of the main block forming arms which enclosed the parade ground. The parade ground was separated from the buildings by two roads which swept round on climbing ramps and joined in front of the main entrance. A flight of steps led from the road outside the main entrance down to the parade ground, parting in its descent to accommodate a stone rampart in the middle which served as a saluting base and as the nearest the architect could approach to a ship's bridge, hampered as he was by being on dry land. A flagstaff flying the White Ensign stood where the two roads met at the bottom of the ramps. Behind and around the main blocks were the subsidiary instructional blocks, the hospital, the gymnasium and swimming pool, the shooting range, the squash and tennis courts, and the pavilion.

The College impressed summer excursionists on the River Dart with a feeling that here indeed was the cradle of Nelson's descendants and the breeding ground of future sea-dogs. It left in their goggling eyes and ears a composite of Drake drumming up the Channel, Nelson shattering the French, and the chorus of 'Hearts of Oak' sung by a watch of bluejackets resembling the man on the Player's packet. Seen dispassionately from the Kingswear side of the river on a bright summer's day, the effect was indeed one of dignity and the spirit of Nelson, lightly coated with icing sugar.

When the eighty cadets of several nationalities stood in Kingswear station and waited for the ferry to take them across the river the effect was not one of the spirit of Nelson, but of deep depression. It was raining gently but steadily, and the town of Dartmouth had achieved that chilling appearance of grey hopelessness and damp despair which is nowhere in the world achieved so successfully as by a Devon town in the rain.

The cadets were met on the Dartmouth side by three damp and embittered-looking Chief Petty Officers.

'Get fell in now!' bawled the biggest and most embittered-looking Chief Petty Officer. 'Chop chop now! Slap it about! Them as is keen gets fell in previous!'

'How can any of us get fell in previous when we all arrived at the same time?' wondered Paul.

'Keep silence! Get fell in three deep tallest on the right shortest in the centre!'

The cadets shuffled into three approximate ranks. The three Chief Petty Officers ranged themselves around the squad, as though to prevent any cadet bolting, and counted. After the count, the squad turned right and began to march up the hill towards the College.

'Swing them arms!' bawled the large Chief Petty Officer.

As punishment for making the mistake of delaying their entry until the age of eighteen and thus depriving the Navy of its right to educate and train them from the age of thirteen, the Special Entry Cadets, known collectively under the house-name of Beattys, were not housed in the main College at all but in a barracks halfway down the hill towards the river at Sandquay. There, the accommodation and amenities would have excited the admiration of a native Spartan. It was to these barracks that the Beattys marched, swinging their arms, in a long straggling column.

As they marched, the Beattys had their first opportunity to see each other together. Michael Hobbes was amazed at the different nationalities. Besides the R.N. cadets, whom he had expected to see, there were Indians, Pakistanis, Sikhs, Burmese, Egyptians, Canadians, Australians and New Zealanders. Michael himself marched between a small Sikh and a tall R.N. cadet whom he later discovered was named Cleghorn. Michael was secretly impressed by the confident manner in which Cleghorn wore his uniform; his cap already had a nautical tilt and looked as though it had borne the brunt of several arctic whaling seasons.

When the Beattys arrived in front of their barracks they were counted again, presumably to check whether any cadets had broken ship already. Then the largest Chief Petty Officer called out each cadet's name from a list and allotted them divisions, chest flats and bed numbers. Cleghorn was ordered to get a new cap, and the parade was dismissed.

The chest flats were long, bare, forbidding rooms which accommodated twenty cadets in each. A line of beds ran down each side and a line of chests ran down the middle. Single light bulbs hung down from the ceiling. The bare wooden floor had been scrubbed and trodden into an undulating, splintered surface. The windows were high and wide open.

'Dotheboys Hall,' said Paul.

On their beds the Beattys found a pile of clothes and assorted gear; it was the complete kit laid down by the Admiralty to be issued to subordinate officers on joining. Trousers, jumpers, shirts, sheets, socks, boots, collars, lanyards, pyjamas, brushes, badges and underwear lay on each bed in a vast amorphous heap. The compilers of the heap had foreseen the cadets' every need down to the most intimate articles including toothbrushes and razors. The inference was that the Navy regarded each new intake of cadets as being on the mental level of savages; not only had they

32

to be taught the rudiments of their profession but also how to wash. The Navy was starting from the very beginning, as though their future officers had been freshly caged and shipped from the Belgian Congo, like specimens for a zoo.

Michael looked round his chest flat. On his side of the room were George Dewberry, a New Zealander, three Sikhs, a Burmese, two more R.N. cadets whom Michael did not know, and Maconochie. On the other side were Paul, Cleghorn, a Canadian, an Indian, four Egyptians and another R.N. cadet.

Michael crossed over to Paul's bed, where Paul was busy stowing his clothes away in his chest.

'Quite a mixed lot in here,' he said.

Paul paused and looked up.

'Like a bloody United Nations. We'd better not start any arguments or we'll have a holy war or something before we know where we are.'

'This is not quite what I expected, I must say,' said Michael.

'What in hell *did* you expect then?'

'I don't know. Not this. It seems all terribly, I don't know, business-like.'

'Well, it *is* a business.'

'I suppose so.'

Michael went back to his bed and began to put away his gear. It took him some time. He was puzzled why they had been left in peace for so long. Michael could only think that perhaps the task of sorting and putting away their clothes was thought to be such a huge one that nothing more was required of them that day. He was vaguely disappointed. He had arrived at the sacrificial taboo ground prepared to undergo the first painful rites of initiation and had found the witch-doctor finished for the day.

But Michael's thoughts were premature. The witch-doctor was at that moment preparing his welcome.

The burliest Chief came into the chest flat and stood watching the Beattys for a few moments. The Chief had a hyphenated way of speaking, as though he were pausing for effect between each word. He inflated his lungs.

'All-right-you-lot! Leave-your-camisoles-for-now-and-muster-

in-the-Gunroom!   Lieutenant-Commander-Badger-wants-to-
speak-to-you! At-the-double-now!'

The Gunroom was a large room provided for the Beattys'
recreation. It was not, however, a room which inspired gaiety.
It was whitewashed and cheerless like the chest flats and contained half a dozen tables and a dozen long wooden forms. The
forms had been arranged to face the door and on them the
eighty Beattys sat down in silence to await the coming of the
man who, for the next three months, would be more powerful
than Jehovah.

Jehovah was preceded by his runner. He was a small, fair-
haired man with the face of an ancient angel and the voice of
a brazen bull-frog. He was Mr Froud, the Cadet Gunner. Mr
Froud had served in the Navy for over twenty years and the
experience had given him the Navy's unique mixture of uncom-
promising official dogmatism and wise tolerance of human eccentricities. There was no provision or regulation concerning the
welfare of men which Mr Froud did not know, no offence
which he had not seen committed before, and no excuse which he
had not heard before. Nothing surprised Mr Froud. He loved
the Navy and he loved his cadets, but he was careful to conceal
his affection. He was more closely concerned with the welfare
and discipline of the Beattys than Lieutenant-Commander
Badger himself; if Lieutenant-Commander Badger was Jove,
then Mr Froud was his thunderbolt.

Mr Froud stood at the head of the room. The Beattys did
not know it, but Mr Froud was thinking the same thoughts as
the President of the Interview Board.

Here, thought Mr Froud, is another shower. God knows
what'll happen to them or to the service before they're finished.

'Pay attention this way!' said Mr Froud. 'My name is Mr
Froud. I'm the Cadet Gunner. I hate cadets. This evening I'll
be kind to you. But from tomorrow onwards I'll be watching
you, so look out! Just before Lieutenant-Commander Badger
comes in, I'll call you to attention. Don't stand up, sit to attention with your arms folded, head and eyes to the front.'

Steps sounded outside the Gunroom.

34

'Attention in the Gunroom!'

'Carry on please,' said Lieutenant-Commander Badger pleasantly. The three lieutenants who had entered with him sat down in chairs placed for them in front.

Lieutenant-Commander Badger surveyed the faces for whom he was responsible, morally and physically, for the next three months.

Lieutenant-Commander Robert Bollinger Badger, D.S.C., R.N., known throughout the Navy as The Artful Bodger, was a stoutish, burly man with a shock of black hair and an air of pleasant detachment from the realities of an unpleasant life; he moved through life unconcernedly but hopefully, as though he expected at any minute to be offered a drink. He had emerged at the end of the war with a splendid record and the rank of lieutenant-commander at an early age, but because of his failure to observe what his contemporaries considered to be the cardinal primary rule of a successful naval officer, namely, the ability to say the right thing at the right time to the right person, The Bodger was likely, unless he looked sharp, to remain a lieutenant-commander with a splendid war record until a late age. The Bodger's contemporaries said that he had been given the appointment of Officer in Charge of Special Entry Cadets because Their Lordships wanted the poor beggars to know the worst first.

'I've called you all together here on your first night,' said The Bodger, 'to give you an idea of what we intend to do with you while you are at Dartmouth. I want to give you the set-up here. My name is Lieutenant-Commander Badger and I am responsible for your training. To help me I have Lieutenants Brakeherst, Chipperd and Mathewson who will be your divisional officers, and Mr Froud, whom you have met already. Also on the staff we have the Chief G.I., the Chief Yeoman and the Chief Bosun's Mate whom you met this afternoon.'

The Bodger felt in his pocket and took out a piece of paper. He unfolded it and laid it on the desk in front of him.

'Now a bit about the organisation of this place. For drill purposes and for sports you will be divided into three divisions named, in the best traditions of the service, after parts of a ship, Foc'sle, Top and Quarterdeck. You will be able to see which division you are in from a notice in the Cadet Office, if you have not already seen it. For parades and for leave, not that you will be concerned much with leave while you're here, you will be divided into watches, also named in the best traditions of the service, Port and Starboard. You will also find a class list on your notice board. Do not read any significance into the composition of the classes. We have not put all the geniuses into one class and all the bombheads in another. Mr Froud worked out the class lists according to an unfathomable system of his own. What that system is nobody knows. What is your system by the way, Mr Froud?'

Mr Froud grinned. 'I permed any twenty out of eighty, sir.'

'Precisely,' continued The Bodger. 'You can see from the start, gentlemen, the place mathematics holds in the complex modern Navy.'

The Beattys found themselves warming to The Bodger. He had a dry, poker-faced humour which they had not expected.

'So much for the mechanics of this place. You will pick up the rest as you go along. Now for the reasons why you're here and what you are going to do while you're here.'

The Bodger felt again in his pocket and took out another piece of paper. He smoothed it with his fingers and the suspicion of a grin crossed his face.

'Yes. What you will learn here is only the very beginning of all you will eventually learn before you start paying back the Admiralty for all the time and trouble they've spent on you. This is the first rung of a long and slippery ladder. You have just set your foot, or rather your parents have just set your foot, on the bottom rung. You are now at the very beginning. I cannot find the words to express, gentlemen, your complete *basicness* at this point. From now on you are on your own. How far you get up the ladder depends on you. You are here to start to learn how to be leaders. There are some people who are born with the art. But they are very few and I don't expect there are any here tonight. There's normally one every other century. Napoleon was the last. Most of us have to learn and go on learning until we die. Some of us will *never* learn, but we'll find out who they are in due course. You are here to learn how to be leaders. That is your vocation. That is what you will eventually be paid to do. You will find that the art of leadership in a young officer lies largely in making other men, some of them considerably older than yourself, do the things you want them to do against their better judgment. Don't be coy about it. You will have plenty of examples set before you. The chances are that you will go through your service career being made to do things against *your* better judgment by other officers senior to yourself. But remember this. If you are always sincere, if you always do your best according to your lights, if you always say what you mean and do what you say and stick to it whatever the consequences, then there will always be someone to put in a good word for you at the court-martial.'

The Bodger knew his subject. He had been himself twice court-martialled, once as a sub-lieutenant in Hong Kong when he attended a dance dressed as a girl and was chased twice round the Hongkong-Shanghai Bank building by a Royal Marine, and again as a lieutenant after a collision in Penzance harbour when The Bodger, in command of an M.L., broke up a Rogation-tide service on the mole with the words : 'Won't one of you bastards throw a poor sinner a line?'

'You are all starting equally here. There may be some of you who come from naval families or were pillars of the local Sea Cadet Force, who think you know it all already.'

Colin Stacforth, whose father was C.-in-C. Rockall and Malin Approaches, blushed.

'Get that idea out of your heads right now. The things you will do here and the pace you will do them at will be no more like the Sea Cadets or what your old man told you than rummy with the family is like contract bridge with Culbertson. You will have to cultivate a professional outlook on life and the sooner you start the better. Your future job will be to so lead your men that in time of war you and they will be able to kill the maximum number of the enemy in the most efficient way. And that applies to officers in any branch. All the officers and the ship's company in a ship have one object, no matter what their particular personal duty may be, and that is to destroy the enemy. Forget what your old aunt told you or what you read in the newspapers. *I* am telling you now what your job will be. You're going to learn it starting right now.

'You will find that there is a cult in the Navy, you will meet it more when you get out into the Fleet, which regards the Navy as a place to mark time in before getting a job with more pay outside. Forget it! You have no other job and you have no other life. *This* is your life!'

With a stout Cortesian gesture, The Bodger indicated the walls of the Gunroom, the picture of H.M.S. *Victory* beating close-hauled out of a cocoa stain and, in passing, the faces of the Chief G.I., the Chief Yeoman and the Chief Bosun's mate standing along the wall.

'You must reconcile yourself to the fact that you will be underpaid for your responsibilities for most of your service career and particularly as you get more senior. Your motto must therefore be to give and not to count the cost, to fight and not to heed the wounds, to labour and not to seek for rest, to toil and not to seek for any reward save that of knowing that if you *don't*, someone will come along and see that you bloody well *do*. Any questions? No. Good. That's all I'm going to . . . Yes?'

The Bodger had noticed a cadet who appeared to have a question.

'Please, sir,' said Maconochie.

'Yes?'

'I read in the papers the other day that the Navy was out of date already. Is that true, sir?'

Lieutenants Chipperd, Brakehurst and Mathewson craned round to look at Maconochie, like men in church turning round to see who it was who shouted 'Liar!' during the sermon. The Chief G.I., the Chief Yeoman and the Chief Bosun's Mate looked hard at Maconochie, as though they were memorising his face. The Bodger himself was temporarily taken aback.

'You must not believe all the articles you read in the papers,' he said, 'particularly when they're founded on logic. Right. That's all I want to say tonight. Carry on please, Mr Froud.'

'Attention in the Gunroom!'

The Beattys stood up while The Bodger and his three satellites left the Gunroom.

'Carry on to your chest flats and turn in! No skylarking or we'll meet sooner than we expected!'

The Beattys filed out quietly under Mr Froud's eye.

On his way out Paul picked up a piece of paper lying by the door. It was part of The Bodger's lecture notes. The notes were not exhaustive. They consisted simply of the words: 'Shake them rigid!' in capitals and underlined.

Paul turned the paper over and saw that it was part of a letter.

'Dear Lieutenant-Commander Badger,' Paul read, 'With reference to your letter of the 18th inst., we are pleased to inform you that we have room for men of ability and integrity in our sales and personnel welfare departments. In view of your considerable service in the Royal Navy, particularly in the command of men, we should be pleased to arrange an interview for you....'

There the letter was torn off.

'Well, I'll be damned!' said Paul.

Meanwhile, The Bodger and his three lieutenants were reviving themselves in the College wardroom.

'Thank God that's over for another term,' The Bodger was saying. 'Soda, please. Do you think *any* of them believed a word of it?'

'If they did, then they'll be the first term who have,' said Lieutenant Brakehurst.

'Don't be so cynical, John,' said Lieutenant Chipperd. 'They lapped it up, particularly the bit about killing the enemy. That was right up their street. Just what they've run away to sea to do. You've got to remember that at the moment they're like ninety per cent of the population of this country. All they know about the Navy they've learned from Ealing Studios. One thing I must say for Noël Coward, he's probably the best recruiter the Navy's ever had.'

'Now who's being cynical. Though they're a rough looking lot of hoods, I must say. The old codgers at the Interview must be losing their grip.

'I wonder what this mob will be like,' pondered The Bodger. 'I hope to God they don't go in for mass hypnotism like the last lot.'

'Anyway,' said The Bodger, 'they'll be too busy keeping out of Froud's way to worry about anything else for a while.'

3

'CARRY on, Chief Cadet!' shouted Mr Froud.

'Aye aye sir!' yelled Peter Cleghorn, Chief Cadet for the day. 'Port Watch to the river, Starboard Watch to P.T., Beattys, right and left . . . *turn*! By the right . . . double . . . *march*!'

It was six o'clock in the morning. A grey Devon dawn had just established itself and its wan and cheerless light illuminated the Port Watch, in shorts and singlets, percolating down the steps towards the river and the Starboard Watch, also in shorts and singlets, panting up the hill towards the gymnasium. It was the start of a new day at Dartmouth and the Beattys, who experienced each on alternate days, could never decide which start, the river or the gymnasium, was the worse.

The river normally took the shorter time. A skilful crew could occupy so much time manning their boat, getting out their oars, and starting to pull, that it was breakfast time before they had pulled more than a hundred yards from the buoy. After some practice Tom Bowles and Paul could arrange it so that they never left the buoy at all but appeared to Lieutenant Chipperd, the Beattys' Boat Officer, on the jetty, to be waiting for Maconochie to untangle himself and get out his oar.

The gymnasium, however, was warmer and it was easier there to go through the motions of intensive physical effort without in fact extending a muscle. But the gymnasium had one disadvantage. The P.T. Instructor was no fonder of P.T. at 6 a.m. than the Beattys. Term after term of cadets had suffered under his early morning sarcasm. He conducted his classes with a ferocity which appalled such dilettante gymnasts as the Beattys who had hitherto regarded P.T. as a means to an end, as football training in wet weather or as a stop-gap while the rest of the school paraded with the cadet corps. The idea of P.T. for its own sake, as a fetish, almost as a religion, was foreign to them and many times as they hung from the wall-bars the Beattys cursed the P.T.I. and prayed that the gods would look down in pity and strike this barbaric man in his pride.

One morning their prayers were answered. The exercises that morning had been particularly fatiguing and after one of them the Starboard Watch were standing about in attitudes of resigned exhaustion.

The P.T.I. was scornful.

'Tired?' he asked. 'Look at you. Lolling about like a lot of pregnant prawns. Anyone would think you'd been taking some exercise. You've only had kid's stuff. Watch the next exercise.'

The P.T.I. ran lightly up to a vaulting-horse and somersaulted over, without touching it. The Starboard Watch looked at him silently.

'There.'

The P.T.I. smirked.

Suddenly there was a stir in the ranks and out stepped a challenger, a White Hope. It was the chosen instrument of the gods, Cartwright, an Australian cadet who until this moment of destiny had been less energetic than most.

'Fair crack,' said the White Hope. 'Any joker can do that.'

Cartwright ran up to the horse, sprang into the air like his native kangaroo and somersaulted twice before landing neatly and quietly on the other side.

The P.T.I.'s jaw drooped. He looked at Cartwright, quietly resuming his place in the class. Not since the day he told a New Zealand cadet to do a dozen press-ups and the lad did them one-handed had the P.T.I. been so dumbfounded.

'Watch the next exercise,' said the P.T.I. . . . 'Knees bending with arms stretching.'

Afterwards, the Beattys discovered that Cartwright had been

42

Junior Gymnastics Champion of South Australia and Tasmania before he matured and turned his energies in other directions.

The violent early morning exercise was symbolical of the whole of the Beattys' Dartmouth training. From their first day the Beattys were plunged headlong into a rush of new experiences. They were weighed as carefuly as though they were title-fight contenders. They were carefully measured, as for a sarcophagus. They were medically examined from head to foot as though the Navy wished to satisfy itself that their physical condition had not deteriorated since their acceptance and it was not therefore accepting soiled goods. Their eyesight was tested for day and night vision. Their hair was cut and their teeth were inspected and pulled out or filled in as necessary. They were issued with text-books and note-books, pay books and identity cards, arctic clothing and tropical clothing, and respirators. Dartmouth took nothing on trust. They signed for the books and they signed for the clothing; they were enclosed in a gas-chamber to test the respirators; they swam two lengths of the swimming-bath, clothed and unclothed, to prove that they could swim; they ran two lengths of a football pitch, clothed, to prove that they could run; and they were photographed, presumably to prove that they were still unscarred.

The Beattys were marched, doubled, halted, turned about, marched, doubled, halted and turned about once more. They were left no time for reflection, no time to wonder to what mysterious professional goal they were being hastened, no time to consider what changes in body and mind were being placed upon them. They could barely find time to write letters home. From early in the morning until late at night they were chased, hustled, hurried and hurtled, pell-mell. It was as though the Navy were vigorously shaking off the dust and lethargy of civilian life so that they could begin afresh. The mental condition peculiar to a regular naval officer was not cultivated easily nor quickly; the necessary reflexes took time to train and Dartmouth was only the beginning of the Beattys' indoctrination. No young head-hunter, no prospective pupil of a political creed, ever submitted to so long or so intensive an initiation as a junior naval officer before he is considered to be trained.

The instructional course at Dartmouth took the form of lectures supported by practical work. The best lecturers, as pure lecturers, were the Chief Petty Officers. Their subjects were limited, but they taught them with the despotic assurance of men who knew their briefs absolutely and whose dicta in the lecture-room were seldom or never questioned. They were experts in their own fields and they crushed easily any who doubted it.

'The Navy,' said the Chief Bosun's Mate, 'runs on three things. Rum, Bum, and Baccy. You lot remember that and you'll all be admirals. Now pay attention this way! The *Reef Knot*! If you don't know how to tie a reef knot, you'll never be an admiral. To make a reef knot you holds your length of line in your hands, holding the left end in your left hand and the right end in your right hand. Let's see if you've got that.'

The Chief Bosun's Mate passed along the row of cadets.

'Right. Now you passes the right over the left, and under, then left over right, and under. Pull it tight and what've you got? You've got a reef knot. Try it. Right over left and under, left over right and under. Right. Right over left and under, left over right and under. That's right. Right over left and under, left over right and under. Then you pulls it taut and what've you got? You've got it all balled up! Let's have a look 'ere you!'

'I can't seem to do it your way, Chief,' wailed Maconochie plaintively. 'When Wise Owl taught us, he always told us to . . .'

'I don't care if it was Wise Owl, Blue Bird or ruddy Scarlet O'Hara 'oo taught you,' said the Chief Bosun's Mate. 'Now you're '*ere* you'll do it *my* way. Try it again. Right over left and under, left over right and under, and Christ. . . . Give it 'ere! I don't see as how you *could* get it wrong! A ruddy Boy Scout could do it better.'

A wrongly-tied knot hurt the Chief Bosun's Mate as keenly as though it had been tied with the strings of his heart. He lived for his knots and his splices. His proudest possession was a Double Matthew Walker Knot mounted on a varnished board which had attracted the commendation of King George V during an inspection of the old *Royal Oak*. It was the Chief Bosun's Mate's considered opinion that if They—meaning the mysterious and all-powerful Lords who administered the Navy from their fastnesses in Whitehall—paid more attention to knots and rigging and less to being nice to foreigners the Navy would not be in the state it was.

'The Navy,' said the Chief Yeoman of Signals, 'is run by the Communications Branch. The Navy only works now because one admiral in ten knows what's going on. If it weren't for the signalmen, none of them would know what was going on.

'The first thing about the Communications Branch is Accuracy. What's fair enough for the Gunnery Branch, a near miss or a straddle, is not good enough for the Communications Branch. You've got to be accurate and say what you mean. I'll tell you a little story. It's in every book of memoirs about the Navy and it might as well be in your'n. An admiral on the China station used to send his dhobeying ashore to be done by a washer-woman. The washer-woman used to come off every Monday morning with the Admiral's dhobeying. One Monday the boat didn't turn up. So they sent a signal—'P.S.B. for admiral's woman.' When the Flag Jack saw it he didn't half shave off. So they sent another signal. Reference my, then they give the date time group, please insert washer between admiral and woman.'

The Chief Yeoman's face gave no sign that he acknowledged or even noticed the laughter of the class. The Chief Yeoman had a complexion like shrivelled parchment. His nose was sharp and beaked and his eyes were narrow and keen. He looked like a disillusioned vulture. Long years of close contact with senior officers on the bridges of H.M. Ships and Vessels had embittered the Chief Yeoman to the point where, like Cassius, he mocked himself and scorned his spirit that he could be moved to laugh at anything. It was the Chief Yeoman's considered opinion that if They paid more attention to signals and less to politicians the Navy would not be in the state it was.

* * *

'The Navy!' said the Chief Gunnery Instructor, in exclamation marks, 'is not proud to have you! Don't you go getting that idea in your little heads! You're here under probation! You're supposed to be the cream of England's youth, and if you're the cream all I say is God-Help-England! I do! Take-that-grin-off-of-your-silly-face! This morning, pay attention, we're going to try and learn something which boy seamen learn with ease! So I expect it'll take you lot a little time to get the hang of it! This morning we're going to learn how to turn about! Detail for turning about! When turning about the cautionary order in your case 'about' and the hexecutive order in this case 'turn' are given on two right feet when you take a check pace to the old front with your left foot and turn round in three paces raising the knees and keeping your arms to your sides and stepping off with a full pace of your left foot and swinging the arms to the height of the shoulders! Watch me!'

The Chief G.I. placed himself in front of the squad and gave himself the orders for turning about.

'Squad! Squad . . . by the right quick . . . *march!* Squad will turn aye-bout! Move to the right in threes squad aye-bout . . . *turn*-check-one-two-three-*off* with the left foot! Now let's see how you do it!'

The Chief G.I. was a huge man, in stature and in voice. He was a renowned beer-drinker; a notice still hangs in a Sliema bar testifying to his ability to drink thirty-eight Hopleaf beers and walk back to his ship unaided. He watched the Beattys' attempts to turn about with a disdainful smile, as a Norse King in Valhalla might have watched the antics of mortals below him. When the Beattys finally halted in front of him, breathless but conscious that they had done as well as ordinary mortals could, the Chief G.I. was ready with comment.

'All I hope is that the Captain wasn't watching that! He's not strong, you know! I wouldn't like to be the cause of him having a stroke and being brought to a bed of pain through watching you! I seen some squads! I thought I'd seen 'em all! But *you* lot are worse than a man deserves! They've given me the cream that's paying you a compliment! They've given me the cream of of England all right! All the clots!'

Spink, always nervous when close to the Chief G.I. or to any authority, let out a high hysterical laugh.

'What's your name? Up the hill and back! *Double* march, you human gash-shoot!'

The lectures by the Chief Petty Officers were only a small part of the syllabus. The major part was taught by The Bodger, the three divisional lieutenants and the College Instructor Officers. The instruction covered seamanship, navigation, engineering, communications, torpedoes and gunnery and was supported by the latest information from the Fleet. Several of the Beattys discovered that their Dartmouth notebooks contained more detailed and complete information on some subjects than they received anywhere else, even in establishments specialising in those subjects.

On the Beattys' staff, The Bodger was the most competent lecturer.

'The Beaufort Scale,' he said one morning, 'is a convenient method of expressing the forces of winds. Naval officers are supposed to be like fishermen. They exaggerate everything. What you and I would call a howling gale, having been through it, some civil servant sitting on his bottom in a safe office ashore will call a slight chop. But if they see a number, they might possibly believe you. It's all done by numbers. Nought is defined as calm with a wind speed of less than one knot. Smoke rises vertically, branches of trees are motionless, whole day's play at Old Trafford, farmers complain of drought, and so on. Six is a strong breeze. Wind twenty-two to twenty-seven knots. Smacks have double reefs, large branches in motion, telegraph wires whistle, you can't put up an umbrella, farmers complain about the apple crop, and so on. Twelve is a hurricane and if you're ever in one you won't need a Beaufort or any other kind of scale to tell you about it. Defined as wind speeds above sixty-five knots, widespread damage inland, Air Ministry roof blown off, yacht crews take up dry-fly fishing, Wilfred Pickles organises Relief Fund, farmers complain of floods and so on. So much for the Beaufort Scale. Any questions? Maconochie?'

'Have you ever been in one, sir?'

'Hurricane? A couple. During the war.'

'Which war was that, sir?'

'Ha bloody ha ha,' said The Bodger grimly.

'But sir, I didn't mean—!'

'Never mind.'

The Bodger knew some worth two of that. Later in the lecture he dealt with lights.

'When you see a light at sea, the *first* thing you do is take a bearing of it. Don't worry about whether it's the *Queen Mary* on a collision course or a seagull all lit up. Take a bearing *first*, and then take action. Maconochie, what's the first thing you do when you sight a light at sea?'

'Take a bearing, sir.'

'Correct. Now, the different types of light. Navigational lights can be red, white or green. No other lights are allowed. So if you see a ship exhibiting purple, blue or puce lights it's probably the Dartmouth ferry or an American liner. Now open your Seamanship Manuals at the section devoted to lights and you will see some pages of beautifully coloured examples.'

The Beattys opened their books and studied the examples.

'You will see that they are all quite logical. Are they not, Maconochie?'

'Yes, sir.'

'Now, Maconochie, supposing you are in a ship and you wish to indicate that you are a vessel over a hundred and fifty feet in length aground on a reef at night having just previously been streaming seine nets to starboard and acting as plane-guard for *Ark Royal*, what lights would *you*, Maconochie, as Officer of the Watch, immediately and unhesitatingly order to be hoisted?'

'Two black balls, sir?'

'Two black balls, Maconochie, indicate that your ship is not under control, which would be a reasonable assumption, but there would hardly be much object in hoisting two black balls at night, would there? Now Maconochie, leaving your personal feelings aside, double round the parade ground repeating slowly and reverently the while—"I must exhibit two black balls when out of control in the daytime *only*"—until I tell you to come back.

'And now, gentlemen, where were we? Lights, black balls, yes. Incidentally the sort of time you hoist black balls is when the steering gear breaks down or the quartermaster has a fit. You hoist them when you're temporarily out of control . . . yes?'

'Would you hoist them when you're refuelling at sea, sir?' asked Tom Bowles.

'Yes, good question, you certainly would. You're not a free agent and to a certain extent you're not under control so while you're actually connected by hose or line to another vessel you would hoist them. Right now. . . .'

Maconochie had the unfortunate faculty of being, when out of sight, out of mind also. Half an hour later, the Matron of the College was surprised to see a cadet approaching a state of exhaustion staggering round the parade ground, muttering.

'I'm sorry, Matron,' panted Maconochie. 'But I've got to exhibit two black balls when I'm out of control.'

Lieutenant Mathewson was divisional officer for the Quarter-deck and responsible for the Beattys' engineering instruction. He lectured on one morning a week to all the Beattys at once. The sight of eighty cadets gathered together in one room would have daunted most men. Lieutenant Mathewson was in the position of lecturing on subjects which he had never quite understood himself. He found the Beattys awkward. Nor was he such a facile speaker as The Bodger.

'The Closed Feed System,' he said, 'is the main artery of the ship's main engines. If anything happens to the Closed Feed System the ship immediately comes to a grinding halt, all the lights go out and there's a great shouting and tumult.'

Lieutenant Mathewson paused. It had been a good opening. He wondered how to go on.

'In the old days ships had Open Feed Systems but they found that the stokers used to tip fag ends and whatnot into it so they scrubbed round and fitted a Closed Feed System. We'll deal with the feed system in the Boiler Room first. You all know the difference between a Boiler Room and Engine Room, I suppose? I told you last week? Good. Now if you look at the drawing on the board you'll see. . . . It's no good asking me questions, you at the back, I haven't told you anything to ask questions *about* yet. Where was I? Feed System in the Boiler Room. First of all, you've got a doofah thing, this *valve* which admits feed water to the boiler. . . . Yes, what *is* it? Do you want to go outside or something?'

'Sir, that drawing on the board says Feed System in the *Engine Room,* sir.'

'So it does. Sandy must have got the drawings mixed up. *Sandy!'*

An elderly man wearing blue overalls looked through a small door at the side of the lecture room. Sandy was one of the battalion of pensioners, the hall-porters, gardeners, boilermen, storekeepers, boats' crews, stewards and sweepers without whom the internal domestic workings of Dartmouth and of every other shore establishment in the Navy would quietly, but surely, have come to a halt. They were the men who knew the local tides and the local tradesmen. They remembered where the swings and slides had been put after last year's children's party. They also knew where the drawings for Lieutenant Mathewson's lectures were kept.

'Never mind, Sandy. I'll make do with this one.'

'No, I'll get it, sir, I'll get it.'

Sandy ferreted about in a small cupboard behind his door. He took out a rolled drawing, carried it across to the blackboard, and hung it over the other drawing.

'Sorry, Sandy.'

'If yew doan't tell me, sir, how kin I know? I say, if yew doan't tell me nothin', how'm I to know?'

Sandy retreated behind the small door.

'Well, we're all set now. Feed system in the Boiler Room. You know, I've changed my mind. I think we'll do the Engine Room first, after all. You at the end of the front row. Come up and take this drawing down. Don't let Sandy hear you, for God's sake.

'That's right. Engine Room. In the Engine Room you have a condenser, that's this doofah here, a closed feed controller, that's this little widger here, and an extraction pump. The condenser, as its name implies, condenses steam into water after it's left the turbine. I forget now whether I told you about turbines? I did? Good. These whatsits here are tubes. The main circulators push sea water through the tubes to condense the steam. If you get a leak in one of those tubes there's a real nausea. You get salt water in the closed feed system. Condenseritis, it's called. Keeps Senior Engineers awake at night. . . .'

The Beattys were as closely supervised out of their working hours as they were in the class-room. Each cadet had to take part in one of the College activities in the evenings. The cadets noted their activities in a log which The Bodger inspected once a week. Any cadet who had spent more than one day in the week skulking, by which The Bodger meant not playing cricket or sailing, was summoned to The Bodger's office.

Spink was the most frequent skulker.

'Look here, Spink,' said The Bodger. 'On Monday last you went shooting and a week ago on Thursday you went on the river. That's fair enough. I'm not complaining about that. But every other day for the last fortnight you've been bird-watching, butterfly-catching, or fossil-hunting. What's all this about?'

'There are some very interesting specimens in this part of the country, sir,' said Spink.

'Spink, my dear old *chap*. When I was at Dartmouth I was the best bird-watcher in my term. There wasn't a bird for miles around I hadn't watched. And as for butterfly-catching, no butterfly from here to Totnes was safe until I passed out of Dartmouth. I must admit I never thought of fossil-hunting, but what I'm getting at is this . . . there's nothing anybody can teach me about bird-watching, butterfly-catching, fossil-hunting or any other kind of watching, catching or hunting. You people seem to think that I and all the staff came out of the egg the day before yesterday. Now listen, Spink. I'm not interested in your private

51

hobbies. That's not what you're here for. You can do that during your leave. While you're here you will join in the College activities as laid down by the College. Is that understood?'

'Yes, sir.'

'And you can tell Dewberry and the other nature boys what I've told you. Right?'

'Yes, sir.'

'Carry on, Spink.'

Spink was in the minority. Most of the Beattys needed no urging to take part in the sports provided by the College. It was, perhaps, the only part of their training on which they and the College were completely in agreement. Most of them had played games at school and now played them at Dartmouth, if not with an excess of zeal at least out of a hope that some astonishing feat of athletics would lift them for a short time from the general ruck of the term. The Bodger was not so impressed by these feats as the Beattys imagined, but he recognised the part games could play in transforming the Beattys from a crowd of schoolboys of different schools into a composite term of cadets with a feeling of comradeship in their term and, eventually, in the Navy.

Almost half the Beattys went regularly on the river and half normally played cricket. Tom Bowles was attracted to the river as soon as he came to Dartmouth. He had seldom sailed a boat before, but within a month on the River Dart he had learnt more about sailing small boats than most naval officers learn in a lifetime. Tom Bowles was able to sense the smallest quirk of wind and current and quickly became the best coxswain in the term except for David Bowie, a New Zealander, who had started with advantages, having been able to swim before he could walk and having spent a large part of his childhood sailing in Auckland harbour.

Michael Hobbes and Paul Vincent played cricket, Paul for the reason he had given the Interview Board, that it was his only sport, and Michael because it was summer. Michael had played cricket in the summer at school and it would have seemed peculiar to him not to do so now that he was at Dartmouth.

Maconochie also played cricket. He could not bat, neither

could he bowl, but he could field. After some practice and the confidence of a few catches, Maconochie developed into a quite remarkable fielder close to the bat.

Cleghorn and Stacforth played tennis and Dewberry, the College orchestra having no french horn, learnt to play the trumpet. He noted it in the log as 'athletic training.'

Some College activities were held after supper. One of them was the Dancing Class.

The Dancing Class was taught by the wife of a College master. Partners were provided by other masters' wives, by the nursing sisters from the hospital and by various other ladies in the College whom The Bodger loftily referred to as 'the camp-followers one gets in any great establishment.'

The dancing took place to the music of a gramophone. The College had a limited stock of records and cadets who went to the classes for any length of time became accustomed to them and to no others. The Dartmouth Dancing Class was thus responsible for the widely held belief amongst naval wives that naval officers can only dance to certain tunes and only then when they have had sufficient to drink.

None of the Beattys except Raymond Ball attended the Dancing Class. One or two of them tried, Michael among them, because they felt that dancing, however repugnant, was an accomplishment they should possess.

On the one occasion when Michael attended the Dancing Class he was ordered, on entering the room, to take up his position for what sounded to him to be The Promenade Whisk with Sideways Chassé. Michael turned and bolted and never returned. It seemed that the Dancing Class had been going on since the College was built. Michael had no doubt that at one time, possibly between the wars, the class had been learning simple steps. But they had now progressed into the realms of fantasy and there seemed no way of bringing them back.

Raymond Ball was the exception. He was an experienced chevalier of the chassé, a paladin of the palais, a hardened veteran of many campaigns, from the Lyceum to Hammersmith. He was probably the first cadet ever to have come to Dartmouth with a Gold Medal for Ballroom Dancing. He was a triton amongst the minnows at the College class and even the class teacher, who was holding perspiring cadets at arm's length before Raymond Ball was born, had to admit herself outclassed.

But for most of the Beattys the time between supper and going to bed was the only time of the day which they could call their own and they preferred not to spend it in such cold-blooded pursuits as ballroom dancing. Evening was the time for reflection, for unbuckling the spirit after the exertions of the day. It was the only time when the Beattys could attempt to take stock of what was happening to them at Dartmouth.

'What amazes me,' Paul said in the chest flat one evening, 'is the emphasis they put on trivial things. If you can climb a rope, you're made. If you can tie bloody silly knots, you've got a great future in the service. What are they getting at? What's it all leading up to? Do they *want* a lot of performing monkeys or what do they want?'

'It's almost like a continuation of school,' said Michael. 'But not quite. They seem to put a kind of pressure on you which school never did.'

'They take it so *seriously*, too. This place must cost thousands to keep up. What've we got tomorrow?'

Michael consulted a timetable which he made out for each week. He was a methodical boy and wrote on his timetable his work and recreation for every hour of every day. The timetable was neatly ruled off and gave times to the nearest minute. Paul and the rest of the chest flat found it invaluable.

'P.T. tomorrow. . . .'

'Oh Lord.'

'. . . Then The Bodger for Ship Organisation, Chipperd for Anchors and Cables, Chief G.I. for Parade Training. In the afternoon we've got the Schooly for navigation. In the Dogs we've got that match against the Officers and Masters. After supper the Bodger again on Leadership. Tomorrow's also the day we've got to enter our marks for throwing the heaving line. . . .'

'Enough, enough. 'Tis not so deep as a well or so wide as a church door but 'tis enough. 'Twill serve. Will there be time for me to go to the heads sometime, do you think? Still, we must just take each day as it comes. Does the road wind uphill all the way?'

'To the bitter end,' said Michael, who was now used to Paul, and recognised his cue.

'And shall we find other Beattys on the way?'

'Day and night, my friend,' said Michael.

A long low note on a bosun's call sounded outside the window of the chest flat. It was the Night Rounds Party and Isaiah Nine Smith, the Chief Cadet of the Day, sounding the Still. The long low note ended and was succeeded by the voice of Mr Froud, chastising the author of the note. Clearly, the Still should be a long, high note.

Spink was standing rounds for the chest flat. He rehearsed his report, repeating it to himself over and over again.

'Number one chest flat cleared for rounds, sir, nineteen cadets present, temperature fifty-five degrees Fahrenheit. Number one chest flat cleared for rounds, sir, nineteen cadets present, temperature fifty-five degrees Fahrenheit, sir.'

The Still, now wavering between high and low, came nearer and stopped outside. Spink braced himself. The Night Rounds Party, a small cavalcade led by Isaiah Nine Smith carrying a lighted lantern, followed by Mr Froud with the Chief G.I. bringing up the rear, came into the chest flat.

'This lantern doth the horned moon present,' murmured Paul, under the blankets.

Spink saluted.

'Number one chest flat cleared for rounds, sir, fifty-five cadets present, temperature nineteen degrees Fahrenheit, sir.'

'Oh blessed Bottom, thou art translated.'

Paul's silent laughter stopped when Mr Froud stood at the foot of his bed.

'All right, Vincent. Up to the surface.'

'Sir?'

'Were you bathroom sweeper tonight?'

'Sir.'

'Turn out and swab the deck again and square off the basins.'

'Sir.'

The Night Rounds Party disappeared towards the other chest flats, their progress marked by the banshee wailing of Isaiah Nine Smith's bosun's call.

Paul turned out. Five minutes later he was back again.

'See what I mean,' he whispered to Michael as he climbed back into bed.

Their new life reacted on individual Beattys in markedly different ways. Those who had been first to preparatory and then to public schools found the transition easiest. They merely exchanged the petty tyrannies and traditional idiosyncrasies of their schools for those of the Navy. They were not mature enough to understand that the fads of a public school may be left behind with the school but those fads inculcated by the Navy could become lifetime habits. They did not feel the separation from their families keenly because they had been separated from their families for long periods before they joined the Navy. The lack of privacy did not trouble them because they had never known privacy except in the short holidays they had spent at home. Theirs was a simple transition from the semi-monastic existence of a public school to the semi-monastic existence of Dartmouth.

Michael and Paul were among this group. Michael in particular found the adjustment to Dartmouth easy as though, as he said, it were a continuation of school. The Bodger regarded Michael Hobbes as almost the norm of the Beattys. He was still diffident but eager to do well. He was intelligent enough to do all that was asked of him but not intelligent enough to enquire into motives. Properly led and carefully taught, he would make a servant who would serve the Navy faithfully and according to its demands upon him as long as he was able. Since he had been at Dartmouth The Bodger had developed the knack of picking out boys who were ideal subjects for training, as a salesman learns to pick out a genuine customer. Michael Hobbes was, in The Bodger's opinion, a genuine customer.

Paul, on the other hand, adjusted himself to Dartmouth just

as easily but was more critical of its motives. He appeared to the staff to be looking at the Navy with quizzical eyes. He was sure that he could make a success of it but he was not yet sure that it was worth making a success of. He was apparently suspending judgment on the Navy until it had proved to him that, behind the façade, it provided a satisfying fulfilment. He carried out his duties as well as any cadet in the term but The Bodger gained the impression that he was doing his best only through allegiance to himself and not yet through any allegiance to the Navy. The boy was balanced on an edge. He could make the best type of officer of all, or he could grow embittered later, lose his ambitions and, because he was a forceful and persuasive character, cause others to lose theirs.

The cadets who had been to day schools, or to schools which do not give their pupils the same early experience of human foibles as the major public schools, found Dartmouth more difficult. Dartmouth seemed to these cadets a series of furious and seemingly pointless rushes from place to place. They were always one of a herd of milling bodies. They were always pestered. They were always late. Their lives had become a succession of sorties from one period of futile occupation to another, the whole mad stampede being carried out at the whim of a group of insane megalomaniacs in uniform.

Maconochie and Raymond Ball were typical. Maconochie had the further disadvantage that he suffered from illusions of personal grandeur. He had come into the Navy prepared to take it in his stride with his own charm and polished personality. Maconochie considered himself a finished product and found it impossible to accept the Navy's view of him, as the rawest of raw material. Dartmouth took his self-assurance by storm, trapped him, and exposed the inexperience underneath. The process of destroying Maconochie's egotism, which Paul had begun almost instinctively in the train on the way to Dartmouth, was completed by the Navy so quickly that Maconochie found himself struggling to maintain his place in the term after a few months.

Raymond Ball was superficially the same as Maconochie but he differed in one important aspect. Maconochie's self-confidence

57

was easily shattered; Raymond Ball's never would be. The Bodger thought him very promising material for that reason. Raymond Ball's allegiance was, like Paul's, to himself but unlike Paul's it would never be to anything else. Raymond Ball would make a successful naval officer until the time came for him to make a choice between the Navy and himself.

Tom Bowles was in a class quite by himself. Once in twenty years there arrives at a gymnasium a boy whom the trainers and managers recognise immediately as a natural fighter and a probable champion. Similarly at Dartmouth, in about the same period of time, a boy joins the Navy whom the training staff know is the one they have been looking for. Such a boy is the final goal of the interviewing board and the consummation of their hopes, the boy cut out, marked and destined for the highest rewards the Royal Navy offered.

One last and very small category of Beattys, headed by Dewberry and Spink, allowed nothing to trouble them. They plunged from place to place as they were directed but they neither hurried nor did they fuss. They had already decided that joining the Navy had been a ghastly mistake and nothing now could make it any more so. The Bodger worried about these cadets but saw no solution except to ease them out of the Navy as soon as possible.

4

'SOME time next week you are all going to spend a day in an aircraft carrier. Those of you who want to be pilots, and there are bound to be some, I suppose, will have a chance to see the kind of thing a Fleet Air Arm pilot does. Those of you who don't want to be pilots will see what you're escaping. Now I'm not going to try to influence you one way or the other about flying. It's quite immaterial to me how you end your miserable existences but speaking as a small ship man myself, I personally want to see my grandchildren running round my knees and piping in childish treble voices: "What did *you* do during the war, Grandaddy?" and I shall say: "Say thank you now to Grandaddy for not being a pilot during the war else you wouldn't be here to ask that".'

The Bodger paused and regarded his audience. The Beattys stared back solemnly. It was impossible to tell from their expressions whether they were contemplating the life of an aviator or merely imagining one of The Bodger's grandchildren.

'Whether you like the idea of flying or not,' continued The Bodger, 'there isn't one of you here who won't be directly concerned with the Fleet Air Arm some time during your service career. Some of you will actually be pilots or observers. Some of you will serve on air stations. Most of you will go to carriers when you go to sea. You will all be concerned in some way. Flying now is the main armament of the Navy. It's here to stay in a big way and you'd better get used to it.'

The Bodger need not have used such emphasis. He was addressing members of a generation who had never known a world without aircraft, to whom the most refined techniques of aerial warfare, up to and including the nuclear bomb, were commonplace. They had been in their cradles when Kingsford-Smith flew the Pacific and Byrd flew over the South Pole, toddlers when Amy Johnson reached Australia, and they were starting kindergarten when the Luftwaffe were trying their wings over Spain. They had been the first generation in the history of the world to look out of a class-room window on a summer afternoon and see a fleet of heavy bombers in the sky. Their lessons were learnt to the running undertone, like distant gunfire, of the great deeds of Taranto, *Ark Royal,* the hunt for the *Bismarck,* the bursting of the dams, Midway and the Battle of the Coral Sea. They had collected pieces of shrapnel and the tailfins of incendiary bombs as assiduously as they had earlier collected sea-shells and pebbles and they had all wanted to be pilots when they grew up with as fierce a desire as they had previously wanted to be engine-drivers. The techniques of survival had become as familiar to them as the school time-table. They marched by classes down to the shelters, in dressing-gowns and carrying their cocoa-cups, as unconcernedly as though they were filing into morning prayers. They enjoyed air raids and a boy who was fortunate enough to have his home bombed became a school celebrity and was pointed out as such to visiting parents.

Although the Beattys had forgotten details, traces of their knowledge, like the last instinctive remnants of an ancient lore, still remained and taken as an average the Beattys knew more about aircraft than The Bodger—a small ship man on his own admission—knew himself.

The question of whether or not to be a pilot caused sharp differences of opinion amongst the Beattys. Although The Bodger's speech could hardly qualify as a recruiting talk, it reminded the Beattys that sooner or later in the Navy they would be called upon to choose the particular specialisation, within their present branch, in which they wished to serve.

Tom Bowles was the leader of the faction who wanted to be pilots. He was supported by Isaiah Nine Smith.

'What attracts you so much about it, Tom?' asked Michael.

'I don't know. It's exciting, and it needs a lot of skill. It gives you a chance to be independent and act on your own a bit. I just know I want to do it.'

'You get paid more, too,' said Isaiah Nine Smith.

'Judging by what The Bodger said, I imagine they pay you more because they don't have to pay you for so long,' said Paul.

'Oh, go and get knotted,' said Tom.

The aircraft carrier anchored off Dartmouth in the early morning and the cadets were taken off to her by drifter. They were met on board by midshipmen who split the Beattys up into parties of ten and guided them up to the island to watch the flight deck being prepared for flying.

The midshipman looking after Paul and Michael was more friendly than they had expected. He was an ex-Beatty himself.

'I'm Tim Castlewood,' he said. 'I'm supposed to show you characters what gives in this mighty vessel. How's Beatty these days? Is old Froud still spitting fire and brimstone?'

'He is,' said Paul.

'He's O.K. when you get to know him. You should hear him singing "The Harlot of Jerusalem".'

Paul tried to imagine Mr Froud singing 'The Harlot of Jerusalem,' but his imagination jibbed. It was easier to imagine the Loch Ness Monster singing 'Annie Laurie.'

Tim Castlewood led the way out on to a narrow platform jutting out from the island. He took off his cap.

'Off caps, fellows. No caps allowed while flying is in progress.'

'What's the idea of that?' asked Maconochie.

'It might blow off and get in a pilot's way or get caught in something. It's safer to take them off and hold them in your hands while you're goofing.'

'Goofing?'

'Watching the flying. Anyone who watches the flying is known as a goofer. Where you're standing now is a goofing position.'

61

Down below, the flight deck was being made ready for flying. Men in coloured flight deck helmets were handling aircraft off the lifts and on to the flight deck. Small red trucks drove in and out, towing aircraft to be ranged aft where more men stood waiting with chocks. Other parties were preparing the catapult loaders, laying out bridles and hold-backs, trundling starting trolleys and tail-wheel forks, and unreeling fuelling hoses. Two men in heavy white suits and steel helmets with axes thrust in their belts stood by the large flight deck mobile crane at the after end of the island. The work was directed by unintelligible barks over the flight deck broadcast.

The aircraft were ranged in two lines down each side of the after end of the flight deck. The pilots walked out from a door in the island, carrying their helmets in their hands, and manned their aircraft. A pilot's mate in overalls leant over each cockpit and strapped the pilot in.

The carrier had increased speed and turned into the wind. The wind buffeted the island with increasing strength. The ship's wake curved in a long crescent of eddies fringed on its outside edge by small tumbling waves.

'We've got to turn into the wind,' said Tim Castlewood. 'We need about thirty knots over the deck. There's quite a lot of wind today. Sometimes we boil up and down the Channel for a whole day looking for wind.'

The flight deck was silent and ready. Everything now depended upon the wind. A meteorological rating stood by the catapults with an anemometer and signalled the wind speed to the bridge.

'When Flyco gives them the tip they'll taxi up one by one to the catapults and be boosted off. The catapults are those two tracks you can see running up to the forrard end of the flight deck.' Tim Castlewood was watching the wind speed signals. 'That's it. They'll start up any minute now. Of course, you've got to remember that we're in no hurry today. If this was an operational strike this would all be done much faster.'

A voice counted out the last seconds over the broadcast.

'*Five. Four. Three. Two. One. . . . Start!*'

Puffs of smoke appeared at the cowlings. An engine fired and

62

was joined by two or three more and finally by all. The sound expanded and beat against the island until the Beattys could feel it through their shoes and in their bones. The propeller blades swung slowly and idly, spun faster, until their individual profiles merged in a shimmering disc. The two rows of inanimate aircraft were alive and throbbing. The flight deck had come to life.

Yellow-jacketed directors signalled the chocks away and motioned the aircraft forward, round and up the flight deck towards the catapults. The directors stood at intervals to accept the aircraft from each other and pass it on to their successors.

The sound grew to an almost unbearable crescendo as the first aircraft came past the island and jolted on to the catapult. The bridle and hold-back were hooked on. The Flight Deck Officer held up a green flag. The aircraft flattened its wheels on the flight deck and strained against the hold-back while the pilot opened the throttle. At full throttle the aircraft crouched on the catapult with its engine screaming, quivering in an attitude of restrained power. The group of handlers squatting between the catapults put their hands to their ears. The Flight Deck Officer whirled the green flag.

The Flight Deck Officer glanced forward, then aft, and dropped the flag. The hold-back flew apart. The aircraft shot away, skimmed along the flight deck, out over the sea and climbed away from the ship. The Flight Deck Officer turned and held up the green flag again for the next aircraft already waiting on the other catapult.

One after the other the aircraft were secured on the catapult, worked up to full power and launched from the ship. The last aircraft dipped over the end of the flight deck, while the Beattys caught their breaths, and slowly climbed again, flying in a crab-like motion sideways and upwards. The flight deck was silent again.

'Not good,' murmured Tim Castlewood.

'Does anyone ever get launched straight into the sea?' asked Maconochie.

'Occasionally someone gets a cold shot but it's only very occasionally and even then nine times out of ten it's something to do with the engine. It's not normally the catapults. This ship has never yet given anyone a cold shot. Touch wood. Most of the cheap thrills come when they're landing on. This particular lot are pretty good though. I don't expect we'll see any expensive sights today.'

The flying display continued. Aircraft took off and were put through their paces. They dropped bombs and fired rockets at a splash target. They power-dived and flattened out just over the ship. They flew past the ship in formation. Every hour a fresh detail took off and the previous detail landed on. The show was beautifully timed and carried out. The flight deck drill was impeccable.

'It's been a good day,' said Tim Castlewood as they watched the last aircraft fly low over the ship and turn into the landing circuit.

The batsman stood out on his small platform, shaking his flags to stream them in the wind, and waited, arms stretched and feet straddled to receive the aircraft.

As the aircraft crossed the round-down the batsman's flags cut sharply out of sight. The aircraft appeared to hang in the air, then dropped and a burst of vapour flew from each side of the wheels as they touched the deck. The aircraft bounced, struck the deck again, missed all the wires and in a slow lazy glide curved into the barrier.

After the first sound of tearing metal there was a moment of silence, a total suspension of movement like the sudden holding of a breath. Then simultaneously the shape of the aircraft dissolved in a gout of fire and the flight deck swarmed with running figures.

Hoses were run out by men who stumbled and scrambled in their haste. Two jets of foam soared out over the fire and were followed by two more and by two more until their streams merged and covered the aircraft in a blanket of foam. The heat of the fire was intense enough to touch the cheeks of the men watching from the island. A cap dropped from the island and floated downwards. It landed in front of one of the men in fireproof suits who trod on it, kicked it into the foam, and advanced

64

onwards into the fire. The two men in the ponderous suits vanished into the smoke and re-emerged with the pilot between them. Standing dwarfed by the helmeted inhuman figures on either side of him, the pilot looked up into the island and smiled. Paul thought it a terrible smile, like Christian's after the death of Apollyon.

'Jesus!' breathed Paul. 'I thought he'd had it.'

Tim Castlewood nodded. 'So did he, I guess. The Martians in the suits were pretty quick or he would have had his chips. Lucky it stayed the right way up. If it had turned upside down, I reckon that character would have had the chop.'

'Bloody idiot,' said a pilot wearing a beret who was standing near the Beattys.

'Why, sir?' asked Paul.

'Playing to the gallery. Who does he think he is, a bloody gladiator? He's damned lucky he didn't bounce over the side, poling his stick about like a ——.'

'You there! You with that bloody idiotic grin on your face! That *trog* there!'

The Beattys and the other goofers turned to see who was shouting.

It was the carrier's Commander (Air). He was a tubby man with white hair and cheeks the colour and roundness of a peony. He was known as the best children's party Santa Claus from Lee-on-Solent to Lossiemouth but now, as he stood at the door of Flyco and shouted at the Beattys, it was hard to picture him in the part.

'You, halfway down there! Stand *back* the rest of you!'

'Me, sir?' asked Maconochie.

'Yes, YOU, blast you! What the hell's the use of our making you trogs take your scrofulous caps off if you're going to let go of them every time you hear a bang? Like a bloody girls' school giggling and chattering and dropping your handbags! I don't know where you're going in the future, trog, but keep out of the Fleet Air Arm!'

Commander (Air) stumped back into Flyco and slammed the door.

'Golly yes,' said Tim Castlewood, 'I'd forgotten about the cap. I knew there'd be a nausea about it. Get a grip, for God's sake,' he said to Maconochie. *'Trog!'*

The last flames had already been extinguished and the blackened, foam-smothered aircraft was surrounded by men with cranes and lifting tackle like scavenging ants, who hoisted the carcass up and dropped it over the side into the sea. Other men with brooms and hoses swept and hosed the foam off the flight deck and down into the scuppers. A third party removed the wrecked barrier and erected a new one. In half an hour no trace of the crash remained except a damp patch on the flight deck and a heap of torn wire near the starboard walkway.

The crash had been more spectacular than serious; less dramatic crashes had done more damage to other aircraft and had killed the pilots. But it made a deep impression on the Beattys. Those like Paul who did not wish to be pilots had had their objections given concrete and spectacular form and those who did, like Tom Bowles, were given food for thought.

A few days after the visit to the carrier, four Motor Torpedo Boats came to Dartmouth. They were under the command of a large black-bearded Lieutenant-Commander whom The Bodger greeted as an old friend and drinking partner. Although he had only come to Dartmouth for the night because he did not like the weather report and wished to renew his acquaintance with a few of the local hostelries, Blackbeard consented, after some talk and several beers, to take the Beattys out in his boats for a forenoon.

'Provided,' he said, 'they're not sick, don't tread on my toes and don't ask bloody silly questions. For you, Bodger, I'll do it. Now tell me, Bodger, how the hell did you get this job at Dartmouth. . . .?'

Once out of the harbour, the boats opened up to forty knots, flinging clouds of spray to either side and leaving a broad path of boiling water behind them. Blackbeard showed off his boats as though they were chorus-girls. He made them turn in line ahead and abreast, keep close station at full speed, weave and dodge between each other, and split apart and come together in station again. They practised torpedo and gun attacks on each other and exercised man overboard with a buoy.

After two hours at forty knots, the initial thrill had worn off. The boats had finished their evolutions and the cadets had been shown the torpedo tubes, the guns and the depth charges. There seemed nothing more to do except go back to Dartmouth. The Beattys were therefore relieved rather than alarmed when Maconochie created a diversion by falling overboard when the boats were turning at high speed.

When Blackbeard's attention had been drawn to Maconochie's head bobbing in the wake, his first proposal was apparently to leave him there. But when he saw that the other boats had also sighted Maconochie and were turning to pick him up, Blackbeard thrust his quartermaster aside and seized the wheel himself. He flexed his mighty fingers on the spokes, hauled the boat round by main force, and directed it towards the now sounding Maconochie.

The four Motor Torpedo Boats converged on Maconochie at a combined speed of more than seventy miles an hour. Just as it seemed that Maconochie was certain to have his head removed from his shoulders, Blackbeard throttled down and stopped. The other boats bucketed by, throwing sheets of spray and derisive shouts over Blackbeard, his boat, and Maconochie. Blackbeard tightened his lips.

Maconochie was hauled on board, dripping.

Blackbeard leaned out of his tiny bridge.

'Come here, excrement!'

'Cadet Maconochie, sir,' said Maconochie, saluting.

'I don't care what your bloody name is,' growled Blackbeard. 'You listen to me. I didn't want you in my ship anyway and it's only because your training officer is a friend of mine and you're on his slop-chit that I didn't run you down just now. I don't know which branch of the service you're thinking of joining but don't come in boats! Understand?

'Yes, sir!'

* * *

67

The third visit of the term involved the Beattys in more personal effort. It was a four-day cruise in a destroyer of the Plymouth Local Flotilla. The Beattys were to join on Friday morning and leave late on Monday evening.

The cruise was treated as an evolution. The Beattys were prepared for it with lectures, demonstrations and extra kit as carefully as though they were all about to embark on a polar expedition.

The Chief Bosun's Mate gave a lecture and demonstration of that most intricate piece of naval architecture, the hammock.

'When you've got your 'mick slung between two hooks, you stand on the right side of the 'mick, that's the left side looking towards the head, with your lashing in your right hand. Let's see if you've got that.'

The Chief Bosun's Mate passed along the row of cadets and still unlashed hammocks.

'Get a bit closer, lad. That's right. Then you takes your lashing in your *left* hand and you pass the end over your 'mick with your right hand, bring it under and back to your left hand making half hitches all the way down the 'mick as you go. Seven half hitches there should be, one for each day of the week. Now you try it. Pass it over, half hitch, pass it over. *Half* hitch Monday, passitover, alfitch Tuesday, passitover, alfitch Wednesday, passitover. Alfitch Thursday. Alfitch Friday. I knew it. I *knew* it! You've got it all balled up. I don't see as how you *could* get it wrong, I don't. Cor, what a bunch o' coconuts. Never seen such a bunch o' knitting. Now stand back a bit! Let's have a look'ere you, for Chrissakes. Mention Wise Owl once more and I'll crown you, I will!'

The Bodger lectured on ship life in general. He outlined the appropriate Beatty action for every major disaster, from abandoning the ship to an outbreak of scurvy. The Bodger enjoyed his lectures.

'The sharp end at the front is called the bows and the blunt end at the back is called the stern.

'Don't call them lavatories, they're heads, and they're not portholes, you only have port-holes in P. & O. boats, they're scuttles.

'Don't forget to salute the quarterdeck when you go on board. It's a very old service custom, the kind of thing people outside the Navy spend their time trying to find the origin of. Keeps 'em out of mischief. For you and me it's sufficient that it's an old service custom. There's no need to salute twice and ask permission to come on board like they do in American films, just salute and get out of the way and keep out of the way. I've heard that some of you haven't been too successful in keeping out of the way of senior officers on previous visits. I recommend you do it this time. Keep out of the Captain's way until after breakfast, in fact if I were you I'd keep out of his way all the time. He's a very old friend of mine and he doesn't like cadets, least of all Special Entry cadets. The Engineer Officer is called the "Chief" but don't let me hear any of you calling him that. He doesn't like cadets either.

'You will live on one of the messdecks and pretty sordid it will be too, I can promise you. Try to learn as much as you can from the ship's company although I don't imagine they're very fond of cadets either.

'If you have to abandon ship, it's no good rushing for the Carley floats, there are only enough for the ship's company. Wait for the pipe "Abandon ship, stand fast cadets" and then jump.

'There's nothing you can do about an attack of scurvy, anyway. You should have been drinking lime juice for the last six months and as they haven't got any limers for you to drink in any case you'll just have to lump it.'

The Beattys wondered what manner of ship this was, which seemed to combine the most sinister characteristics of an Arab slave trading dhow and the *Altmark,* and what sort of man commanded her, who appeared to be a crossbred of Captain Bligh and the Angel of the Lord.

The ship was the *Rowbottom,* a wartime emergency class destroyer in need of a good scrub down and a coat of paint. Her Captain was a pale Lieutenant-Commander with hair as red as Swinburne's and a delicate complexion, as though he had just stepped from a pre-Raphaelite painting.

In spite of his saintly appearance, the Captain was hailed by

The Bodger with an ecstatic roar of greeting as the Dartmouth boat came alongside.

'*Poggles,* old wineskin! How's life?'

Poggles looked down from his bridge, whither he had retreated to watch the advance of the cadets, and smiled weakly. He waved a weary hand.

'Passing fair,' murmured Poggles wanly. He raised the hand which he had not previously waved and took a sip out of the beer tankard he held in it. 'Bearing up, you know. How's yourself?'

'Fine, you old lecher!' roared The Bodger.

Poggles winced.

'Come up and have a grog.'

Poggles had another glass of beer ready for The Bodger.

'Cheers, Poggles.'

'Cheers, Bodger.'

'Where are the proletariat going to live?'

'After messdeck. Same as last time. Not very palatial but there isn't anywhere else.'

Poggles looked over the bridge parapet at the cadets coming on board. There seemed to be hundreds of them. They were swarming up out of the boat, humping their bags and hammocks. The iron deck was already alive with overawed cadets wondering where to go without getting in the way.

Poggles cupped his hands.

'Petty Officer Moody!'

A tall Petty Officer who had been forced against the guard-rail by the press of cadets looked up.

'Show these cadets their messdeck.'

Poggles came back and resumed his beer.

'Bolshie-looking lot you've got this time, Bodger?'

'That's the cream of England you've got there, boy.'

'Don't joke,' said Poggles.

He sipped his beer meditatively. He was an imaginative man. He imagined the Beattys living in their messdeck. He closed his eyes and a faint shudder shook his frame. So might Bishop Hatto have thought of the rats swarming into his tower, knowing that the tower was stiff with rat poison.

Petty Officer Moody made no comment on the messdeck. He indicated it with his thumb and stood back for the cadets to go down.

Rowbottom operated with a reduced complement and the after messdeck was normally used for storing equipment. It had not been used as a human habitation for some time, not in fact since the previous term of Beattys had lived there, four months before.

One corner of the compartment contained several sacks of potatoes. In the opposite corner were three rusty valves and a red bicycle. A light dusting of dried peas covered the floor except by the ladder where there was an unidentifiable but sinister red stain.

The Beattys were left alone to stow away their gear while *Rowbottom* put to sea. It was not until the ship was outside the harbour that the silent Petty Officer Moody returned and made spasmodic visits to the messdeck. On each visit he selected several cadets with a jerk of his thumb and led them off.

Petty Officer Moody showed the cadets tiny hutch-like compartments in the bridge superstructure which were filled with machines which clicked and whirred. The machines were guarded by troglodytic little men stripped to the waist who perched on stools like gnomes and glared malevolently at the Beattys over the pages of paper-backed novels. Petty Officer Moody did not venture any explanation of the functions of either the machines or the men. The visit, if visit it could be called, was conducted in complete silence.

After a quarter of an hour of muteness, Tom Bowles asked: 'How many gyro compasses has this ship got, P.O.?'

Petty Officer Moody stopped in his tracks. Then he turned and fixed Tom with a basilisk stare. He gazed at Tom menacingly for a few moments. Finally, and reluctantly, he spoke.

'An officer doesn't have to *know* anything,' he said witheringly, as though he were addressing a child who was being wilfully stupid. 'All *you* have to do is stand up there and say "Port Thirty" and then when we're swinging good and proper say "Steer three-two-zero, Quartermaster".'

There were no more questions.

71

Meanwhile, the cadets' messdeck had a new visitor. A grim-visaged Chief Stoker with a complexion like weathered brass poked his head down the hatchway and silently nodded to half a dozen cadets.

The Chief Stoker led the cadets down into tiny hutch-like compartments in the bottom of the ship which were filled with machines which thumped and hissed and spurted clouds of steam. The machines were guarded by troglodytic little men who glared malevolently at the cadets from behind pipes and out of holes in the deck. The Chief Stoker did not venture any explanation of the functions of either the machines or the men. The visit, if visit it could be called, was conducted in complete silence.

After a quarter of an hour of muteness, Maconochie asked: 'What's the horsepower of this ship, Chief?'

The Chief Stoker stopped suddenly, halfway up a ladder, as though he had just felt an excruciating pain in the back. Then he slowly and carefully descended again.

'An officer doesn't have to *know* anything,' he said witheringly as though he were addressing a child who was being wilfully stupid. 'All *you* have to do is say "Carry on, Chief," and shout down and tell me when I'm making smoke.'

There were no more questions.

Back in their messdeck, the Beattys compared notes.

'What did your Petty Officer tell you?'

'Nothing. What did your Chief Stoker tell you?'

'Nothing except an officer doesn't have to know anything.'

'Same here. Chummy lot, aren't they?'

'What I like about these conducted tours,' said Paul, 'is the continual flow of merry chatter and fascinating anecdote from the guide. Never a dull moment, customers kept amused all the time.'

A voice shouted down the hatch.

'Hey! You there!'

'Great heavens!' said Paul. 'A human voice!'

'Who's cook of this mess?'

The Beattys looked at each other.

'Maconochie,' said Paul.

'Well, grub's up!'

'Away you go, Trog,' said Paul encouragingly.

In the afternoon The Bodger produced a timetable and organised tours of the ship. Ratings of various branches called at the cadets' messdeck to conduct the tours. None of them was quite as silent as Petty Officer Moody and the Chief Stoker but on the other hand none of them was talkative. The Beattys could only get them to answer questions with the greatest difficulty. As far as normal human contact was concerned the ship's company of *Rowbottom* were as unco-operative as the men who sailed with the Ancient Mariner. It was as though the entire ship's company had successfully graduated by correspondence course from a Trappist monastery.

While the tours were going on, *Rowbottom* was steadily nearing the island of Guernsey. She anchored there in the calm of a beautiful summer evening. Six Beattys were present on the bridge when Poggles anchored his ship.

'Cox'n,' said Poggles, down the voicepipe.

'Sir?' said Petty Officer Moody.

'See that Bass Bitter advertisement dead ahead?'

'Sir.'

'Steady on that.'

'Steady on Bass Bitter, sir. Aye aye, sir.'

'Slow ahead both engines.'

'Slow ahead together.'

'Slow ahead together, sir. Both engines answered slow ahead, sir.'

'Very good.'

Poggles leaned on the parapet and sniffed the evening air.

'Good night for a run ashore, I think, Bodger. We might take a glass or three of the local vino, what do you think?'

'*Splendid* idea!' replied The Bodger.

'Yes, I think so. A few tots won't do us any harm.'

'Alka-Seltzer bearing one-four-zero, sir,' said *Rowbottom's* Navigating Officer.

'*Alka*-Seltzer?' said Poggles. 'What's Alka-Seltzer got to do with it?'

'Sorry, sir. Hennessy. Three Star, two-five-two, sir.'

'*That's* better. Steady on Guinness, Cox'n.'

'Steady on Guinness, sir. Aye aye, sir.'

'Just coming up to the transit between Martini and Sandeman's Port, sir.'

'Very good. Let me know when we reach Johnny Walker.'

'Aye aye, sir.'

'Stop together. I seem to remember a little popsy the last time we were in here . . . what in hell was her name now? Said she loved naval officers and would go miles to get one. . . .'

'Johnny Walker, sir!'

'Very good. Half astern together.'

Poggles languidly let go a small green flag. Down on the cable deck the blacksmith swung his hammer. The blake slip parted, the cable thundered up out of the locker, thumped over the scotsman and down through the hawsepipe. A gesticulating signalman began to make signs with flags.

'Stop together.'

'Stop together, sir. Both engines answered stop sir.'

'Very good.'

The cable stopped rattling. The signalman held one flag out at rest. The Cable Officer looked out over the guardrail at the water and held up his thumb. Poggles stretched wearily. *Rowbottom* had anchored.

'That was neatly done, if I may say so, Poggles,' said The Bodger.

Poggles shrugged his shoulders modestly.

'Aw shucks,' he said.

The Beattys, too, were impressed. The Captain had found his way to an exact spot on the chart, guided unerringly not by radar, echo-sounders, light-houses, buoys or leading marks, but by brewers' signs. It had been a magnificent performance.

'That'll do for now,' said Poggles. 'Come on, Bodger, shift into your glad rags and we'll have a couple before we go.'

Within half an hour, most of *Rowbottom's* ship's company and all her officers except the officer of the day had gone ashore. The Beattys too were anxious to get ashore. The houses ashore glowed yellow and crimson in the setting sun and formed a fringe of colour in front of the soft violet hills of Guernsey in the distance. It was an exciting prospect. But the Beattys did not get ashore immediately.

Petty Officer Moody was *Rowbottom's* duty petty officer. The Bodger had left instructions with him to see that the Beattys who did not go ashore were kept occupied.

Petty Officer Moody thought of a long time ago when he had been a boy seaman at *Ganges*. He had done a considerable amount of extra boat-pulling in those days. He walked to the hatch of the cadets' messdeck.

'Away seaboat,' he said.

The seaboat was manned and lowered, pulled round the ship and back to the davits, hooked on, hoisted and secured. The Beattys looked at Petty Officer Moody.

'Away seaboat,' said Petty Officer Moody.

With a fresh crew the seaboat was lowered, pulled round the ship, hooked on, hoisted and secured.

'Away seaboat,' said Petty Officer Moody.

Before long the Beattys had lost count of the number of times the seaboat had been manned, lowered, pulled round the ship, hooked on and hoisted again. They reached that state of exhaustion familiar to the galley-slaves of old Rome where they saw only the oar and the rope and heard only the monotonous word of command which regulated their fatigue. When the seaboat was finally secured, very few of the Beattys still wished to go ashore. But Tom Bowles went to enquire about a boat.

He found the Quartermaster, a stout Leading Seaman from the west country, drinking tea with the Bosun's Mate.

'*Cadets*' liberty boats?'

The Quartermaster looked blankly at the Bosun's Mate.

'The first Lootenant, eh said nothin' aboat cadets' liberty boats. There's *awficers*' boats, and there's *ship's coompany's* boats, but *cadets*, he doan't say nothin' aboat them. Nor-r, there's nothin' aboat tha-at. Did the First Lootenant say anyhin' to *yew* aboat cadets' liberty boats, Jan?'

'Yar-r, noaw ma lover-r,' said the Bosun's Mate. 'Yers the boat rewtine, sir-r, but it doan't say nothin' aboat cadets.'

The Quartermaster and the Bosun's Mate gazed at Tom Bowles with interest, as though a cadet of any sort was a new phenomenon to them but a cadet who talked of going ashore was a thing completely rich and strange.

'All right,' said Tom. 'Thank you very much.'

Dawn broke on a grey sea and a heavy swell. Long sweeping waves hissed past *Rowbottom's* scuttles. *Rowbottom* rose and dropped uneasily over them. The shore was hidden in a thick opaque mist. Droplets of fine rain drifted over the decks and hung in rows along the guardrails. It was the weather the shepherd shuns and every holidaymaker in England recognises.

When The Bodger awoke at seven o'clock he stared about him in amazement. Then he remembered where he was and thought of his cadets.

'Ten thousand maledictions,' he said. 'They're supposed to be on a training cruise and here they are loafing. Have been loafing since the cruise started.'

The Bodger looked out of the scuttle and decided to exercise the seaboat as soon as the swell died down.

The swell did not die down. It grew livelier and more troublesome and pitched *Rowbottom* to and fro on its crests. The fine droplets became steady rain and the mists were cleared by squalls which swept down and lashed the ship from end to end. At noon *Rowbottom* was forced to raise steam and put to sea in a rising gale.

The Beattys were totally ignorant of the appalling effect of even a moderately rough sea upon living conditions in a small ship and they had not taken any precautions to guard themselves or their belongings. *Rowbottom's* first swoop as she left the shelter of the land and dug into a heavy sea sent a torrent of water through the open scuttles and brought every cup, plate, knife, fork and spoon on the tables cascading on to the deck in a cacophony of sounding crockery and tinkling cutlery. The reverse roll brought a further cascade of trousers, caps, socks, shoes, shirts, and a tennis racquet belonging to an optimistic Indian cadet.

76

Maconochie was suddenly and comprehensively sick on the deck. The others climbed into their hammocks and stayed there except those who had already been detailed for watches. These climbed unsteadily up the ladder into the outer air, thankful to leave the messdeck. Three Burmese cadets, whose names The Bodger was unable to remember and whom he referred to as Port Tak, Starboard Tak and Tin Tak, crept on to a pile of spare bedding in a corner of the messdeck and lay down there to die. Their feet were swilled by the water which flowed back and forth over the deck carrying its flotsam with it. Winds might blow and crack their cheeks, cataracts and hurricanes might spout until they drenched the steeples, but the Burmese contingent lay immobile, their faces the colour of Irrawaddy river mud, and their thoughts impossible to divine.

The cruise was cancelled on Sunday afternoon because of the weather. *Rowbottom* had steamed slowly up and down the Channel for thirty-six hours, sometimes heaving to for hours at a time, waiting for the gale to blow out. But it showed no signs of doing so and *Rowbottom* anchored in Dartmouth on Sunday evening.

The Beattys emerged on deck, looking pale and tired. Some of them needed help with their hammocks. Poggles stood on his bridge and watched them go, with a sense of wonder that human beings could change so much in so short a time. So might Surajah Dowlah have watched the survivors emerging from the Black Hole of Calcutta.

The last visit of the term was to a submarine. The visit was distinguished by its lack of incident. The Beattys embarked, were taken to sea, submerged, surfaced and brought back again. The whole operation was performed by so few men and with such a lack of apparent effort that the Beattys were unable to appreciate the amount of skill and training involved. Maconochie was not sick, neither did he fall overboard. Nor was the commanding officer of the submarine an old friend of The Bodger's.

5

IN later years the Beattys looked back on their Dartmouth days as halcyon days, when the sun shone, when the Navy was new and mysterious, when their horizons had not yet been clouded over by examinations, responsibility, the cares of a family, and promotion. It was summer and every day was warm, long and full of promise. It was a novel, green world and they danced like sprites in it, before the Navy and the Fleet claimed their youth. Dartmouth was like the early hours of a cricket match. The sun was still climbing, the grass still damp and hopes high. It was not yet the heat of the afternoon when the sun reached its height and runs and wickets preoccupied the minds of the players.

Dartmouth let them dance, let them win small victories, knowing that it had already won the most important victory. The Admiral had been right. The Navy did not want normal boys but boys who would carry out their duty without questioning the ultimate end, like special tools which, once moulded, would carry the shape of their calling for ever. The Navy required its officers to have a way of thinking and a way of life of its own and though hampered by lack of money and badgered by politicians and the press it set about getting them at Dartmouth, hiding its true purpose under a camouflage of tiny false purposes like the branches over a hunter's pit.

Each day at Dartmouth was new and different and contained some fresh experience, but the sum of the days, looked back upon afterwards, appeared as a homogeneous whole, each day inseparable from the others. But there were landmarks, days which stood out in every Beatty's memory. One such landmark was the Royal Visit to Dartmouth.

The event had been on the Dartmouth social calendar for some time, but the Beattys were only made aware of it when Mr Froud took over their drill periods from the Chief G.I. That in itself was enough to convince them of the gravity of the occasion.

At the beginning of the term the Royal Visit had seemed to The Bodger like a small cloud the size of a man's hand. It remained there until The Bodger realised that the increased parade ground activity by other terms showed that the cloud was now the size of a camel or an elephant.

'In two weeks' time,' The Bodger said to Mr Froud, 'Royalty will be inspecting the Royal Naval College, Dartmouth. They will inspect the cadets. They will inspect the Beattys. And what will they find? They will find the biggest shower of lazy, idle, scruffy, slack and mutinous trogs there ever was! One look at them and the cry will go up—"*Who* can be their divisional officer?" The answer will come—"The Bodger." "Off with his head!" shouts the Red Queen and another lieutenant-commander bites the dust. James, you must do something. You must personally regard these cadets. Cherish them. Watch over them. *Breathe* over them like the voice over Eden.'

'I'll do my best, sir,' said Mr Froud. 'Heaven knows, I watch 'em enough already. The Chief says they're making him old before his time.'

'You must lighten his darkness then, James,' said The Bodger.

Mr Froud's task was not so formidable as that which the Chief G.I. had faced a few weeks before. The Beattys now knew at least the rudiments of the Naval Drill Book. By patient and never-ceasing admonishment and example the Chief G.I. had worn the roughness off the Beattys' movements and had cured their more marked idiosyncrasies; he had even cured Maconochie of his habit of giving the Boy Scout salute in moments of stress. But much had to be done before the Beattys were adequate for a Royal Occasion.

The Beattys were conscious of their inadequacy. They were determined to impress Mr Froud, but when he first appeared they were not confident enough to avoid some considerable shuffling before they aligned themselves on three markers in lines which, if not straight, were the best they could do with Mr Froud looking at them like that.

'Like a lot of bloody old women!' observed Mr Froud succinctly. 'Four, rear rank! Get those arms in!'

Paul stiffened into a posture similar to the once-fashionable Grecian bend. But Mr Froud did not think it fashionable. He walked behind Paul and spoke in his ear.

'WHEN YOU STAND TO ATTENTION YOU STAND WITH THE BODY BRACED CHEST OUT STOMACH IN HEELS TOGETHER AT AN ANGLE OF FORTY-FIVE DEGREES HEAD UP EYES STRAIGHT TO THE FRONT BOTH EYES LOOKING IN THE SAME DIRECTION,' Mr Froud said to Paul. 'My small daughter of three could do better. Blindfolded.'

Mr Froud walked in front of the Beattys and surveyed them.

'Two weeks tomorrow,' he said, 'Royalty will be coming down here to have a look at us. You're not fit to be seen. If we could hide you somewhere for the day, we would. I've heard some *horrible* things about you lot on this parade ground. Let's see if you can prove they're not true.'

Mr Froud had a beautiful word of command. It had been trained from an early age, practised on the prairies of Whale Island, and was now reaching its full time of fruition. From the first command, the Beattys knew they were in the hands of a parade prima donna, a drill-book diva.

They plunged forward together and headed for the centre of the parade ground as solidly as a Zulu impi. They marched in line, swinging their arms, keeping their dressings, in step with each other. Mr Froud wondered whether the Chief G.I. had been mistaken.

But at the turn, where Mr Froud achieved a high soaring B Flat which would have tested Dame Melba herself, Mr Froud saw the cross which he, like the Chief G.I. before him, had to bear.

Before marching off the Beattys had been sized, the tallest on the left and the shortest on the right. This arrangement always left three small Sikhs in the right-hand file.

The three small Sikhs had the individuality and the proud independence of spirit which have always made their nation good friends and bad enemies. They were incapable of marching with the rest. They were of the main body, but not with it. Time and again, when the division wheeled and crunched off in a new direction, three turbaned figures marched away on another line.

The erratic behaviour of the Sikhs affected the other Beattys. They saw three Sikhs approaching them, first from one side and then from the other; they saw three Sikhs receding into the distance; and they saw three Sikhs struggling through the ranks after the rest had turned about. The Beattys grew nervous. Such was the Sikhs' co-ordination and so determinedly did they manoeuvre that several of their neighbours were hypnotised into following them. The remainder lost the step, missed orders, forgot their right and left, and their proper file and their proper direction. When Mr Froud halted them, the Beattys were no longer a division, or a squad, or a platoon, or any known symmetrical formation of men. They were a shapeless, rankless, straggling rabble.

Mr Froud watched blankly. Seldom had he seen such an exhibition. He dug deep into his memory for a comparison.

'Once, when I was a little boy,' he said, 'a circus came to our town. In that circus was a three-legged woman. My dad wouldn't let me have a look at her and from that day to this I've wondered what she looked like. Now I know. Now I know what *eighty-one* three-legged old women look like! I wish my small daughter of three was here to see you lot. I really do. She'd laugh like a mad thing just looking at you.'

As the drill periods wore on, the Beattys concluded that Mr Froud's small daughter of three was something of an infant parade-ground prodigy, who not only knew the Naval Drill Book by heart, but had written it.

After a fortnight the Beattys felt that they had improved. But Mr Froud shook his head.

'I don't know who's going to teach you. I can't.'

'How about your small daughter of three, Chief?'

The Beattys rested while Maconochie doubled twice round the parade-ground, once for blasphemy, which was calling a Cadet Gunner 'Chief,' and again for impertinence to a Cadet Gunner (a crime comparable only to defacing a statue of Nelson). However, Maconochie's protest seemed to cheer the Beattys, for when they next halted Mr Froud admitted that he had once long ago seen a squad of Nigerian thermometer glass-blowers give a worse exhibition than the circus act with which the Beattys had just offended his tired old eyes. The Beattys felt that they could have received no higher praise.

'But don't run away with the idea that you're any *good*. You're not. But at least I'm not ashamed to be seen on the same parade-ground now.'

The sun shone for Divisions on the day of the Royal Visit. It was the social climax of the summer term and several hundred parents and friends were present. From their positions on the ramparts they looked down on a brave picture of lines of cadets in their best uniforms and white caps, and the sparkling gold lace and polished swords of their divisional officers. It was a picture of hope and enthusiasm and eagerness for life which thrilled the hearts and moved the tears of the watching parents, friends and masters and even of the newsreel cameramen who had been invited for the occasion.

Whilst the Parade waited for the Guard to appear, Mr Froud walked slowly behind the Beattys' ranks giving advice in a low, growling stage whisper.

'Don't let me see any of you fainting like a shower of Fannys. Remember what I told you. If you've got to move something, wriggle your toes. Don't move anything that shows, because I'm *watching you*. If you feel the sky beginning to close in on you, wriggle your toes. If you hear a buzzing in your ears, wriggle your toes. If your legs go all weak and you see everything going grey and hazy. . . .'

Soundlessly, George Dewberry toppled like a felled tree and lay prone at Mr Froud's feet.

' . . . just wriggle your toes and you'll be all right!'

Mr Froud passed along the ranks repeating his advice and smelling out the weaker members who, one by one, fainted; far better that they should faint now than later. He worked especially hard on the three small Sikhs but the Sikhs resisted. They wriggled their toes until their boots creaked, but they stayed upright.

The last Beattys had hardly regained their places after carrying one of their number, legs trailing, to the side, when the Guard appeared and the ceremony began.

The Guard halted opposite the flagstaff. The Colours were marched in slow time from the main doors of the College, down the steps and across the parade-ground to a place in the middle of the Guard.

When the Royal Visitors appeared on the parapet, the Guard presented arms, the band played the National Anthem, and the Colours dipped. Fathers removed their hats, mothers wiped their eyes, the cameras whirred and the cadets, their officers and the spectators were held together in a few moments of traditional pride and personal loyalty.

The Royal Visitors acknowledged the salute and descended to the parade-ground to begin the inspection. The parade relaxed. The divisions were stood at ease and the band played excerpts from the operas of Gilbert and Sullivan.

The inspection took some time. When the inspecting party, heavy with medals and weighted with gold lace, at last reached the Beattys in the rear the band had long since exhausted its repertoire from 'The Mikado,' 'The Gondoliers' and 'Trial by Jury' and were playing excerpts from 'Chu Chin Chow' and—in a fit of unaccustomed and daring modernity on the part of the Bandmaster—a selection of tunes by Ivor Novello.

The most distinctive figure in the Beattys' front rank was Mehibash, a tall bronzed Egyptian who stood as rigidly to attention as an obelisk. No inspecting party could pass such a figure by without a word and because Mehibash's English was known to be rudimentary and to consist largely of profanities taught him by the Beattys, The Bodger was afraid that Mehibash might be at a loss for a suitable reply; it was a point which The Bodger had forgotten to arrange beforehand. But The Bodger had no need to worry. Paul had anticipated the question and had coached Mehibash in his answer.

'How long have you been in England?'

Mehibash swivelled a golden-tawny eye downwards.

'Too blahdy lawng, thang you verree moch!' said Mehibash and grinned generously. He was obviously confident that he had upheld the reputation of the Pharaohs in this barbaric land whose inhabitants had been painting themselves blue and burning their prisoners in wicker cages whilst his ancestors had been building the Pyramids.

The College marched past, led by the Guard and the Colours, and afterwards went to church. The cadets filed into the College chapel in the same order as they had marched past the saluting base and wearing superficially the same expressions. The service was as much an evolution as a parade, as though it had been designed to give the maximum number of cadets the maximum amount of religion in the shortest time.

The visiting Bishop who conducted the service had once been told as a theological student that no sailor could be an atheist since he lived too close to one of God's instruments, but a period in a Portsmouth parish and experience as a naval padre in two wars had made the Bishop sceptical. But now, as he looked over his huge congregation, the Bishop felt again that heart-warming quality which all naval services have, whether they are held in a church, or on the quarterdeck of a ship at sea. Used as he was to the empty churches and elderly congregations of his own diocese, the Bishop beamed at the youngest, most hopeful and certainly the largest congregation he had had for years.

The cadets too felt the exaltation of the moment. The words of the Naval Prayer gave them a vision of the line of ships and men which they and their future ships would continue. It was one of the few times while they were at Dartmouth, indeed while they were in the service, when they were permitted a glimpse of the final end of their labours.

After starting on a crest of such high exaltation, the day dropped into a trough of low comedy. The Day of the Royal Visit passed into the Night of George Dewberry's Run Ashore.

Having avoided Mr Froud all day, George Dewberry dressed himself in his best uniform at supper time, presented himself to the Chief Cadet of the Day for inspection and proceeded ashore.

It was George Dewberry's first, last, and only expedition outside the College. He went alone and this was in itself unusual, for the naval custom whereby officers proceed ashore in parties of not less than two, often a prudent custom abroad, is normally still observed at home, where the natives might have been supposed to be friendly. George Dewberry told nobody why he went ashore on that particular night or where he had been, but from the moment he stepped inside the Beatty barracks it was obvious what he had been doing. George Dewberry was splendidly, unashamedly, roaring drunk.

It was Michael who first heard the voice outside the chest flat window, and a sound of scuffling.

'Goosh!' roared the voice. 'Goosh! Gorright! Clumsy fool! Whatcha think you're doing, eh? He he! Goosh, hup! Goosh me.'

Michael looked out of the chest flat window and saw George Dewberry standing astride, calmly and with an air of satisfaction passing his water against the base of the Beattys' flagstaff. Michael thought of The Bodger's face in the morning and shook Paul.

'What the hell's the matter?'

Paul looked at his watch.

'Good God, Mike, do you know what the time is?'

'Quick Paul. George Dewberry's tight.'

'How tight?'

'As a newt.'

'Good for him.'

Paul turned over but Michael shook him again.

'Oh for Christ's sake!'

'We can't leave him there.'

'Why *not*? Look, let me get some sleep, will you? Please?'

'You've got to give me a hand to get him to bed. He might hurt himself.'

'Hope he does.'

'No, come on, Paul. We've got to get him to bed. There'll be the most frightful nausea if The Bodger or old Froud or someone finds out.'

'Oh all right.'

Paul got out of bed and they both looked through the window. George Dewberry was just finishing. Having finished, he stepped back, solemnly saluted, turned and saw his audience.

'Hi fellows!' he said cheerily and waved. 'No s-satisfaction without urination y'know.' His cheery look changed to one of bewilderment. When Michael and Paul reached him, he was staring about him with a puzzled air, as though he were searching for someone. Here is Dewberry, he appeared to be thinking, but where is Bohun, where are De Vere and Mowbray, nay, what is first and greatest of all, where is Plantagenet? They caught him as he fell and dragged him into the chest flat.

'Y'know,' he said, 'I feel *really* good. I never felt as good as this before. Everythin's goin' to be *O*.K.!'

'No wonder,' said Paul. 'You smell like a bloody brewery. What've you been drinking?'

'*Drinking?*'

'You're as honked as an owl.'

'Y-you may think *I'm* honked,' George Dewberry said with a seraphic smile as they sat him on his bed, 'but you should see the other blokes!'

Paul removed George Dewberry's clothes, with no protest from him; indeed he co-operated, giggling, as though he were performing some form of party forfeit. When he was naked, George Dewberry sat up and examined his toes as though he had never seen them before.

'Thish little piggy went to market—hup!'

'Up,' said Paul. He lifted George Dewberry on to his feet.

86

George Dewberry staggered along, willing to go wherever his benefactors cared to lead him. He was still reciting 'This little piggy went to market' when Paul turned on the cold shower.

The effect of the ice-cold water was immediate and appalling. George Dewberry brought his fist sharply down on the bridge of Michael's nose and let out a roar of shocked, and sober, fury which would have brought the Seven Sleepers doubling out of their cave in Ephesus.

'Shut up, you idiot!' whispered Paul fiercely through gritted teeth as he fought to control George Dewberry who was plunging and kicking like a young buffalo in the springtime. 'You'll have Mr Froud in here!'

'—— Mr Froud!' George Dewberry bellowed. '—— Froud!'
He was struck by the alliteration.

'—— Froud, —— Froud, —— Froud,' he carolled.

Paul and Michael were both knocked aghast by this blasphemy. The rest of the chest flat, all now wide awake, wondered whether it was worth while getting up to look at the iconoclast George Dewberry before he was struck down by heavenly wrath.

They were given no more time to decide. As if he had materialised in answer to George Dewberry's frenzied incantations, Mr Froud appeared at the door of the bathroom and shone a torch round inside.

Dewberry was transfixed in the beam, goggling like a rabbit in the headlights. Aladdin rousing the Genie for the first time, Semele confronted by Jupiter in radiance, could never have been so taken aback and utterly confounded as was George Dewberry by the appearance of Mr Froud.

Mr Froud looked coolly at the figures in front of him, George Dewberry in the centre and Paul and Michael with his eyes streaming standing beside him like heraldic supporters, and was conscious that he had made a dramatic entrance.

'Get him to bed,' Mr Froud said quietly and vanished as suddenly as he had come.

Afterwards, when he was a watchkeeping lieutenant at sea,

Michael realised that he had witnessed that night only one of the many techniques for carrying out an important part of a naval officer's profession.

The theory and practice of dealing with drunks was considered so important that it received a special mention in The Bodger's lectures.

'It all boils down to one thing,' said The Bodger. '*Never*, on any account, put yourself in such a position that they can strike you or insult you in any way. If you see a boat-load of drunks coming off, don't stick your head over the guardrail and shout down to them or as sure as *fate* some witty Jolly Jack will answer you. Make the boat lie off. They can lie off all night if necessary. They'll calm down when they see they're not going to get on board until they've quietened down. When they do come on board, get away out of it and let the Royal Marine fisting party take charge of them. You'll hear dozens of stories, though most of them are apocryphal, of Officers of the Watch being chased round and round the quarterdeck by intoxicated matelots armed with razors, knives, stilettos, bill-hooks or pickaxes, depending on the locality. The object of the chase is not, as you might well suppose, to provide the Quartermaster and the Bosun's Mate with a source of innocent merriment nor is it to give exercise to the constipated and enervated officers of H.M. Ships. The idea is simply to prevent the man increasing the seriousness of the charge against him from one of drunkenness to one of striking an officer. Coming off shore drunk is classed as a regrettable but human failing. The chap loses one day's pay. But striking an officer is another thing altogether. It used to be punishable by what was called flogging round the fleet, so many lashes at the gangway of each ship. Even now it carries the heaviest penalties in the Naval Discipline Act, formulated and instrumented by the Articles of War. The chap is placed under Close Arrest at once and will be damn lucky to escape a court martial. So be warned. If you see a drunk coming, don't stand in front of him flaunting your gold lace or you'll get thumped and rightly so. I can guarantee that if you're ever Officer of the Watch and you get clobbered by a libertyman *you'll* see the Commander the next morning as well and he'll give you the biggest bollocking you ever had in your life for being such a bloody fool as to let him do it. Who decides when a man is drunk? Dewberry?'

'The Medical Officer, sir.'

'Wrong. The *Officer of the Watch* decides whether a man is capable of carrying out his duty. He can consult the Medical Officer if he thinks the man's ill or the man claims to be drugged, but the Officer of the Watch, and the Officer of the Watch *only*, decides whether a man is drunk. So remember that. If you are the Officer of the Watch at the time then you will be the man the Commander will ask. Not the Medical Officer.'

The cadets who remembered The Bodger's advice found it sound when the time came to test it. They found this was true of all The Bodger's advice. The Bodger had been a midshipman when war broke out and in the following six years he had learned more than he could have done in twenty years of peace time service. His acute observation and wry sense of humour had built up a fund of anecdotes and epigrams which the Beattys understood and remembered more easily than text-book diagrams. The Bodger had no patience with books and had the greatest difficulty in imparting information through a set series of lectures. But once The Bodger began to reminisce the Beattys were allowed a glimpse of their future lives and problems.

The Bodger taught the Beattys how to run a wardroom wine account at a profit and not be court martialled for securing the mess funds; how to maintain a tailor's bill so that the tailors never threatened through their solicitors, although the bill was never actually cleared; how to appear to be drinking drink for drink with an official guest and remain sober; and how to play golf with Admirals and tennis with their daughters, without blighting their own careers or becoming engaged. The Bodger told the Beattys the classical opening conversational gambits for an official cocktail party in a foreign port; the proper facial expression and demeanour of an officer trying to reach a difficult decision in public watched by critical ratings; and the appropriate words of condolence, congratulation or enthusiasm when addressing a senior officer who has been passed over for promotion, become a father, or had an idea. The Bodger warned the Beattys of paper collars, of mixing the malt and the grape, of not drawing trumps, of backing ante-post, of marrying too early, and of drinking alone or when they had work to do. The Bodger gave freely of his own experience and the Beattys began to see him, not as a man disinterested in the service and in cadets, but as a man who had learned by bitter trial and error and who was interested in the cadets' welfare and anxious that they should do well. The Bodger was perhaps the best sort of officer, one who served the Navy with no illusions but still with love.

The Beattys themselves were by now a recognised term of personalities instead of a list of names and an anonymous mass of faces. Although The Bodger was not a sporting man in any expert sense he knew the good effect on a divisional officer's reputation of his term's success at sport, and The Bodger realised that this present term of Beattys, although lazy, although unquestionably the worst term at drill in living memory, and although they had the longest defaulters' list the College had known for twenty years, were exceptional at all games.

The progress of the summer term's sporting events was a series of triumphs which provided The Bodger with a constant source of pride and gratification. There was the day when the Beattys beat the rest of the College by five runs. This was the match in which Paul opened the Beatty innings and carried his bat for an exquisite century. It was also the match in which the inimitable Maconochie, fielding very close to the bat, brought the Dartmouth innings to an end by catching the ball in his groin.

Another memorable day for The Bodger was the Sailing Regatta. The River Dart became for that day a scene of seething nautical activity, with much bending on of lines, hoisting of sails, dipping of lugs and casting off of painters to a running accompaniment of shouts of 'Luff up!' 'Check that sheet!', 'Lee-oh!' and even 'Fore!' David Bowie and Tom Bowles carried off the dinghy races between them, Peter Cleghorn showed an unsuspected—and unrepeated—talent for sailing in winning the whaler race, while Mr Froud won the Officers and Masters Race with a crew of Beattys.

Mr Froud's crew included Michael and Paul who normally went to the river only when forced but who, finding themselves temporarily in the House of Rimmon, philosophically hauled on lines and shifted their weights forward or aft as directed by the Cadet Gunner. They found that Mr Froud, out of uniform and into a boat, suffered a sea-change and became one of the most kindly and charming of men.

Mr Froud was not a sailing enthusiast. He sailed a boat once a year, at the Regatta. His boat was always a cutter and his crew always six Beattys whom he had singled out as being unlikely to become Gunnery Officers. Mr Froud cared nothing for the subtleties of sailing. One starting gun was very like another and Mr Froud watched with almost oriental detachment whilst other boats, manned by officers, masters and cadets who were conscious that the eye of the world was upon them, made a sliding, drifting melee at the starting line. Meanwhile Mr Froud concentrated on the cold chicken and bottled beer which his wife had provided and ordered his crew to do likewise.

When his race started and Mr Froud looked about him at the blue water, the curve of the sail and the green combes of Devon on either side he said : 'I wish my small daughter was here,' and his crew understood him.

It was Mr Froud's custom to sing as the end of the race came near, and when he crossed the finishing line with the tiller in one hand and a bottle of Pale Ale in the other, chanting the opening staves of 'The Harlot of Jerusalem,' the Beattys in his boat felt that for an afternoon they had shared the company of a great and good man.

The Beattys' own private sporting events also made The Bodger hug his sides. There was the Obstacle Race in the gymnasium when Spink, who had never before mastered the science of climbing a rope, amazed the P.T.I. by swarming with galvanic speed using his hands only to the top of the rope and sticking there, petrified with fright. When the P.T.I. exhorted him to—
'Come *down*, lad. Come down 'and over 'and like I showed you' Spink slid to the bottom and was led away to the Sick Bay with rope burns.

Spink was not the only casualty. The Beattys' success had not been achieved without cost. In the Sick Bay Spink joined Maconochie who had lain spreadeagled in bed since the day of the cricket match; the india-rubber Cartwright whom Nemesis had overtaken and thrown from the high bar, with a broken collar-bone; and the Burmese Starboard Tak, who had nearly drowned at the Swimming Regatta. Starboard Tak had been carried to the Sick Bay after the P.T.I. had forced from his lungs a quantity of liquid which resembled muddy Irrawaddy river water.

The last landmarks of the summer term were the Passing Out Divisions and the Prizegiving after it. The Beattys were not eligible for most of the prizes and watched unmoved while diminutive cadets from other terms doubled up to receive prizes for the winning Prize Essay on 'Nelson in Naples' and the award for the Fastest-Tied Reef Knot of the term. The prizegiving Admiral's speech afterwards, however, affected everybody.

The visiting Admiral was one of that handful of naval officers who have been in the public eye for as long as the public can remember. His exploits about Town as a young lieutenant, his Victoria Cross, his eye-patch and his aquiline shaving cream advertisement type of features had made for him a place in the public affection seldom equalled by any officer. At the time of speaking he was the nearest thing to Beatty since Beatty himself. Privately, inside the service, he was known as the man who was determined, when the time came, to shake the base of the old saw that First Sea Lords may come and First Sea Lords may go, but civil servants go on for ever.

This was the man who faced the cadets from his dais, looking quizzically at the rows of faces, as though he were already casting them for the film of his life story.

The cadets were just as interested in looking at the Admiral. They all knew that this man was above the common run of Admirals, an international celebrity whose personality commanded a place not only in the headlines of the *Daily Disaster* but also in the more exclusive captions of *The Tatler and*

Bystander. The cadets were keen to hear what this magnificent man, who bore the palm before the majestic world, would have to say to such insignificant dross as themselves; they were curious to know upon what meat had this Caesar fed that he had grown so great.

The Admiral distributed the last prizes, shot his cuffs, glanced at the clock and prepared to speak.

'Very soon, gentlemen,' said the Admiral, 'you will be serving as midshipmen in the fleet. I don't think any of you realise at the moment just what an important part you have to play in the fleet. When I was Captain of my own ship I paid very close attention to my midshipmen, closer than they welcomed. When you're a midshipman you're nearer to the sailors than you will ever be again in your service career. If there's any trouble in the ship, the midshipmen will know about it. If there is anything wrong in a ship which the officers don't know about, then it's the midshipmen's fault for not knowing.

'That position brings its responsibilities. Nobody expects a midshipman to know very much. I didn't expect mine to know anything. I was very pleased when they showed that they did. They were young and they made plenty of mistakes. That didn't matter. I've made plenty myself.'

The senior officers, masters and other important people who were seated behind the Admiral like subsidiary gods ranged behind Jove on Olympus, looked incredulous, as though they had just heard Jove admit that his thunderbolts sometimes missed.

'I didn't mind them making mistakes. But what I did mind and what did annoy me very much was them failing to try to do their duty as leaders. All of you are going to be leaders in the Navy. Your duty will be to lead men by your personal example and your own officer-like qualities. And don't think you're home and dry already and you know it all. You've only got the uniform so far and you're only here through the efforts of your parents. From here on, it's up to you and nobody else. Your men will never follow you if they don't respect you. If my midshipmen had the courage to do their best all the time, to stick to their principles and to speak out when the time came,

93

then I backed them up. I'll give you an example of what I mean.'

The subsidiary gods showed interest. A ripple of preparation ran through them. As clearly as though the words had been spoken, the message ran—'Funny story coming up!'

'Early in the war when we were at action stations in the Channel I wanted to speak to my ship's company over the main broadcast. I began to speak and I was surprised that I couldn't hear my voice coming over the bridge repeater. I tried again and still nothing happened. Just as I was giving up in disgust and deciding to send for my Electrical Officer, a young midshipman, I think he was Navigating Officer's Tanky, stepped up and said: "If you took the microphone cover off, sir, and switched on the transmitter, I think it would work, sir." And so it was. I'd forgotten in the heat of the moment. I didn't say anything to that midshipman myself but afterwards I overheard my Navigating Officer take that midshipman aside and say: "I know you're new to this and don't know the form, old man, but let me tell you that it's an old service custom that Captains are not given bottles by midshipmen!"'

The cadets rocked with laughter. The lesser gods howled, rolled in their seats, hooting, holding their sides and wiping tears from their eyes. When the Admiral laughs, all laugh.

'Now I expect you're all saying that it's all very well for me to talk, but how does one become a leader? There are no hard and fast rules, I'm afraid. It's not a thing you can teach by correspondence course. You learn by experience, and I can't give you that experience and I don't think I would even if I could. But I can give you some hints.

'First of all, you must know what you're doing. You must know your job. It's no good leading men if you don't know where you're leading them. You'll be like the grand old Duke of York who marched his men to the top of the hill and then marched them down again.

'You must *know* your men. You must try and understand that you're not dealing with machines but with people who feel and react and behave in different ways in different circumstances.

94

Unless you take the trouble to get to know them, you're wasting your time. I don't mean just a chap's name and official number and whether he's G or T. I mean what sort of a person is he, what is his background, and what's he thinking about the ship and his job and his mess.

'You must look after your men. There are no bad ratings, only bad officers. You must make it your business to see to their welfare. Never be too tired to speak to a chap when he wants your advice, never dismiss a complaint without investigating it, and never neglect an opportunity for advancing a rating or helping him in his job. And don't try to be popular. It's the curse of the Navy. There are too many *nice* officers in the Navy as it is.

'Above all, keep your sense of humour. This is really vital. Given two men of the same ability, the man with the sense of humour will go furthest. By that I don't mean a nasty, vicious, carping sense of humour. You must still be loyal to your men and to those above you. What I mean is the ability to recover from setbacks, the ability to take each day as it comes, and the ability to see the funny side whatever happens. It's a priceless asset. Value it above gold. I well remember when my ship was torpedoed, I found myself floating about in the water next to my Sergeant-Major of Royal Marines, my Regulating Chief Stoker, and one of my Lieutenants. The Chief Stoker wiped the oil out of his eyes, looked around him, saw the Lieutenant and me, grinned and said to the Sergeant-Major: "Gawd, ain't it amazin' how all the scum comes to the top!" '

Again a concerted paroxysm of laughter swept down and across the hall and back. Once more the senior officers turned and looked wonderingly at each other, their faces crinkled with laughter.

'Now I know that on these occasions the best moment of all comes when the Admiral gets what he's got to say off his chest and goes. Gentlemen, that great moment is now at hand. Good luck to you all, and thank you.'

*   *   *

Afterwards, the Admiral circulated with a drink in his hand among the College officers.

'Let me see now. *Badger,* isn't it?'

'Yes, sir.'

'Do you remember that microphone cover?'

'Very well indeed, sir. I shake when I think back on it.'

'Never mind. It was a perfect example of the kind of thing I was trying to put across. Do they still call you The Bodger?'

'I'm afraid they do, sir.'

'Must be something in it. What are you doing here?'

'I'm in charge of the Beattys, sir.'

'How do you find them?'

'Great fun, sir. Quite a promising lot. They can be infuriating, of course, but on the whole I find them very rewarding, sir.'

'Do you like training jobs?'

'It's a very great responsibility, sir. More than almost any job. I'm very fond of it.'

'I'm glad you find it so. I think you're quite right, too. We need officers with a sense of vocation to fill these jobs. Well, I'm glad to have met you again, Badger.'

'Thank you, sir.'

The Admiral moved on.

Others closed round The Bodger.

'Well, I don't know what you're all getting on about,' said The Bodger indignantly. 'What was I to say? The man asks me if I enjoy it. I do. So I tell him so. That's not to say I want another job like this one. It would kill me. Anyway, they're a bloody good crowd. Beat your lot at tennis last Sunday, anyway.'

'Oh well, if you're going to bring that up.'

The night before the Beattys left Dartmouth, The Bodger intimated that he and his staff would be in 'The Floating Bridge' and there would be beer for anyone who cared to come. Lieutenant Mathewson sang a song about lunatic asylums which had the refrain: 'Come inside you silly bastards, come inside.' Lieutenant Chipperd sang a song with the refrain: 'And the pig

96

got up and slowly walked away.' Lieutenant Brakeherst recited a version of 'The Boy on the Burning Deck,' with gestures. Mr Froud sang 'The Harlot of Jerusalem.'

The Bodger made a speech. Mr Froud was the toast-master.

'My lords, ladies and gentlemen, pray silence for Lieutenant-Commander Robert Bollinger Badger, Royal Navy, otherwise known as The Bodger!'

There was a tempest of clapping and shouts of 'Bodger for king!' as The Bodger climbed laboriously on to a table and waved his tankard.

'Gentlemen, this is for me a sad, *sad* moment. When I think of this splendid College of ours, the amount of taxpayers' money lavished upon it, the equipment it has for turning reasonable officer material out of the raw natural state, when I consider that I am now looking round at the survivors of the worst that College can do, when I realise that I see before me the Navy's future officers and leaders, the sifted and graded results of three months' work, the cream of a proud mother country, then I think to myself—"God help us!"'

The Bodger took a huge swallow from his tankard.

'But do not be dismayed. Worse men than you have reached flag rank. The path to the top is *lined* with stinkers. The game is to outstink the next bastard, to out-Herod the er—next bastard. People will tell you the Navy's going to the dogs. And so it is. It's been going to the dogs ever since I can remember, certainly since I joined. My father was a naval officer and the Navy was going to the dogs in his day. My grandfather was a naval officer and he left the Navy because it was going to the dogs. They were thinking of introducing steam or something. My *great*-grandfather—now what the hell did my great-grandfather do?—oh, yes, he refused to *join* the Navy in spite of all my great-great-grandfather could do because he thought the Navy had *gone* to the dogs. He didn't approve of Lady Hamilton. My great-great-grandfather . . . so don't be alarmed when people tell you the Navy's going to the dogs. It's *always* going to the dogs. It's when people stop saying it's going to the dogs and start telling you what a splendid service it is and how much better and better it's going to be in the future, *that's* when you start worrying. As long as everybody is saying the Navy is going to the dogs then you've nothing to worry about. All is well.

'Having said that, I will now give you a toast. I want you to drink with me to the future. The future's in your hands and may you have as good a time making as big a mess of it as your fathers and grandfathers before you. Good luck to you all in the future and particularly in the Training Cruiser where you'll need it, believe me. I don't know who will be in charge of you in the Training Cruiser but I wish him luck as well!'

The Beattys made a strange picture on the station platform. They had been issued with one trunk and enough kit to fill three. Those cadets who had not taken the advice of the pensioners who cleaned out the chest flats and sent home for extra luggage found themselves in difficulties. Maconochie travelled up to London looking as though he had been evicted by the bailiffs with his trunk, a canvas hold-all, three laundry bags full of shoes, five paper parcels and a pair of boots hung over his arm by their laces.

Michael went up to London with three trunks and no very clear idea of what he had learnt at Dartmouth or even why he had been sent there.

'Never mind, Mike,' said Paul. 'All things come to those who wait. Think what you know now that you didn't know before. I can't think of anything offhand but there must be something. I know! You're a leader, boy! You've got the uniform to prove it!'

6

H.M.S. *Barsetshire*, the Cadet Training Cruiser, was a comfortable ship, at least in the opinion of her officers and her ship's company. The cadets' opinion of her was not known, nor was it consulted. She had been built in the spacious days before Hitler, when it was not unusual for a naval officer to have a private income and when recruiting for the Navy was not a subject of party recrimination in Parliament but depended on more mundane influences, such as the end of the hop-picking and harvesting seasons and the decline of local industries. Her high speed and four funnels made her ideal for service on the China Station where the one enabled her to return from Wei Hai Wei in record time for the Hong Kong Races and the other four impressed the Chinese. Her peacetime service in the tropics evidently demonstrated her admirable qualities for wartime service in the Arctic, for she never steamed south of the British Isles throughout the war except after D-Day when she was attacked off the Normandy coast by a group of Messerschmitts who, it was assumed, mistook her for the newly constructed Mulberry Harbour.

After the war, most of *Barsetshire's* armament was removed and extra superstructure built in its place. The re-distribution of weights gave her plenty of living and class-room space and a capacity for rolling immoderately in quite moderate seas. She was therefore re-classified and re-commissioned as a Cadet Training Cruiser.

* * *

It was raining, gently but steadily, when the new cadets first saw *Barsetshire* lying alongside the dockyard wall. She was a depressing sight and her grey bulk in the rain, the dreary jetty littered with the bones and intestines of other ships, and the concealed fear of an unknown life ahead of them combined to chill the hearts of the newly-joining cadets.

If the cadets were not glad to see *Barsetshire*, *Barsetshire* was not glad to see them. The Junior Cadets were met by the Cadet of the Watch and the Bosun's Mate standing, sodden and dripping, at the salute.

'Buck up, you guys,' pleaded the Cadet of the Watch. 'I'm catching my death of pneumonia standing here.'

The Junior Cadets, sensing like new boys at school that it would not be wise to offend their seniors from the start, hurried on board and stood in a miserable huddle on the quarterdeck. In his haste Ted Maconochie accidentally trod on a red setter dog which had been inspecting the new cadets from the side of the quarterdeck. The dog gave a howl and flashed out of sight down a hatch.

'*Look,* you fellows,' said the Cadet of the Watch. 'Thin out a bit, will you? Get *going*. You worry me. You bring back my horrible past. Hey Bluey!'

The Bosun's Mate, who was already halfway towards the snugness of the quartermaster's lobby, turned reluctantly.

'Show the sprogs the messdecks, will you?'

'O.K. Whacker.' Bluey nodded to the cadets. 'This way, you guys.'

Bluey led them forward and down a ladder to a large compartment. The deck of the compartment was covered with corticene of a depressing sickly green colour. Pipes, cables, trunkings and hammock bars ran overhead. Bare tables and benches were placed in rows on either side. A couple of Royal Marines looked morosely at the new cadets from a serving hatch. The atmosphere of the compartment was one of utility; it was plainly a space to be used and quitted as quickly as possible. It had the odour of Oliver Twist's workhouse. It was not a room for the enjoyment of meals but a site for the eating of sufficient basic food for survival against a pitiless life. It was the Cadets' Messdeck.

The problem of accommodating over 200 cadets in a limited space was solved by strict allocation. Every cadet was fitted into a niche, a cell in the honeycomb, from which he was not allowed to move. *Barsetshire's* Chief G.I. met the cadets on the messdeck and organised their joining routine. He portioned them out into divisions, into classes, into watches, and into parts and subs of watches. He allotted them a gunroom in which to stow their books and instruments, a mess table at which to eat, a slinging billet for their hammocks, a chest for their clothes, and a bathroom to wash in. The Chief G.I. impressed on the cadets that they were not to stow their books, sling their hammocks, eat their meals, keep their clothes or wash themselves in any other place than that allotted to them. The Chief G.I. gave each cadet a ship's book number, a gunroom number, a mess number, a slinging billet number, a chest number and a bathroom number to help him remember. Finally, each cadet was given a name tally which he pinned on his jersey so that any officer or petty officer could know his name without troubling to ask him.

'All I need now is a suit covered in broad arrows and a pick for breaking stones,' said Paul and straightaway learnt the first lesson of the Cadet Training Cruiser which was that idle jokes always recoiled on their author's head. The Junior Cadets were ordered to shift into overalls, given hammers, and spent the afternoon chipping paintwork on the upper deck in the rain.

After tea the Juniors mustered on the messdeck for a speech of welcome by the Cadet Training Officer. They had heard that *Barsetshire* had a new Cadet Training Officer, a man keen on training, who had arrived with the intention of setting *Barsetshire* and its cadets to rights. The Juniors awaited his arrival with almost as much trepidation as they had awaited the arrival of The Bodger, long ago on their first evening at Dartmouth, although their anxiety was now tempered by the knowledge they had gained from Dartmouth, that nothing in the Navy would ever turn out to be as bad as it sounded in the speech of welcome.

The Cadet Training Officer's arrival in *Barsetshire* was preceded by almost the same preliminaries as The Bodger's had been at Dartmouth. The Chief G.I. first ran a disillusioned eye over the rows of cadets and reported to the Cadet Gunner, Mr Piles. Mr Piles then came and glanced round the messdeck, presumably to test the evidence of the Chief G.I.'s eyes, and went away to report to the Cadet Training Officer. A file of assistant training officers, divisional officers and instructor officers came in and sat down in the front row. After them came the new Cadet Training Officer; he was, unmistakably and without any shadow of doubt, The Bodger.

The Bodger appeared to enjoy the mingled astonishment and consternation which his familiar figure had caused. He himself had only just recovered from the shock of his new appointment. He had received the appointment because he had broken one of his own stoutest maxims. The Bodger had done a thing which he himself had warned the Beattys never to do. He had spoken idly to an Admiral and he was now reaping the consequences.

'I've cast my bread on the waters,' The Bodger said to his wife when he opened the envelope and read his appointment, 'and it's come back like a bloody boomerang and caught me a dastardly blow behind the ear.'

The Bodger looked round at the faces of the cadets who had been Beattys as though he were refreshing his memory of them.

'Well,' he said, grinning, 'this is as big a surprise to me as it is to you. I don't think there's any need for me to introduce myself. Those of you who were Beattys are old enemies and should know my name by now and those of you other lesser breeds, without the law, will soon be able to find out. I don't know very much more about this ship than you do. I only joined it myself three days ago. So I can't tell you much about the details. You're going to do two cruises in this vessel. This time we're going to the Mediterranean, next cruise to the West Indies. You're here to learn some of the practical side of your profession. You learnt a lot of theory at Dartmouth, here you're going to put in into practice. There are very few seamen in this ship. You're the seamen and you will have to live and work as they would have done if they had been on board. I can't tell you much more than that just now. I'll speak to you all again later. All I can do now is welcome you to the ship and hope that you get full value from your time here. Your divisional officers and I will do our best to see that you do whether you intend to or not. I think that's all. Unless you've got anything to add, Mr Piles? No? Well, that's that.'

The cadets rose as The Bodger put on his cap.

'Oh, one more thing,' said The Bodger at the door. 'The cadet who kicked the Captain's dog immediately on joining the ship, report to my office.'

The senior cadets had rejoined *Barsetshire* a day before the juniors and once the junior cadets were on board the ship lost no time in leaving England. It was as though, having once let the new cadets have a glimpse of *Barsetshire*, the Captain was anxious to put to sea before any of them had an opportunity to break ship.

Passers-by on the dockside the next morning observed intense activity in *Barsetshire*. The ship swarmed and hummed with life from stem to stern and from masthead to waterline. Parties of cadets were doubling from the quarterdeck to the fo'c'sle, milling about for a few minutes, and doubling aft again. Other cadets were playing an endless game of tag up and down the ladders leading to the bridge. One group of cadets by A turret were hauling on a rope, unknown to a further group on the other side of the turret who were hauling on the other end of the rope. Periodically a cadet with a piece of paper in his hand doubled forward along the upper deck, disappeared round the other side of the ship and reappeared a few moments later still doubling forward and still carrying the piece of paper. Boats were being lowered, hoisted, re-lowered and again hoisted. Flags were run up to the yardarm and hauled down again. Decks were scrubbed, covered in ropes, tackle and grease, and again re-scrubbed. The whole scene was orchestrated by shouts, cries, oaths, pipes and bugle calls.

After half an hour, the spectators on the dockside had split into two main groups. The first thought that it was all some form of new evolution connected with defence against atomic attack and the second—with a taste for the dramatic—maintained that

103

the officers and ship's company of H.M.S. *Barsetshire* were preparing to abandon ship. Neither party, who had perhaps been influenced by the Merchant Navy practice of entering and leaving harbour with two men and a dog on the fo'c'sle and a cat on the quarterdeck, guessed that *Barsetshire* was, in fact, preparing for sea.

Four hours earlier, a brown haze had crept from the funnels, followed by a thick black pall from one of them which had continued in ever-increasing density and volume until the Chief Stoker in that boiler room found time to get across and cuff the ear of the stoker who had turned on a sprayer without lighting it. The boilers had been flashed, steam had been raised and the main engines had been warmed and turned to ensure that they still worked. The Engine Room Branch had then confessed themselves satisfied and the Chief Stokers and Chief E.R.A.s had settled back to suck their teeth and predict that something would go wrong.

The yeast of preparation which had been fermenting in the bowels of the ship then boiled over and effervesced into the light of day, filling the decks with the running, pulling, shouting figures, jerking to and fro like the puppets on a screen, which afforded the dockside audience with such unexpected diversion.

Peter Cleghorn was a Screw-Flagsman. He was given a pair of flags by the Chief G.I. and ordered to hold them out from a small platform by the mainmast.

One of the flags was red and the other was white but Peter Cleghorn was not told their significance. He began to experiment. He observed that when he held out the white flag the panorama below him was one of organised and controlled movement. But when he held out the red flag the pattern broke up and dissolved into chaos. Men ran, stopped short, and pointed, as at a comet, pulled on ropes, dropped them, and pulled again; and telephoned, put down the receiver, and almost immediately seized it again.

A feeling of omnipotence swept over Peter Cleghorn. He felt like a god, commanding the world below. Merely by holding out a flag he could alter the natural course of events. When Cleghorn

104

chose to hold out the white flag, the law of gravity and the principles of physics held sway. But when Cleghorn showed the red flag, all was anarchy. He held out the white flag and the red alternately and observed their effect. Just as he was determining to hold them both out simultaneously, he was knocked to the ground by a colossal blow on the back. The flags fluttered impotently down to the upper deck.

Peter Cleghorn looked up and saw the Gunnery Officer standing over him.

'WHAT do you think you're doing, fluttering your flags about like that? When you hold out the red flag it means there's a wire fouling the screws. You've been holding that flag out and we've had all the wires in ten minutes ago! Where do you think you are, a bloody Palio?'

As the ship moved down harbour, the ship's broadcast kept up a stream of growling unintelligible remarks, like those of a caged but ungagged lunatic, interspersed with notes on the bugle, when The Hands who had fallen in by their parts of the ship for leaving harbour came to attention and gazed out over the water at solemn dockyard workmen and, later, waving holiday-makers.

Halfway down the harbour, *Barsetshire* fired a gun salute to the Commander-in-Chief.

Gun salutes were Mr Piles' responsibility. They were for him the supreme moments of a cruise. Mr Piles approached a gun salute as a conductor approaches the performance of a sacred oratorio, with awe and humility. Although no conductor ever had so inexperienced an orchestra, for the Saluting Gun's Crews included Dewberry and Spink, Mr Piles persevered and rehearsed every movement and when he raised his voice to start the salute it was like the opening bars of a stupendous overture.

'Saluting Gun's Crews, stand to your guns! One Round— Load!'

Mr Piles watched while the crews loaded their guns.

'If-I-wasn't-a-Gunner-I-wouldn't-be-here-fire-*one!*'

The shot boomed out across the water.

'If-I-wasn't-a-Gunner-I-wouldn't-be-here-fire-*two!*'

Again the reverberations rolled back and forward between ship and shore.

'If-I-wasn't-a-Gunner-I-wouldn't-be-here-fire-*three!*'

A third time a delicious smoke clouded Mr Piles' eyes and an exquisite concussion wrung his ears. Mr Piles smiled. The first movement was going according to rehearsal.

The fourth gun was manned by George Dewberry who was gazing at the shoreline slipping past.

'If-I-wasn't-a-Gunner-I-wouldn't-be-here-fire-*four!*'

There was silence after Mr Piles' voice. It was as though a soloist had missed his entry. There was no sound except the flapping of the ensign halliard against the mast and the scream of the seagulls.

'If-I-wasn't-a-Gunner-I-wouldn't-be-here-fire-four-*clot!*'

George Dewberry awoke and fired. Simultaneously Spink, the next cadet, startled by the ferocity in Mr Piles' voice, involuntarily fired. There was a shattering double explosion.

'If-I-wasn't-a-Gunner-I-wouldn't-be-here-fire-*five!*'

Once more there was silence.

'If-I-wasn't-a-Gun—'

'Please sir, do I count that last one as four or five?'

'*Out* of my way!'

The orchestra jumped back as the conductor sprang at them.

Alone, Mr Piles loaded and fired every shot, running round from gun to gun and muttering 'If-I-wasn't etc-*six!*' up to seventeen, when he stood back triumphantly.

'Checkcheckcheck!'

Mr Piles strutted off the saluting gun deck, clucking like a hen who has just laid seventeen eggs.

Outside the breakwater, the special sea dutymen fell out and were relieved by the normal sea watch. The anchor cables were secured so that they swung just enough to disturb the men in the messdecks below. The hands lining the upper deck were dismissed and the ship settled down for the passage to Gibraltar.

The First Lieutenant came down from the cable deck and ordered himself a large gin.

'I thought that wasn't too bad at all, Jimmie, for the first time,' said the Communications Officer to him. 'Bit slow over that last spring though.'

'What can you expect,' growled the First Lieutenant, 'with only two men and a dog up there.'

The principle of the Cadet Training Cruiser was similar to that of a corrective school for juvenile delinquents. The cadets were hardened to their first serious experience of life at sea by shock tactics. Their time was portioned out to the last minute. Their lives were ruled by bosun's call and bugle which were the audible instruments of a routine as inexorable as time itself. Never again in their lives would the cadets perform manual and repetitive tasks for such sustained periods and never again would they be expected to assimilate the material of lectures under such difficult conditions. Their lives were a combination of officer and seaman. They were called upon to entertain guests and to scrub decks, to act as Officer of the Watch and to paint the ship's side, to waltz and to pull a boat, like sociable galley-slaves.

No cadet had any excuse for not knowing where to go or what to do at any time on any day. A large notice-board stood outside the Cadet Office with every cadet's name upon it and his watch, class, special duty and time of duty. The board showed the prophesied life of any cadet throughout the day and by looking at the symbols against his name a cadet could see his day's programme. The notice-board combined the functions of score-board, employment exchange and horoscope.

The cadets' day began at a quarter to six when they were wakened by Reveille. The Duty Petty Officer followed and completed the harm done to the fabric of sleep by walking among the lines of hammocks, prodding any remaining occupants and calling out: 'Wakey wakey! Rise and Shine! The sun's burning yore eyes out!'

At six o'clock the Port and Starboard watches of cadets, or a sufficient number of both watches to convince the Commander that they were a quorum, mustered on the quarterdeck to scrub decks. Water was hosed over the upper deck and lines of cadets marched up and down with brooms, scrubbing up, turning round, and scrubbing back in obedience to the chanted words of command: 'Scrub Forrard, Scrub Aft, Scrub Forrard, Scrub Aft!' Afterwards, when the cadets looked back on their service in *Barsetshire,* scrub decks became the symbol of the Cadet Training Cruiser. It was the trade mark of the ship, the common starting point for all reminiscences; the words 'Scrub Forrard' and 'Scrub Aft' became embedded in the subconscious memories of every cadet who passed through *Barsetshire* and were remembered long after they might have been forgotten, instinctively, like a primitive invocation to a savage African rain-god.

After breakfast, half the cadets went to instruction in the class-rooms and the other half remained on deck to work in their part of ship. The cadets did instruction or worked in their parts of ship on alternate days.

Class-room instruction was normally given by the divisional officers. Michael and Paul's divisional officer was a Lieutenant du Pont, a Fleet Air Arm pilot doing two years as a seaman executive officer and considering himself to be dwelling in the tabernacles of the uncircumcised in doing so. His seamanship was of the empirical school and he shared The Bodger's distrust of the printed word, preferring to place his faith in his own judgment and in his own view of a situation as he saw it at the time. He conducted his seamanship, in his own phrase, off the cuff. He was a raconteur of some notoriety, having an inexhaustible fund of the anecdotes which the rest of the wardroom referred to as the 'there was I, upside down, nothing on the clock and *still* climbing . . .' variety. He was known as Pontius the Pilot and listening to one of his stories, suffering under Pontius the Pilot.

Pontius the Pilot was supported by two other divisional officers, Lieutenant (E) Piggant, who lectured on engineering subjects, and Instructor Lieutenant Evans, who lectured on navigation and mathematics. They played stand-off and scrum half respectively for the ship's rugby team.

Lieutenant (E) Piggant, known as Ginger, was not an exceptional engineer officer. His lectures, like those of Pontius the

Pilot, tended to be rough and ready. He had originally volunteered to be an engineer officer, not because of any driving ambition to be an engineer, but because his training included four years ashore where he could play rugby football. His final passing-out from the engineering college had not been so much a reward for his technical ability as a recognition of his services to the college fifteen and his five Navy caps.

Instructor Lieutenant Evans, known as Evans the Slide Rule, owed his entry into the Navy to ability rather than to football, though he played football with a Welshman's national fervour. He had won a Cambridge scholarship from a Welsh mining valley school and he treated his commission in the Navy as a pleasant but hardly serious interlude before taking up his true work in research physics. He looked upon the Navy as a harmless pastime for amiable eccentrics and he found the company of naval officers fascinating, but unreal, as he would have found the company of charming lunatics. He did not properly understand his colleagues in the wardroom, and particularly The Bodger, and they did not understand him, but they appreciated his service from the base of the scrum and for that they would have tolerated anything.

The cadets' work in their parts of ship was supervised by the Captains of the Tops. The cadets in the Quarterdeck Division who had been Beattys recognised their Captain of Top at once. He was the taciturn Petty Officer Moody in *Rowbottom*.

Petty Officer Moody was a Diver, First Class. He had requested to be drafted for diving duties and had been drafted to *Rowbottom*. On leaving *Rowbottom* he had again requested to be drafted for diving duties and had been drafted to *Barsetshire*. He had never been kindly disposed to cadets and he now walked the decks of *Barsetshire* with the temperament and outlook of a man allergic to bees who has been imprisoned in an apiary. It was his custom to restrict his use of words to a minimum. He would silently indicate to a cadet to follow him, lead him to a bulkhead or a rope and silently point to it. The cadet was then left to decide what operation Petty Officer Moody required to be done.

'I didn't know whether to chip it, paint it, or pee on it,' said Paul one day in the cruise after Petty Officer Moody had shown him a bulkhead.

'So what did you do?' asked Maconochie.

'I got a bucket of water and scrubbed it. It seemed the safest thing to do.'

'How did you manage to get a bucket from Froggins?'

'Asked him for it.'

'And he gave it to you?'

'Yes. Mind you, he acted as though he was giving me his first-born child."

Able Seaman Froggins was the divisional lockerman. He lived a crustacean existence in the darkness of the tiny compartment on the upper deck from which he dispensed metal polish, cotton waste, scrubbers and general cleaning gear. He was very seldom seen to leave his locker but lurked behind the coiled ropes and tackles, invisible except for his beard, like a hermit crab. Every new cadet joining the division believed that Able Seaman Froggins had personally paid for every item of cleaning gear issued, for he portioned each tin of metal polish out as reluctantly as though its contents had been siphoned from his own veins and each scrubber as warily as though it were one of his own limbs.

Able Seaman Froggins had a magnetic effect on cleaning gear. It leapt into his hands. Scrapers, brushes, buckets and squeegees collected round him as readily as animals around St Francis of Assisi. He conducted a perpetual war with the other lockermen, and his rare sorties from his locker were invariably bandit raids from which he returned laden with gear which re-appeared a few days later freshly painted and inscribed with new initials. In the course of time Able Seaman Froggins's locker had become an Aladdin's Cave of all the implements necessary to keep a ship clean and it was curious that while other parts of the ship were reduced to their last scraper and their ultimate bale of waste, Able Seaman Froggins was able to issue every cadet in his division with a scraper and provide waste up to the last day of the week.

However rich his treasure-house was, Able Seaman Froggins

parted with nothing without a struggle. When Maconochie was ordered to clean and grease all door clips in his part of the ship and went to the locker for cleaning gear, Able Seaman Froggins gave him half a tin of polish and a handful of cotton waste.

'I can't clean much with that,' Maconochie said.

Able Seaman Froggins leaned out of the gloom and fixed Maconochie with an eye like the Ancient Mariner's.

'I could —— clean the whole —— Forth Bridge with that —— lot,' he said. 'Any —— could.'

'Well, *I* can't.'

'You must be —— wet as a —— scrubber,' said Able Seaman Froggins and retreated into the gloom.

Maconochie, however, had a consolation. He may have been wet but he was not unique. In Able Seaman Froggins's opinion all cadets were as wet as scrubbers.

After supper on *Barsetshire's* first night at sea, Michael noticed a small blue button numbered 'Eleven' pinned beside his name on the Cadet's Notice Board. A legend on one side showed Eleven as Port Look-out and a small tally at the top of the list of names which included Michael's read : '0200-0400.' The Notice Board's system was at work. It showed that Michael's sub of the watch were on watch from two until four in the morning and furthermore that Michael himself was one of the lookouts on the port side of the bridge for the same period.

Paul had a number Nine and Maconochie a number Sixteen.

'What's yours, Mike?' asked Paul.

'Lookout.'

'That's tough. I'll bet it'll be bloody cold up there.'

'What's yours?'

'Telegraphsman. What's old Trog Maconochie got?'

'Bosun's Mate.'

'They're playing it safe. I don't see how he can make a mistake with that. They'll hardly want any pipes made in the middle of the night.'

'I think I'll turn in now,' said Michael. 'If we've got to get up at two in the morning we'd better get some sleep first.'

Michael lay awake for some time thinking over his first day at sea in *Barsetshire*. He was glad that The Bodger was the new Cadet Training Officer. The Bodger's face on the Cadet's Mess-deck had somehow seemed reassuring, introducing a touch of familiarity in completely strange surroundings. Michael knew from the little he had seen of *Barsetshire* that it would demand more of him than Dartmouth. He could compare Dartmouth with school but *Barsetshire* was outside his experience. She was closer to the real Navy than the cadets had been before and Michael was more afraid of her, now that he was actually on board, than he had been of Dartmouth, once he was there.

He woke to a tug on his hammock and the light of a torch in his eyes. Denis Hubert, a Senior Cadet who was the leading cadet of Michael's sub of the watch, was peering in over the edge of the hammock.

'Are you Hobbes? Time to get up. Quarter to two. Chop chop, the poor bastard up there's probably freezing to death.'

Michael relieved Isaiah Nine Smith on the port wing of the bridge at two o'clock.

'Thank God you've come, Mike. I was beginning to feel like an iceberg. Can you see anything?'

'Not a sausage.'

'Well, there're only two lights in sight. One's jolly nearly astern now and the other's at red three zero. They've both been reported. The one out there's a ship going the same way as us. Been there all watch just about. Can you see it?'

Michael stared out to sea but could see nothing. But as his eyes grew accustomed to the darkness, he made out a faint wink of light.

'O.K., I've got it.'

'Good. Here're the binoculars. Got the weight?'

'Yes.'

'See you in the morning.'

Lookout was a comparatively minor duty, allotted to junior cadets because it was cold and monotonous and possibly because junior cadets were more likely to see something than cadets who had had their physical properties impaired by a previous cruise in *Barsetshire*. Michael had been on watch for half an hour before he saw a new light. His hands were almost too numbed to hold up the binoculars and tears wrung from his eyes by the cold wind streamed down his cheeks but he was sure about the light. It was a pale glimmer bobbing close to the water and it looked like a fishing vessel.

'Hey!' Michael shouted.

The head of the Officer of the Watch appeared at the port side of the bridge.

'There's a light out there to the left, sir! I think it's a fishing vessel, sir.'

The head of the Officer of the Watch remained at the port side of the bridge, staring at Michael. It was the Gunnery Officer.

'You,' said the Gunnery Officer, coldly. 'What's your name?'

'Hobbes, sir.'

'Hobbes, the Officer of the Watch in one of H.M. Ships is not addressed as "Hey" by the Port Lookout.'

'I'm sorry, sir.'

'When you see something and you want to report it you sing out "Port Lookout to Compass Platform" and wait until you get an answer. Then make your report, in this case—"Red Five, steady white light." And in case I didn't hear you the first time, you repeat it.'

'Aye aye, sir.'

'Well, go on then.'

'Port Lookout to Compass Platform?'

'Compass Platform.'

'Red Five, steady white light, sir. Red Five, steady white light.'

'Very good. That light has been in sight now for something like ten minutes. Resume your search.'

'Aye aye, sir.'

Michael resumed his search, discouraged.

Nevertheless, the Gunnery Officer made a careful note in a small book of the fishing vessel's bearing and distance from *Barsetshire* and *Barsetshire's* own course and speed. When Michael saw the book he thought it a lot of trouble to take over one small fishing boat, more than five miles away. He ventured to ask the Gunnery Officer.

'Hobbes,' said the Gunnery Officer, 'as you get on in the service you will meet a lot of things which seem to you rather pointless. You may rest assured that everything in the Navy has a point although you may not see it. Tortuous it may be, long-winded it may be, a lot of extra trouble it most certainly will be, but deep down there is a point. This book is the Fishing Vessels Log. There's been a feud between the Admiralty and fishermen for years. It's like one of those Sicilian vendettas handed down from father to son. Whenever one of H.M. Ships passes within miles of a fishing fleet the Admiralty are immediately flooded with claims for broken nets and lost catches. The fishermen tell the newspapers about financial ruin, bailiffs in the house, fisher-men's wives and helpless infants turned out into the snow and a slow death in the gutter amongst the herring heads for all con-cerned. It's a very poignant story and to protect themselves from its poignancy Their Lordships give us all a little book so that They can produce it in court and say : "Look, you so-and-so's, we weren't anywhere near you." So when you get to the stage of being an officer of the watch you want to keep this book up to date. It may save you a lot of nausea if you do. Does that explain it? Now push off and don't let me hear you making another report like that again or I'll have your clappers for a necktie.'

'Yes, sir,' said Michael, conscious that he had received what were, from a Gunnery Officer, kindly words.

The new cadets settled in to their life in *Barsetshire* very rapidly. After three days they found it hard to visualise any other way of life than their present one and after a week they felt as though they had been in *Barsetshire* all their lives. In a short time the junior cadets learned ways of making their lives easier. Certain animals and insects employ camouflage, armour or speed for survival, each species evolving a certain means of protection upon which it gambles its life. So the junior cadets in *Barsetshire* rapidly accumulated a store of self-protective knowledge which acted as a hard shell against the climate of existence in the Cadet

114

Training Cruiser. This knowledge was useless in any other society and became useless as soon as the cadets left *Barsetshire* but while they were in *Barsetshire* it was vital. They learnt exactly how long it took to lash up a hammock, stow it away and be up on the quarterdeck for Both Watches. They learnt which lecturers were normally late, which part of a table was generally served first, which of the Petty Officer Instructors were more easy-going, and which end of a squad of cadets was more likely to be detailed for the most unpleasant work. It was beyond the power of even the most zealous Cadet Instructor to check up on all the cadets all the time; the cadets' problem then became one of estimating the mathematical probability of being discovered.

Some cadets developed a sixth sense which warned them of danger. Paul, in particular, was one of those who became hyper-sensitive to the approach of a petty officer. In the matter of Guard and Steerage he was almost superhumanly clairvoyant.

Guard and Steerage was the most bitterly fought and most closely contested struggle of all between the cadets and their superior officers in *Barsetshire*. Any cadet who kept a watch or who had been detained on duty after midnight was entitled to a Guard and Steerage and was at liberty to stay in his hammock for half an hour after the rest of the cadets had gone to Both Watches. It was the most highly prized privilege of all and most cadets would willingly have worked all night so that they could stay in their hammock between six and half past in the morning while the rest scrubbed decks. The aim of the cadets was to take a Guard and Steerage at every opportunity; the aim of their superior officers was to ensure that only the cadets entitled had the privilege.

Paul's professed object in the training cruiser was to take a Guard and Steerage every morning; the sweetest music in his ears was the sound of decks being scrubbed by others. He would miss Both Watches every morning with impunity and then, for no logical reason, get up, lash up his hammock and scrub decks; that morning the Chief G.I. did rounds of Cadets' Messdeck and Gunrooms.

Maconochie, on the other hand, seemed incapable of avoiding

fate. He would attend Both Watches scrupulously until one morning he tired and stayed in his hammock; that morning the Chief G.I. did rounds of the Cadets' Messdeck and Gunrooms. Maconochie effected a temporary solution by shifting his hammock to a billet near Paul. Maconochie scrubbed decks when Paul scrubbed decks and when Paul stayed in his hammock Maconochie did the same. Maconochie congratulated himself on his system until the morning the Chief G.I. found them both in their hammocks when it was discovered that Paul had been in the sea-boats' crew from 0400-0600 and was entitled to a Guard and Steerage while Maconochie, who had had no watch, was not. Thereafter Maconochie attended Both Watches so regularly that Petty Officer Moody grew accustomed to his face and enquired after its absence on every occasion; it was then impossible for Maconochie to take an illicit Guard and Steerage.

One further solution was employed by Raymond Ball who never scrubbed decks but sat in the cadets' heads and read a book instead. His face had never been seen at Both Watches and consequently its absence was never remarked. Even this solution was finally defeated by the Chief G.I. who, needing some hands one morning to get up spare bedding, went along to the cadets' heads and shouted 'Fire! Fire!' Raymond Ball and a handful of others tumbled headlong into the Chief G.I.'s arms.

On the evening before *Barsetshire* reached Gibraltar, her first foreign port of the cruise, the P.M.O. gave a lecture and film show to the junior cadets. The P.M.O's lecture and film-show was famous in the training cruiser. Some of the officers on the staff attended it every cruise; they looked forward to it, as concert-goers look forward to the Promenade Concerts every year.

The P.M.O. was six feet tall, with iron grey hair and blue eyes. He was an Irishman from County Cork, a gentle and unsuspicious man by nature. Twenty years in the Navy, listening to sailors describe their complaints, had made him cynical, but had not erased the last traces of his native brogue. The P.M.O.

116

still spoke with a slight lisp and occasionally introduced an aspirate into his dental consonants.

'Tomorrow we'll be getting to Gibraltar,' said the P.M.O. to the junior cadets, 'and I've no doubt at all that some of you'll be putting your private parts where I wouldn't be putting my walking-stick. So let me be saying at the start that I'm not meaning to give you any *advice*. Nobody takes the least bit of notice of advice, and nor they should. You'll not be the first to go ashore in Gib and you'll not be the last. I'm telling ye now some of the things I've noticed in the past and which might be of use to you to know. Whether you take any notice of them at all is up to you entirely.'

The P.M.O. opened a sheaf of notes and spread them out on a table.

'There's a very awkward and unpleasant disease which people catch in the Mediterranean. It's a form of dysentery and it's known as the Malta Dog. Some people catch it because they're not used to the water, or because they've eaten something which doesn't agree with them. You can catch it from shellfish or from meat that's a bit too old. So when you go ashore to have a meal, watch out for things like prawns or lobsters or greens that have not been washed. If you do get it, come along to the Sick Bay and we'll give you some cement. Everybody has their own remedies. I always take a glass of equal parts of port and brandy.

'It'll be a bit hotter from now on than most of ye're used to. Whenever you're in a hot climate you have to take extra care to keep yourself clean. You'll have to wash yourself more often or you'll get rashes and toe rot.

'I'll not be telling ye never to sleep with strange women. That's a thing that every man has to decide for himself and the sooner the better. But if you do decide to have a little bit of excitement, don't be thinkin' ye're giving the poor frustrated girl the one night of delirious joy in her drab and dreary existence. Not at all. Ye're a part of the rent, or just a little bit on the groceries bill, or something to keep the butcher happy for a while. There'll be two types. Either she'll tell you the price straight away or she'll stay quiet and look at ye. If it's the first, then you're clear

117

where you stand. It's the second you have to be careful of. She'll be wondering how much you're good for and she'll likely over-estimate a little and you'll have to beat her down and there's no more degrading sight than a naval officer haggling with a woman over the price of a little bit of copulation.'

The Bodger sat in the front row, restraining his laughter. As a newcomer to the ship, he had never before heard the P.M.O.'s lecture and he now realised that he had been missing the perform-ance of a natural showman. The P.M.O.'s droll delivery and perfect timing might have made him famous on the stage.

'Now I'll come to the bit ye'll all be wanting to hear,' said the P.M.O. solemnly. 'The chances of catchin' something. I'll be frank with you. There's no real safeguard against venereal disease except total abstinence, just as there's no real safeguard against getting drunk except not drinkin'. But it would be a poor world without women and drink, would it not? The next best thing to abstinence is continence. If you can't contain yourself, then at least control yourself. And take care. My Chief Nightingale up at the Sick Bay will be delighted to fix you up. I can't be tellin' ye that too often.

The P.M.O. put away his notes in his pocket.

'All I've been tellin' ye,' he went on, 'goes all to hell if you've been drinkin' too much. If you're drunk, you'll behave like an animal and an animal has never heard of birth control. It's easily done. Several of you go ashore together. On the way you have a drop to drink until one of you has a drop too much. He's the one we'll call Paddy. When you all decide to go, Paddy wants to stay where he is, where it's warm and he can see the women. He won't be wantin' to be pushed into the cold where there's no beer and no women. So he stays where he is and the rest of you go on without him. From that minute, Paddy is half-way towards the Sick Bay. Now that'll be enough from me. I've got some films to show you which'll let ye see what happens to Paddy after you've left him. They'll not need any comment from me so I'll leave ye to them. I tried to get you the ones they show to the Wrens but they're booked up for years ahead so you'll just have to make do with these.'

118

The P.M.O. left the messdeck. After everyone else had sat down again The Bodger remained standing.

'Before we see the P.M.O.'s blue films,' he said, 'I want to emphasise what the P.M.O. said on the subject of liquor. Most of the local drinks in the Mediterranean are an acquired taste. Stuff like Spanish brandy, absinthe, ouzo and arrack are drunk by the local inhabitants by the quart. But if you start drinking them you'll get drunk very quickly. Some of the worst stuff will not only make you drunk, it may send you blind. In the old days they used to sell a white stick with every crate of it. Things are not so bad now as they used to be, but even now quite a lot of the local hooch will do you a power of no good. Stick to sherry or beer. Sherry is very cheap in Gibraltar and Spain and you can get some first class stuff for very little compared with what you would have to pay for it in England. That's all I have to say on that. Now for the P.M.O.'s ciné bleu.'

7

As she made her stately way down to her berth, *Barsetshire* bore up under the scrutiny of the other British and American ships in the harbour like a dowager at a reception who knows that she is probably the eldest lady present but is sure that her pearls are still the best in the room. Her white scrubbed quarter-deck, her burnished and brushed guard and band, and the slow ripple of water past the grey side in the golden Mediterranean early morning, completed a picture which had not been wonderfully created by an artist but by a set of instructions embellished by a tradition. Each part of the picture, each member of *Barsetshire's* ship's company was intent on his own role and hardly conscious of the effect which the whole achieved, but together they lifted the heads of the American sailors, leaning over the guard rails and chewing their morning gum, and made them listen to 'The Star-Spangled Banner' which *Barsetshire's* band were playing in their honour, and look at *Barsetshire* herself with respect.

Gibraltar was both the start and the finish of a foreign commission in one of H.M. Ships. Every ship on her way to the Mediterranean, South Atlantic, East Indies or Far Eastern Stations counted her time properly abroad from the day she entered Gibraltar. No ship on her way home passed through the Straits without calling there. It was the first portal to the east and the last milestone before home. Most of the sailors ashore in Gibraltar were therefore fresh from home and enjoying their first taste of a foreign port or on their way back to England and enjoying their last visit to a foreign port. The citizens of Gibraltar were subjected to the constant merry-making of ever-renewing, never-tiring hordes of sailors.

The novelty of the celebrations wore off for the Gibraltarians some time early in the nineteenth century. Since then they have watched the antics of the Royal Navy ashore in their citadel follow an ancient and time-honoured pattern. Beer bottles bearing traditional labels sail through the windows of the same bars. The same cars are overturned. The pavements in Main Street have been worn thin by the waiting boots of innumerable patrols. The Naval Provost Marshal has been issuing identical warnings for over a century and the longest-standing and most eagerly read column in the Gibraltar press is the one dealing with the outrages of sailors. When the Americans began to come to Gibraltar, some of the more wishful-thinking of the Gibraltarians hoped that times would change but experience showed that the American sailors ashore behaved much like the British except that they were, if anything, more thorough in anything they attempted and more generous in the payment of compensation. In the process of time the more philosophical Gibraltarians have grown accustomed to the intoxicated sailor and accept him for the trade he brings; they regard the nightly wassail in Main Street as one of the penalties of living in a gateway to the East. An entrance to a main road must expect its share of traffic incidents.

None of the junior cadets had been to Gibraltar before but they were all inheritors of an extensive folk-lore of visits there in other ships and in other cruises which was passed on to them by the Instructors and by the senior cadets. The Chief G.I., in particular, seemed to have brought so much trade to the local trades and professions of Gibraltar and La Linea that some of the junior cadets wondered why he was not made a Freeman.

The Chief G.I. collected the leave cards when the cadet libertymen mustered on the upper deck for inspection.

'All off ashore?' he asked sardonically, and unnecessarily.

121

'You'll have to go across the border if you want to get your hand on it. You won't get a bit this side. Fifty pesetas, and then you'll be seen off.'

'A bit of what?' asked George Dewberry wonderingly.

'A bit of crumpet,' said Raymond Ball.

'*Crumpet?*'

'Skip it.'

'That reminds me,' said Paul. 'Did you get our passes, Mike?'

'Yep. The Bodger gave them to me. You all owe me two bob.'

'Libertymen carry on down into the boat,' said the Chief G.I. 'Don't all rush at once.'

'I wonder which of us will be Paddy?'

'I reckon George Dewberry is our best bet,' said Raymond Ball.

'I don't see Trog Maconochie anywhere,' said Paul.

'He's looking for his belt. Little does he know I'm wearing it.'

'How shall we play it this evening?'

'Well,' said Paul, 'I vote we have something to drink first, and then something to eat, and then a little more to drink and by that time it'll be time to go across the border.'

'The Bodger told me there's not much point in going across before ten and it's a good idea to get back before the border closes at one. Otherwise they keep you in a Spanish jail for months while they find out from Cadiz what to do with you.'

'I expect he knows by experience. I bet The Bodger'll be good for the woman's rent, rates, laundry and groceries and probably educate one of the children as well.'

In the first few hundred yards from the landing stage the cadets met more American patrols than Gibraltarians, but once up the steps and into Main Street they found themselves swallowed up in the beginnings of an evening which Gibraltar had come to know very well.

The bars were all similar. They had swing doors, a band with a female trumpeter on a dais, and they were full of sailors. The bars sounded the same, with the jarring notes of a trumpet, drums and castanets, shouts and songs and the accumulated sound of voices talking, bottles clinking and shuffling feet. In the street, bullfight posters were pasted on the blank spaces of the wall by a lottery stand. The shops offered highly coloured rugs, cigarette lighters, cameras, clocks, shirts, watches, bales of cloth, handbags, bullfight photographs, toy monkeys and perfume. There were very few cars and those made their way slowly between the crowds who walked in the centre of the narrow street. American and British sailors jostled small, swarthy men in pastel-shaded suits. The women watched from the tiny balconies with latticed and fretted windows on the first floor.

As the sun went down in rose and scarlet and finally indigo far out in the Atlantic beyond the Pillars of Hercules, the noise in Main Street swelled. The music from the bars grew louder and the swing doors belched out a stream of sailors who tumbled into the street, picked themselves up and tottered to the bar next door. The tinkling of broken glass attracted a patrol from the other side of the street and they went into the bar to quell the first fight. Their entrance was the cue for redoubled shouts from inside and higher and more frenzied notes on the trumpet while the castanets carried on their steady ticking without a break in their rhythm. The Gibraltar evening was warming up according to its traditional schedule.

The cadets ate prawn cocktails, swordfish steaks and pineapple fruit salad and afterwards drank beer quietly in bars where girls of fourteen or fifteen in flaring skirts danced the paso doble with dark youths in tight-fitting trousers and short black jackets.

'Come on, George. Don't be a *Paddy!*'

The name struck a chord of memory. George Dewberry straightened up.

'Lord no !' he snorted indignantly. 'Don' wanna be a *Paddy*. Ya know what h-happens to Paddys !'

'Come on then.'

George Dewberry reluctantly followed the others outside. He had been enjoying the heat and the taste of the beer in his throat and the dizzy dancing of the women.

They changed their money into pesetas at the end of Main Street and took a taxi to the border. They walked across into

Spain, where the frontier guards took no more notice of them than if they had been Spanish flies, although they looked concerned when George Dewberry lurched towards a bullfight poster.

George Dewberry led the way by instinct into the first bar.

The walls were tiled with scenes from the bullfight. The bar itself was of hard black wood polished with a wet cloth and barrels of sherry were stacked to the roof behind it. The bartender kept each customer's score chalked on the bar and no money passed until the customer was ready to leave. Each drinker was besieged by a clamouring crowd of shoe-shine boys, men selling fountain pens and postcards, and small girls holding baskets of peanuts and flowers.

The bar was crowded with officers from *Barsetshire,* among them The Bodger, who had his arm round the bartender's wife, and was loudly calling for Fundadore for both of them.

Raymond Ball looked around him.

'Might as well be back in *Barsetshire,*' he said disgustedly. 'Come on, Paul. Let's try somewhere else. This place is too sordid for words.'

They collected George Dewberry, who, in one crowded minute, had had his right shoe polished and had bought three bags of peanuts, a carnation and a postcard of two women wrestling with a donkey, and went outside.

Deeper in the town they came upon a street which reeked of lechery. The air smelt sickly, over-ripe with the smell of offal and garbage. The very houses huddled lewdly together and women in the doorways winked invitingly at the cadets and leapt out into the street to snatch at them.

'Golly!' said Paul. 'This is like something out of Hogarth in one of his juicier moods. Let's get out of the light before we all get raped.'

Raymond Ball might have considered the bar they had just left sordid, but the first bar the cadets tried in this street showed him that there were still depths they had not plumbed.

The bar was small and dark and had a stale smell. It contained two women, one behind the bar and the other in front.

124

Both were past their prime but they had been good-looking in their youth and even now they had preserved a lush maturity of figure which made George Dewberry's eyes pop.

'Ai-yai-*yai!*' he said excitedly.

'Quiet, you bloody idiot!' whispered Paul. 'You're here to drink and that's all. Either of those harridans could eat you alive and come back for more, so keep your eyes in the boat.'

Paul ordered four sherries.

But the woman in front of the bar had already noticed that George Dewberry was the most susceptible member of the party. She sidled up to him.

She was wearing a sagging black dress which drooped low over her breasts.

'What your name, Joe?' she grated in a metallic voice which made George Dewberry start like a spurred stallion.

'Paddy,' answered George Dewberry brightly.

'Come to bed, Paddy.'

'Oh I *say!*'

'Come to bed, Paddy.'

George Dewberry giggled.

'George old man, she's quite serious,' said Raymond Ball.

The woman slid closer to George Dewberry and wound a long serpentine arm round his neck.

'Come to bed, Paddy,' she repeated purposefully.

'Oh, I couldn't! I mean, I hardly know you . . . '

The woman was four inches taller than George Dewberry. She stood fully upright and glared down at him with burning, hypnotic eyes.

The others swallowed the remains of their drinks, seized George Dewberry and hurried outside. The woman pursued them.

'*Come to bed, Paddy! Fifty* pesetas!'

They ran past the next bar, where the Chief Bosun's Mate and the Chief G.I. in plain clothes were drinking.

In the third bar they found Maconochie, who was pinned in a corner by a small woman.

'They all seem to have one track minds in this place,' said Paul.

'Dirt track minds, you mean,' said Raymond Ball.

125

Maconochie looked up and saw them gazing in at him from the window.

'Hey, you guys!' he shouted. 'Come and give us a hand will you? Quick!'

The rest crowded into the bar. The small woman was ecstatic. She released Maconochie and hurried behind the bar to serve them.

Maconochie was glad to see them.

'I never thought I'd be pleased to see you lot,' he said. 'I couldn't see how I was going to get away without assaulting her and she'd probably have had the police in.'

'You nearly didn't see young George here at all. We only just got him out of the last place alive.'

'She was sort of hypnotic. If she'd gone on saying "Come to bed" in that tone of voice much longer I wouldn't have been able to stop myself.'

'The moral is don't come to these places alone.'

'She wasn't bad looking actually,' said Raymond Ball. 'In a reptilian sort of way.'

'Never mind, come on, men. Let's try somewhere else. We're obviously in good company.'

The next bar was also a dance hall. A man and a girl were dancing a form of paso doble in the middle of the floor. It was not the paso doble of Gibraltar. The Gibraltar paso doble was a formal dance executed for the customers. This was the authentic mating dance of man and woman, a wild dance, without inhibitions.

'Name of a name of a name,' said Paul. 'Do you see what I see?'

'It's Pete Cleghorn,' whispered Raymond Ball in a hushed voice.

As a dancer of repute himself, Raymond Ball was both shocked and envious. He had always thought Peter Cleghorn a particularly dull person and had attributed it to his Pangbourne upbringing. Now he saw him dancing in a manner which, in a British dance hall, would have put him in the hands of the constabulary. Raymond Ball also knew that his own technique might be better but he could never match Peter Cleghorn's élan.

The party watched in amazement from the door as he whirled his partner, flung back his head, stamped his foot and brought the dance to an end.

'Ole!' the room shouted, as Cleghorn led his partner back to a table. 'Ole! Ole!'

They crossed over and stood around Peter Cleghorn's table. 'Hi fellows!'

'Pete, I didn't know you could dance like that!'

'I didn't know myself. This is the first time I've tried it. I've watched about four of the bloody things tonight and I thought I might as well have a go at it. What did you think of it?'

'Hot stuff, boy. You'd better let The Bodger have a look. That's right up his street.'

'Heaven forbid. Have you met Conchita?'

Conchita had black hair and very white teeth and looked about sixteen years of age. She smiled at the cadets round the table but she plainly had no eyes for anyone but this phenomenal Englishman who had out-Spaniarded the Spaniards.

'We'll leave you to it,' said Paul.

Raymond Ball was separated from the main party in the next bar. He was much taken with a girl who, until he noticed her, had been sitting by herself and taking no part in the entertainment.

'I say, Mike, lend me thirty pesetas, will you?'

'Surely,' said Michael.

'Thanks.'

Raymond Ball went over to the girl, who looked up enquiringly.

'Hello, my dear,' he said, in his most engaging manner, which made Michael think of the Walrus talking to the Oysters. 'How about a little bit of je ne sais quoi?'

'Eighty-five pesetas,' said the girl briskly.

'Whatever you say, my dear.'

'Well, I'll be goddamned,' said Paul. 'Would you like to take a walk? Let's go and find our own exibeesh, Mike.'

'Good idea,' said Michael.

* * *

Towards midnight, the bars and the curtained spaces behind them began to empty. Paul and Michael walked arm in arm up the street back to the frontier, following in the zigzag wake of Maconochie and George Dewberry just ahead.

As they passed the first bar they had visited, they saw the tall woman in the black dress talking to The Bodger.

'Come to bed, Bodger,' she was saying. 'Forty-five pesetas!'

8

BARSETSHIRE was an elderly lady who needed more time and care than most to make up her face and complete her toilette. Each cruise she retired to a secluded spot to paint ship; in the Mediterranean cruise she anchored in a remote Sardinian bay.

The bay was a desolate spot, with bare brown hills on either side, empty of life or habitation of any kind. In the afternoons the water stretched as smooth as sheet glass and the outline of the shore was distorted by dancing heat vapours. *Barsetshire* lay at anchor, still and motionless, like a painted ship upon a painted ocean. Here, the ship's company settled down to paint ship, or rather, the cadets painted, and the ship's company settled down to watch.

The junior cadets, in their innocence, could not have imagined that there was more to Paint Ship than merely taking paint from a pot and applying it to the ship's side. But they were to learn better. There is more to the art of cosmetics than the mere taking of cream and colour from bottles and putting it on to the skin. Paint Ship in H.M.S. *Barsetshire* was attended with all the rites and ceremonies of a Pompadour's levee.

Able Seaman Froggins and the other lockermen marshalled an awe-inspiring parade of scrapers, buckets and scrubbers (Paint Ship was for them the high moment of a cruise, just as Mr Piles' was a Gun Salute). The Bosun and his party provided a forest of stages, bosun's chairs and ropes. The Painter mustered bundles of brushes and drew off pot after pot of grey paint. The Ship's Band filled a motor cutter and cruised round and about playing excerpts from the operas of Wagner, the Bandmaster conducting from the sternsheets, while the Commander, surrounded by a retinue of divisional officers, captains of tops, the Mate of the Upper Deck and the Chief Bosun's Mate, drove round the ship in the Captain's Motorboat pointing out weak patches in the ship's side with the pomp and authority of a Doge going out to wed the Adriatic.

Before actual painting, there was scrubbing. Stages were lowered over the ship's side, two cadets were lowered on to each stage, and two buckets and two scrubbers were lowered down to each pair of cadets. Every scrubber was attached to a cadet by a lanyard. It might have been assumed that the lanyards were provided so that the scrubbers might in some measure act as marker buoys for cadets who fell from the stages into the sea. Nothing could have been further from the truth. The cadets were intended to act as marker buoys for the scrubbers.

When the ship's side had been scrubbed, bad patches were rubbed with brick and rust marks taken off with scrapers. The canvas was then ready for the paint.

Most of the cadets enjoyed painting. It was one of the few creative pieces of work they were called upon to do in the training cruiser. They found it pleasant to hang over the side on a stage in the sunshine and watch the area of gleaming new paintwork growing overhead.

It was while painting ship that Paul first came into contact with the cadet disciplinary authorities. He was sharing a stage with Maconochie, which was perhaps the root of the trouble. Misfortune hovered over Maconochie as a halo over a saint.

'Don't you feel a certain—how shall I put it?—*atavistic* pleasure in painting, Trog?' asked Paul, of Maconochie.

'Don't call me that,' growled Maconochie.

'But don't you feel something carnally satisfying about it? Dip the brush in, twirl it around, scrape it on the edge, two strokes up, two strokes down, rub it well in and finish on the upward stroke. Don't you sense something vaguely sexually stimulating in it?'

'No,' said Maconochie.

Paul had confirmed early in the cramped space of *Barsetshire* what he had suspected at Dartmouth. Maconochie had no sense of humour. He took everything said to him at its face value. He made a perfect foil for Paul in whimsical mood.

'Like the last lascivious kisses of a dying love, don't you think? The brush moving up and down like the drooping of silken eyelashes against a satin cheek.'

'It's nothing like that.'

'Nor like the caress of a fingertip trailed in tranquil water and sprinkled on a lily-like breast beneath the waving willows?'

'No.'

'Not even the waving willows, Trog?'

'I've told you before, *don't* call me that.'

'You will live to a great age, Trog. I prophesy it. Others may come, dwell their little hour or so, worry a little, and then go. But not Trog. Trog the Inscrutable. The Great Trog, the great-nephew of the Great Chang. Have you ever tried to unscrew the inscrutable, Trog?'

'*No.*'

'Try it. You will find it as rewarding as that wretched band are finding their rendering of The Ride of the Valkyries with the Commander bellowing like a mad thing next door to them. Have you ever ridden with the Valkyries, Trog?'

'Oh, go and get knotted.'

'Tut tut.'

Just then the Captain's red setter, Owen Glendower, looked over the ship's side. Owen Glendower normally enjoyed Paint Ship as much as anyone. There were always interesting pots and cans to sniff at, the decks were always filled with bustle and excitement, there were always ropes and lanyards to gnaw at, and above all there were always more, and more senior, feet to trip over him. Since the day Maconochie had inadvertently trodden on him, Owen Glendower had disliked him; as far as Owen Glendower was concerned, Maconochie's name might as

131

well have been Dr Fell. When Owen Glendower looked over the ship's side and saw Maconochie, his day was spoiled. He seated himself on the beading which ran round the upper deck, immediately above Maconochie's head.

'There's that bloody pooch,' said Maconochie.

Paul looked up and saw a part of Owen Glendower projecting over the sill.

'He doesn't seem to like us very much.'

'It's mutual,' said Maconochie sourly.

Paul looked up at Owen Glendower again. A great temptation seized him. He struggled with it for a time and then gave in. After all, Paul thought, was it not Oscar Wilde who said that the only way to get rid of temptation was to yield to it?

'What would Oscar Wilde have done?' asked Paul rhetorically. Owen Glendower gave a yelp of rage and vanished.

The Cadet Training Officer's Requestmen and Defaulters were held in a special office just off the cadets' messdeck. It was used for nothing else and the inference was that there were normally so many requestmen and defaulters that a separate room was required to hold them. When Paul arrived the only other cadet there was Peter Cleghorn but because he was a requestman and not a defaulter like Paul, Peter Cleghorn was ordered to stand on the other side of the passageway.

Inside the office, The Bodger stood behind a table with Mr Piles at his side to call out the names of the cadets as they were summoned into the presence of the Cadet Training Officer.

'Cadet Cleghorn!'

'Sir!'

Peter Cleghorn sprang to attention and doubled inside. At the door he caught his foot on the sill and fell in a praying attitude in front of The Bodger.

'Get-off-of-your-knees-Cadet-Cleghorn! Cadet Cleghorn, sir, request to discontinue shaving.'

The Bodger beetled his eyebrows.

'So you want to grow a set, Cleghorn?'

132

'Yes sir.'

'Think you can manage it?'

'Yes sir.'

'How often do you have to shave?'

'Once a day, sir.'

'Quietly confident, eh?'

'Yes sir.'

'Well I'm not! Furthermore, even if you did succeed in growing a set, which I doubt, I'm not going to have one of my cadets going about the place looking like a gingerbread Saint. Not granted. Get your hair cut.'

'Not granted. Salute! A-bout turn, double march, get your hair cut!'

Peter Cleghorn doubled away. Mr Piles cleared his throat.

'Cadet Vincent!'

'Sir!'

'Cadet Vincent, off—cap! Cadet Vincent, sir, first charge, did on the third of October, commit an act prejudicial to good order and naval discipline in that he did improperly paint the rectum of one male red setter dog, the property of Captain Sir Douglas Mainwaring Gregson, Royal Navy, Kennel Club Number 426692L. Second charge, did, on the third of October, improperly use one pot of Admiralty pattern grey paint.'

The Bodger studied the charge sheet.

'Mr Piles?'

'I investigated this case, sir. Cadet Vincent was sharing a stage with Cadet Maconochie sir, while painting ship. They were painting ship sir, when the dog made his appearance on the upper deck above them. On seeing the dog, Cadet Vincent reached up and painted the dog's rectum, sir, with Admiralty paint. This action was witnessed by Petty Officer Moody, the Captain of Top. When I asked Cadet Vincent if he had anything to say he was in a very excited state, sir. Kept talking about someone called Oscar Wilde, sir. There is no cadet on board with that name, sir. I've checked.'

'Thank you, Mr Piles. Have you anything to say *now*, Vincent?'

133

'Well, no sir, except that it was purely in self-defence.'

'Self-defence?'

'The dog attacked me, sir.'

'*Attacked* you? What, *arse* first?'

'It was a most threatening attitude, sir.'

'I never heard anything like it. If you go around like this, Vincent, you're going to be a menace to society and I hope I never have to serve with you. Lieutenant du Pont, how does Cadet Vincent do his duty?'

Pontius the Pilot had hurried from the wardroom on hearing that one of his cadets was charged with committing an unnatural offence. He was baffled by the reference to Admiralty paint which he had heard as he came through the door.

'Vincent is generally reliable, sir,' he said. 'I can't say I've noticed any signs of aberration before.'

'Hardly an aberration,' said The Bodger. 'I would call it more of a decoration. Though it was hard luck on the dog.'

'*Dog!*'

'The Captain's dog.'

'The *Captain's* dog!'

'Yes, yes, the Captain's dog,' The Bodger said impatiently. 'Now look here, Vincent. You'd better remember this. You can do what you like with a senior officer's wife but keep clear of his dog, his car and his yacht. Get it?'

'Yes sir.'

'Five days Number Eleven punishment.'

'Five days Number Eleven punishment! *On*-cap! A-bout turn, double march!'

Outside, Paul was met by a deputation.

'How did you get on?' asked Michael.

'Five days number elevens.'

'You were lucky,' said Peter Cleghorn. 'You know how the old man feels about his dog. I'm surprised he didn't personally call for your head on a silver salver.'

'Oh, The Bodger seemed to think it was jolly funny. He gave me a Bodgerism and five days number elevens.'

'Tough luck.'

134

'The only person I'm annoyed with is Maconochie. I reckon it was all his fault anyway.'

'It normally is.'

Paul's punishment was inconvenient rather than arduous. It curtailed his spare time but did not impose any undue hardship. It consisted mainly of extra work which normally devolved to picking cigarette ends and rubbish up from the upper deck. Paul was shaken a quarter of an hour earlier in the morning and spent the time picking up cigarette ends; during the dog watches he picked up cigarette ends for half an hour and did half an hour's drill under the supervision of the Duty Regulating Petty Officer Cadet; and he mustered for evening rounds outside the Cadet Office, having picked up cigarette ends for the previous quarter of an hour.

After two days Paul became as expert as a truffle hound. He knew all the likely places for cigarette ends and visited them periodically, as a hunt draws likely coverts for fox. On the third day there were very few cigarette ends to pick up and Paul was forced to ask the other members of his gunroom to stub out their cigarette ends on the upper deck to give him some employment; even so he frequently found himself faced with endless stretches of deck barren of cigarette ends and he made an arrangement with the gunroom sweepers that they emptied their gunroom spit-kids on to the upper deck as soon as they heard the defaulters call sounded off. On the fifth and last day of his punishment Paul had a fellow defaulter to keep him company and, when he went, to assume his mantle. It was Maconochie, who was given three days Number Eleven punishment by The Bodger for empty-ing his spitkid on to the upper deck instead of down a gash-shute.

Paul's punishment lasted until *Barsetshire* had finished paint-ing ship and sailed to her next port, on the Côte d'Azur.

The bay where *Barsetshire* anchored was cupped in hills which were studded with villas and groves of trees. The small town was built of narrow, red and yellow houses which mounted the hillside to the Corniche above. The harbour was filled with yachts and *Barsetshire* was surrounded by tiny floats paddled by bronzed and near-naked Frenchmen. Monte Carlo lay a few miles to the east, Nice a few miles to the west and the Alpes Maritimes rose up in the blue background.

Michael's first special duty was Main Signals Office Messenger. The duties of M.S.O. Messenger, as described by the Chief G.I., were to deliver signals to the officers addressed, make the tea for the watch, and keep out of the Chief Yeoman's way.

When Michael reported, he found the office deserted but a murmur of voices led him out on to the Flag Deck where several signalmen were gathered round the largest telescope in the ship. Their attention was so close and unwinking that Michael thought that a signal of unusual interest was being passed. Perhaps England had declared war on France, or the Commander been promoted.

'Coo!' said the nearest signalman. 'That's what I want for Christmas, mother dear.'

'Let's have it over here a minute, Johno. I think I can see a good one.'

'You go and get stuffed. This is all mine. Keep your filthy fingers off while I look at what makes the world go round.'

Michael picked up a pair of binoculars, followed the signalman's line of sight, and saw a young woman sunbathing in the garden of a villa. She was wearing a very short bathing costume.

'Left a bit,' said a voice at Michael's elbow.

Michael shifted left and saw another young woman, wearing an even briefer costume; it seemed to Michael that she was not so much wearing it as lying near it.

'Now look right and down a bit at five o'clock,' said the voice.

Michael again obeyed and understood the signalmen's absorption. For there lay a third young woman. There was no costume, merely the young woman. Michael had always thought that the Communications Branch led a dull and miserable existence, but he now saw that they, like everybody else, had their compensations.

'Not bad at all,' said the voice.

'Would you like a look?'

136

'Yes please.'

Michael took the binoculars from his eyes and handed them over.

'Thank you,' said the Communications Officer.

Meanwhile, Ted Maconochie was having difficulty with his special duty. He was bowman of a motor boat.

When a boat approached the gangway, the bowman was required to climb on to the forepeak with his boat-hook and there perform a series of exercises known as boat-hook drill.

'Thump your boat-hook twice on the deck,' said the Chief G.I., 'to give your sternsheetsman the tip. Throw your boat-hook up, catch it at the point of balance, swing it horizontal, and then shift your grip to catch the boat-rope.'

It was not a series of movements which lent itself to grace; Maconochie, even after considerable practice, still looked like a drum-major on stilts.

The coxswain of the boat was an Indian named Rorari who was not a good coxswain.

'The best thing you can do,' said Maconochie to Rorari, 'is fall overboard and let someone else have a go who knows what he's doing.'

Maconochie's advice was apt when Rorari next brought his boat alongside the gangway. Rorari was lying off when the Officer of the Watch, the Gunnery Officer, came out on to the platform of the gangway to motion him with his telescope to come alongside.

Rorari's boat leapt forward, struck the gangway, and bore up on it, goring it like a savage bull. The gangway swayed under the impact like a reed in a storm and a violent shiver passed up its length. The Gunnery Officer lost his balance and plummeted down into the sea. Rorari opened his throttle wide and accelerated so swiftly that the sternsheetsman, who had been gazing compassionately at the spot of bubbling sea where he had last seen the Gunnery Officer, was caught unawares and silently vanished away over the stern. Maconochie laughed scornfully.

Rorari, who was looking for a scapegoat, heard the laugh.

'Mac'notchee!' he screeched. 'I see you! I see you! You say you are not doing anything while all the time you are doing something! All the time you are laughing, joking say "Fall overboard"! You ball me up I ditch you!'

Maconochie gave another scornful laugh. Rorari wrenched the wheel hard over. The boat tilted in a tight circle and Maconochie flew off at a tangent.

The third member of the crew, the stoker, a Sikh named Singh, realised that every man who sailed with Rorari was, like the men who sailed with Hawkins, doomed to a watery grave, kept his eyes down and studied his gauges and was still on board when Rorari came alongside again, which he did by driving the boat at the gangway and allowing the gangway to stop the boat. The Gunnery Officer was waiting on the step.

'Rorari, Rorari, you're an incompetent, dangerous, criminal, nitwitted, blockheaded, thick-skulled, homicidal, bloody idiot!'

'Please sir, it was not my fault! It was not my fault, sir! The bowman balled me up, sir!'

'Who was your bowman?'

'Mac'notchee, sir!'

'Ah yes.'

George Dewberry went ashore to Jimmy's Bar and drank vin blanc. It seemed to him the only sensible thing to do.

Later in the evening The Bodger went ashore to Jimmy's Bar with the Communications Officer. They drank Dubonnet and watched the passers-by.

'Talent's not bad here at all, eh Bodger?'

'Not bad.'

'Not a bad figure at all, that last one.'

'Not bad. Bit shop-soiled.'

The Bodger looked gloomily into his glass.

'Oh come, Bodger. Since when this looking of the gift-horse in the mouth?'

138

'Gift-horse?'

'My dear old Bodger, if you haven't learnt the signals by now, you've no right to call yourself an officer in charge of cadets' training. It's the first thing you should teach them.'

'What are you burbling about, Chris, for God's sake?'

'Forget it.'

The Communications Officer returned to his scrutiny of the local talent. The Bodger looked at his glass.

'Bolshie lot of cadets this cruise, Bodger?'

'Eh?'

'Bolshie this cruise?'

'Who?'

'*Cadets*. Oh, for Pete's sake Bodger, snap out of it! What's troubling you?'

'Sorry, I was just thinking of all those cadets we've got on board.'

'What about them?'

'There they all are, just out of the egg, mad keen, anxious to learn and do well. Most of them, anyway. We encourage them, all of us from Admirals downwards, to *be* keen. And for what? For why? What's going to happen to them all?'

'Well, they'll all grow up and either be promoted and become admirals, or be passed over and grow onions.'

'That's not what I meant at all. We talk to them about officer-like qualities, we tell them all about word of command, lecture to them about leadership, fill them up with bull and they appear to believe it. Or if they don't believe it, they're polite enough to conceal it. Sometimes I think those cadets on board are laughing at us, humouring us as though we were a lot of fat uncles playing bears, and other times I think they believe every word and everything we do or say has the most frightful significance for the future. It's the second alternative which scares me, because not only are we deluding them, we're deluding ourselves.'

'Oh, everybody knows the whole thing is a colossal confidence trick,' the Communications Officer said. 'No cadet could do all he's expected to do in that vessel and come out alive, and any one of us who tried to watch all of them all of the time would go straight round the bend.'

'I mean something much more serious than that. If we go on as we are now, in ten years' time there won't *be* any leaders or anyone whom we can draw on for officers. I don't mean to be snobbish in the least little bit but there used to be a class of people in the country who could be relied on to lead. They may have been queers, they may have seduced all the village girls and barred themselves up in their houses for years. They may have been megalomaniacs, or mad, or obstinate, or eccentric, or downright scoundrels but at least they knew how to *lead*.'

'Bodger, you sound like a curate with doubts! Don't you realise this is blasphemy! Don't you know there is but one God to be worshipped and the First Lord is his prophet and his address is Whitehall?'

The Bodger thumped his fist on the table. 'They're not doubts, they're *certainties*. Look at that cadet sitting over there. I used to know his family when we lived in their part of the world. Dewberry. They used to own a good part of the British Isles and one of his family have represented them in every war the country's had since Agincourt. And look at him. Do you think he wants to be in the Navy? Do you think he wants to lead men? Does he hell! He probably doesn't know what he wants but I'm damned certain he doesn't like what he's got! I can see the day coming in twenty years' time when most of these lads will be coming up for Captain, when the Navy will be run by the people, for the people, on behalf of the people. It's my favourite nightmare. Until there's a war, of course. When that happens command will be left in the hands of a few blokes who know what they're doing and do it without having to account for it, simply because there just isn't time to check up on them. But the minute the shouting and tumult's over, and all the captains and kings have departed, every Tom, Dick and Harry gets a chance to think twice about things and we go back to the good old days of "For why did you do this when you knew so and so had happened?" and "For what did you give that order when surely you were aware of the grave consequences of any continued deterioration in the so on and so on *ad nauseum*?" Then when a war comes along the first thing you've got to do is sack all the peace-time admirals and promote new ones. The wretched fellows have got used to a state where they can't move a finger because one, they haven't got the money, and two, they have to answer for *everything* to the politicians. If a rating wants anything to happen in a hurry all he's got to do is write to his M.P. and then sit back and watch the fur fly. Did I ever tell you about a very great friend of mine called Jimmy Forster-Jones?'

The name registered immediately upon the Communications Officer.

'The character who gassed the ship's company's canary?'

The Bodger thumped the table again.

'That's *exactly* what I'm getting at! Now Jimmy's known as the character who gassed the ship's company's canary. In spite of the fact that Jimmy was probably the finest clearance diver the Navy's ever had. He did more for good publicity for the Navy in those films about under-water warfare than anyone since Noël Coward. Do you know what actually happened about that canary?'

'Well, there were various yarns going about. The one I heard . . .'

'Jimmy's a friend of mine and I heard the whole story from him and from some of the other blokes who were in the ship at the time. Jimmy was a junior two-striper in a cruiser and he had a chap in his division who had a bucket-bird. You can buy them ashore in the Far East. When the bird's hungry it rings a little bell in its cage and you put the grub in a small basket and the bird hauls it up. Quite clever, in a monotonous sort of way. This particular bird didn't sing, dance or recite, it just rang the bell and hauled the bucket up. Well, one day this bird's owner, who was a bit of a bird himself, slapped in a request to see Jimmy about his bucket-bird. This character said his bird was not thriving on the messdeck. The fumes from some machinery space or other under the messdeck were making the bird cough and he wanted permission to hang the cage on the upper deck. Jimmy said O.K. but not until next week. There was an admiral's inspection coming off in a couple of days and the cage would be in the way of cleaning so Jimmy suggested that the bird should be put in the Sick Bay until the inspection was over and then it could go on the upper deck. The bloody bird had been on the messdeck about a year already and a couple more days wouldn't do it any harm. But this character wouldn't have it. He said bucket-birds needed constant care and attention and they'd probably poison it in the Sick Bay or slit its throat or something. So the cage went back on the messdeck. As luck would have it the bird pegged out the very next day. When they looked at it the next morning, there it was, dead. It was probably just old, but there was the most terrible uproar about it! You know what Jolly Jack is like when he thinks the awficers are not respecting his rights.'

'You needn't tell me.'

'They all nattered about it so much that they eventually came round to the idea that Jimmy had actually got up in the middle of the night and poisoned the bloody thing. You know how these things get going once they start. The owner of the bucket-bird wrote to his wife and she wrote to their M.P., complaining of the treatment her husband had received, you know, why couldn't sailors keep their pets like everyone else and what brutes the awficers were, starving and poisoning the sailors' dumb friends. This was just at the time when all the Marshals of the Royal Air Force were sounding off about how redundant the Navy was and this letter was just up the M.P.'s street. He wrote to the First Lord, who tackled the Board of Admiralty about it, who wrote to Jimmy's Captain and before Jimmy could say "bucket-bird" he was up in his best bib and tucker before the Old Man.'

'Poor old toff.'

'Then the newspapers got hold of it. Front page headlines. "Simple Humanities Unknown in Navy." "What Would Nelson Have Said?" "Bucket-Bird Bloodbath." "Canary Carnage." You probably saw them.'

'Yes, I remember them.'

'Clergymen started writing for the Sunday newspapers about

it and the *Daily Disaster* ran a special feature about the Navy bringing in everything from Captain Bligh to the Invergordon Mutiny. They even unearthed some cracked old retired commander living in Leicestershire and psychoanalysed him. The poor old sod found he'd been a sadist all his life and hadn't known anything about it. The Navy got beaten by the Army at Twickenham the next day and the *Daily Disaster* ran a special jubilee *edition* with all the print running sideways. Then the R.S.P.C.A. chimed in and old ladies began to hiss poor Jimmy in the street. Well, inside a week there was a full scale nausea. Chaps coming down from the Admiralty and Jimmy getting into swords and medals every time the bell struck. The part that really hurt Jimmy was when an old lady who ran an aviary wrote him a letter saying that she didn't think he was as bad as everyone said he was and would he come for a day and see over her aviary and see for himself that tiny defenceless birds could be charming companions—what the hell are you laughing at?'

The Communications Officer was leaning back in his chair with an expression of pain on his face. He had some difficulty in speaking.

'Oh . . . Bodger . . . I . . . I'm sorry,' he spluttered, 'but the idea of an N.O. being shown round an aviary by an old lady who thinks he's a monster . . . it's too much !'

'Ha bloody ha,' said The Bodger nastily. 'It's finished Jimmy. I shall be very surprised if he ever gets promoted now. The trouble with a thing like that is that once it starts it gets bigger and the more it goes on, the more people hear about it, the more other people hear about it and the bigger the stink gets. That little episode went on and on until everybody was heartily sick of it. And it didn't do any good either. Jimmy is now known as the Scourge of God in the bird-fanciers' world. That rating certainly did not get recommended for leading hand and will have the reputation of being a sea-lawyer all the time he's in. And the First Lord was shifted to the Ministry of Agriculture. There wasn't even an enquiry into conditions on the messdeck. Apparently it never occurred to anyone that the fumes which gassed a bucket-bird might also do the same to human beings.'

'Ah well,' said the Communications Officer. 'That's life.'

In spite of The Bodger's remarks about him, George Dewberry was enjoying the Mediterranean. It was providing a new and enchanting range of drinks to sample. George Dewberry sampled the local wines so fully that he was almost always drunk on shore. Many of the cadets were confused by the rush and excitement of the new places they visited; frequently their only memory of a town or port was the kind of liquor on which George Dewberry was drunk.

There was Sorrento, a town set in orange and olive trees, monastic calm and cliffs along the sea, where George Dewberry drank Orvieto; Pompeii, where Paul sported amongst buildings and statues, and George Dewberry drank Lacrima Cristi; Vesuvius, where, the funicular having been swept away by an eruption and not yet rebuilt, a guide rushed on up the mountain ahead of the cadets with bottles of vino rosso, which nobody bought at the price except George Dewberry; Capri, where the funicular broke down for half an hour and left the cadets seemingly suspended in a violet sky amongst the scents of jasmine, bougainvillea and poinsettia, and where George Dewberry took the opportunity of finishing a whole flask of Capri wine; and Naples, a city of high buildings on hills and tenements underneath, where George Dewberry drank a bottle and a half of Chianti and slept through an entire performance of 'I Pagliacci' (including two encores of 'Vesti la giubba' and one of 'Non, Pagliacci non son') by the San Carlo Opera Company.

A kindly providence watched over George Dewberry ashore. He was never robbed, nor did he ever lose the way back to some other cadets, nor did he ever fall and hurt himself. Only once was he in the hands of the police.

In Sorrento, George Dewberry was found sitting by himself on a seat late at night trying to sing the soprano part of 'Bella Figlia.' Two men in uniform lifted him to his feet and started walking him back to the ship. As soon as he understood what was happening to him, George Dewberry thrust them away.

'Take your hands off me,' he said. 'You can't do this to me. I'm a British citishen. Take your hands off me this minute or I'll call the Carabinieri.'

'We are the Carabinieri,' said the larger of the two men.

9

IN Malta, George Cross, *Barsetshire* found a stronghold of
the Royal Navy. The Army and the Royal Air Force had foot-
holds which grew stronger every year but the life of the island
still revolved around the comings and goings of the ships and her
pulse was controlled by their movements; her purse also, depended to a large extent upon the tributes of the sailor. It was a
Mediterranean island overlaid with a veneer of England which
showed itself in the menus, in the newspapers, and in the lighter
complexions of many of its children. It was an island of tiny
walled fields, green in summer and brown in the winter; towns
of small houses and huge yellow churches whose towers had two
clocks, one showing the wrong time to confuse the Devil on the
times of the services; church bells in the early morning and heat
off the walls in the early evening; narrow straight streets with a
glimpse of the sea at their endings; purple Melita wine; red and
yellow and green dghaisas in Grand Harbour; small bars with
shade curtains; blue water offshore; carved sacred figures in wall
niches; festivals of banners and processions in the streets; and
Holy Pictures in the public transport vehicles, where old ladies
crossed themselves, putting their souls in the keeping of the
Virgin Mary before trusting their bodies to the care of a Maltese
driver.

The ship was specially cleaned for Malta. Although she had
just been painted, there still remained odd corners which needed
touching up and the Commander spent his day striding about

the upper deck, followed by his Doggie, pointing them out. Pontius the Pilot was seen on deck for an unprecedented length of time, Petty Officer Moody grew almost loquacious under the strain, while Able Seaman Froggins's marauding forays were more frequent and met with stiffer opposition until the day came when Able Seaman Froggins recognised some of his own property in another part of the ship, newly painted and with his own initials erased. When that happened, everyone in the division realised that the heat was on.

Malta was the climax of the Mediterranean cruise, the ship's presentation at Court, and for it she was scrubbed and cleaned and polished as never before until she looked, as the Communications Officer said, like new Jerusalem, a bride adorned for her husband.

Mr Piles and his orchestra fired a gun salute to the Commander-in-Chief as *Barsetshire* entered Grand Harbour, Valletta. There were no mishaps during the salute, the saluting gun's crews perhaps being inspired by their surroundings, the massive bastions of Ricasoli and St. Angelo and the tiers of tawny-yellow buildings on each side rising to the skyline in pinnacles, spires, turrets and balconies. *Barsetshire* secured at the flagship's buoy near Customs House Steps under the critical eyes of the Mediterranean Fleet, gathered for the Fleet Regatta.

As soon as *Barsetshire* had secured, the Captain began his round of official calls and every official call was returned. *Barsetshire* received the Commander-in-Chief, the Flag Officer, Second in Command, the Flag Officer, Malta, the Flag Officer, Flotillas, the Governor, the A.O.C. and G.O.C Malta, and calls from innumerable captains of ships, commanding officers of regiments and dignitaries of the Maltese government.

'Here they come!' said The Bodger, looking through the wardroom scuttle on the morning of the first day, 'all the admirals and their secretaries and their assistant secretaries and their secretaries' secretaries unto the seventh generation.'

'It's like something out of Gilbert and Sullivan,' said the Communications Officer. 'On every side field-marshals gleamed,

147

small beer were lords-lieutenant deemed, with admirals the ocean teemed . . . Pom tiddley om.'

'Hope we don't run out of gin.'

'Ask the P.M.O. He's the wine queen.'

'Where *is* the P.M.O.?'

'In his cabin. Got the dog.'

'Have you fellows thought about the Regatta?' asked the Gunnery Officer.

'*Thought* about it?' said The Bodger. 'One doesn't *think* about Regattas, one *forgets* about Regattas. The sailing should be pretty safe. We've got young Bowles.'

'But what about the pulling?'

'We've got you for that, Guns.'

'Me?'

'Haven't you got the buzz? You're in the wardroom boat. Bow.'

'But that's impossible!'

'Not at all. Dickie asked me had we got a crew and I said we'd got you and Pontius and Chris and Mr Piles would cox.'

'What are you doing?'

'I'm stroke.'

'Ye gods!'

The Regatta held a peculiar position in the affections of the Fleet. Boat-pulling had very little place in the Fleet except as physical training and excited little interest except on one or two days in the year, Regatta Days, when it became the outlet for all surplus energy and the subject of every conversation. Although its detractors said that boat-pulling was only an archaic survival from the Navy of long ago, a ship could romp through her football matches, win all her cricket fixtures, and defeat all comers at the Fleet Athletic Meeting, but only if she won the Regatta was she entitled to call herself Cock Ship.

In *Barsetshire* the Regatta passed through the stage of being a ship's activity and rose to the height of a frenzy. It was an event which aroused fanatical enthusiasm in any ship but in the Cadet Training Cruiser it reached the plane of a religious mania. *Barsetshire* prepared to enjoy the Regatta as a dervish enjoys thrusting knives through his own flesh, approaching a state of exaltation through self-mortification.

The crews were arbitrarily selected by the Chief G.I. in the same way as he selected cadets for other duties. Cadets who found the rare button coloured red and numbered thirty beside their names were plunged into a rigorous training schedule. They pulled a mile in a boat twice a day, did P.T. in the afternoons, and were personally sighted in their hammocks by the Duty Cadet Instructor at nine o'clock every evening. They were encouraged to eat more and discouraged from going ashore. Their only consolation lay in seeing that those who were not in the Regatta crews were just as busy doing evolutions.

Once a cruise, *Barsetshire* indulged in a colossal convulsion of Seamanship. Under the Commander's direction, the cadets ran through the Seamanship Manual. They spread, furled and respread the quarterdeck, foc's'le and waist awnings. They laid out the gear for fuelling at sea, abeam and astern; towing, forward and aft; and for transfer by jackstay, heavy and light. They struck and housed the top mast, hoisted and lowered accommodation ladders, and sent away kedge anchors, sea anchors and the Gunnery Officer's motor-cycle in cutters. They rigged sheer legs. They practised securing to, and slipping from, a buoy, and they rehearsed mooring, cheering, and abandoning ship. They pulled boats away to retrieve buoys, torpedoes and men overboard. They put out fires, electrical and carbonaceous, rigged emergency lighting circuits, shored up bulkheads, and donned breathing sets. They weighed the anchor, moved the rudder, and trained the guns by hand.

'All we've got to do now,' Paul said at the end of a week, 'is raise steam by hand.'

'How do we do that?' asked George Dewberry.

'Haven't you noticed those pulleys on the funnels?'

'You've nothing to complain about,' said Raymond Ball. 'You haven't got to pull a boat miles every day. I shall be damned glad when this bloody Regatta's over. It's so *pointless*. You sweat blood to get a piece of wood from one end of the harbour to the other and when you've got it there you sweat more blood to get it back. It's not as though you were even going to *fetch* something.'

To air such opinions aloud in *Barsetshire* on the eve of the Regatta was tantamount to questioning the validity of the Holy Sacrament in St. Peter's on Easter Day. The rest of the gunroom looked cautiously at the scuttles and drew slightly away from Raymond Ball; cadets had been summoned before the Captain for less.

'You'd better pipe down a bit if you want to pass out of this outfit,' Tom Bowles said.

'I still say it's a waste of time.'

'I know you do, dear boy,' said Paul, 'but if you want to live a bit longer, I should keep quiet about it.'

'I hope it pours with rain.'

Raymond Ball was disappointed. The first day of the Regatta dawned clear and bright. The sun shone and there was a slight breeze, enough to cool but not enough to disturb the surface of the sea. It was a perfect day for boat-pulling.

No ship in the Fleet intended any of its crews to pull without audible support. Every ship lowered all its boats and filled them to the gunwhale with chucking-up crews carrying instruments for producing noise. Some ships had bands, but most were forced to improvise. There were trumpeters, drummers, guitarists, trombonists, men with triangles, hunting horns, washboards and horseshoes, a string quartet, and lines of men holding nothing but empty tins which they struck with mallets, or empty shell-cases which they struck with hammers. When the gun fired for the start of the first race, every band launched a different tune, every sailor with an instrument played, and those with empty tins or shell-cases beat them in time to the oar-strokes of their ship's boats. Those without any instruments shouted through megaphones and cupped hands. All together, the chucking-up crews made a sound like a massacre.

As the Regatta progressed, it was clear that though *Barsetshire's* crews were good, they were not good enough. They were the most stylish crews in the Regatta, but they were not prepared for the sheer ferocity with which some of the other ship's crews pulled. *Barsetshire's* crews led in race after race but were finally beaten by some destroyer or frigate's crew who were pulling on the last shreds of their energy before exhaustion overtook them.

The Officers' Race was typical. *Barsetshire's* boat, the formidable combination stroked by The Bodger and coxed by Mr Piles, led to the finishing line when they were caught by the crew from a Tank Landing Ship, whose boat included their whole wardroom. *Barsetshire* were beaten into third place by the Fleet Tanker *Wave Chiropodist*.

At the end of the second day, *Barsetshire* finished fifth in the final placing, which The Bodger thought was good considering that they had pulled in a standard boat.

'I had a look at that L.S.T.'s boat this afternoon,' he said. 'If I'd pulled in that I could have won that race single-handed. They had the hull sandpapered down and varnished. They'd taken the bottom boards out and planed down the seats. They all had specially fitted cushions. I suggested doing all that to our boat but everyone said it would be setting a bad example to the cadets. Can you beat it?'

'Ah well, that's life.'

The sailing Regatta was held a week later. The Fleet raised steam and steamed round to a bay along the coast of Malta where the course was laid out.

Barsetshire's chief hope for the sailing Regatta was Tom Bowles. He had fulfilled the promise he had shown at Dartmouth and had become the best coxswain in the ship. There are some who have an instinctive sympathy with any boat they sail, just as there are some men whom any horse will obey, and Tom Bowles had matured into such a coxswain. It was a compliment to be asked to crew for him and when Tom asked Michael and Paul if they would crew in his boat they were as flattered as though they had been asked by Drake to make up the numbers in the *Golden Hind,* particularly as neither of them sailed often and knew very little about racing. Maconochie was also asked and was as flattered.

None of Tom's crew knew that he had asked them because he liked to sail an important race with a crew who would do exactly as he told them without any notions of their own.

The weather changed for the sailing races and as the time of the race came nearer, it was clear that all Tom Bowles' skill would be needed. A lively north-east wind, whose local name is the gregale, the Euroclydon which wrecked St. Paul, freshened through the forenoon and showed signs of becoming a gale by the evening. White horses covered the bay and raced down past the ships. The boats at the booms rose and plunged with the send of the sea until it became difficult for the crews to man them. Most of the cadets looked hopefully at the quarterdeck, expecting the races to be cancelled, but the Regatta flags still flew. The races were still on.

Two of *Barsetshire's* dinghies, one sailed by David Bowie, capsized before they had sailed more than a hundred yards from the ship. They were caught by a sudden gust and their coxswains had no time to luff up, no time even to let go the sheets, before they were swimming in the sea. To the cadets watching from the quarterdeck, it was an omen.

The first whaler away sheered from the boom on a reach, forced hard over by the wind. Her crew hung out over the weather gunwhale, their huddled figures disappearing in the sheets of spray which leapt as high as the mast. When the boat came round out of *Barsetshire's* lee the main halliard parted with a crack and the mainsail smothered the crew and pulled the boat broadside on to the sea, almost capsizing her. The watchers on the quarterdeck could see the whaler's coxswain trying to keep the boat head to the wind while his crew rigged a jury sail from the remains of the mainsail.

Tom Bowles' crew were not optimistic as they manned their own boat. Maconochie was openly pessimistic and ostentatiously counted the lifebelts. Michael and Paul felt no better even when they swore at Maconochie. Cartwright and the senior cadet, Denis Hubert, the remaining members of the crew, were resigned; they seemed anxious to get the race over quickly.

Maconochie made the first mistake. Hardly hearing Tom

Bowles' orders over the sound of the wind, he slipped the boat while her bows were swinging in towards *Barsetshire*. In spite of Tom Bowles' efforts to make the boat pay off and the crew's efforts to bear the bows off with boathooks, the boat drifted inexorably along the ship's side and fouled under the gangway.

The heads of the spectators appeared over the guardrail. They saw the boat and began to curse Tom Bowles and all his crew.

Tom Bowles and his crew were cursed by bell, book and candle; they were cursed waking and cursed sleeping, eating and drinking, living and dying. The Bodger and the Communications Officer, in particular, gave a recital of profanity, with recitative and aria, theme and variations, and obbligato for solo oath. When at last Tom Bowles extricated his boat, he and his crew had been cursed as comprehensively as the Jackdaw of Rheims.

Paul decided afterwards, though he never mentioned it to anyone, that the incident at the gangway clouded Tom Bowles' judgment.

Half a mile away from the ship, when Tom Bowles was feeling the capabilities of the boat and establishing his command over her, Paul looked back. The recall flags were flying.

'Tom, they're flying the recall!' he shouted.

Tom glanced over his shoulder.

'Oh hell. I suppose we'd better get back. Ready about!'

Tom put the tiller over and the boat started its swing. But the boat was clumsy and turned too slowly. A gust caught her and she sagged away down wind, tilted on the very top of a wave, and heeled over.

Caught unprepared, the crew slid down to the lee side and tried to climb back again, except Maconochie who was sitting high on the weather gunwhale staring at the water which was beginning to lap over on to his feet. When the water reached his feet he began to pay out the main sheet.

He was still paying out when the water reached his waist and closed over his head. Paul heard him shout as he went down into the water,

The crew swam round the boat and collected a lifebelt each and tied them on. By the time they had all found and put on a lifebelt, only the tip of the mast and the stern of the boat were showing above water. The weight of the sodden sail, still fully rigged, had dragged the bows down.

Paul grasped the stern of the boat next to Tom Bowles. He glanced at Tom's face.

'Never mind, Tom. Don't take it to heart, there's a good chap. It happens to everyone. You saw them all today, going over like ninepins. It happens to everyone sooner or later, *honestly.*'

Michael swam next to them, pushing the hair from his eyes. His teeth were chattering.

'God, it's damn cold, isn't it? It's a good job old Ted counted those lifebelts after all. . . .'

Michael stopped and looked round. He caught the horror stilled in Tom Bowles' eyes. His voice rose shrill and high above the sound of the wind.

'*Ted!* Where's Maconochie?'

They dived together. Their lifebelts buoyed them up. They tried to untie them but their fingers were wet and cold and shaking with haste and they could not unfasten the knots which were already swelling in the water.

Tom Bowles succeeded in slipping out of his lifebelt and disappeared. When he came up and shook his head, Denis Hubert dived. They all tried, one after the other. Cartwright stayed under longest but when he too came up alone, they lost hope.

Cartwright shook the water from his eyes.

'He's not there now, I'll swear,' he said breathlessly. 'Must have got caught under the sail, poor joker.'

10

COMMANDER Richard St. Clair Gilpin, D.S.C., Royal Navy, the Executive Officer of H.M.S. *Barsetshire,* strode up and down the quarterdeck, his telescope clasped behind his back.

The Commander paced the quarterdeck alone. Cadets working nearby avoided his eye. The quartermaster, the bosun's mate and the sideboys had vanished into the lobby. The Cadet of the Watch had taken the opportunity to go forward to look at the boats. Only Pontius the Pilot, the Officer of the Watch, stood waiting anxiously for the Commander to speak.

It was half past six on a cold morning, the first morning of a new cruise. The Commander, who was an impatient man, had not yet had his breakfast and his temper had not been improved by the sight of the new cadets who had joined the day before.

The Commander roused himself and glared about the quarterdeck. Pontius the Pilot tensed.

'Officer of the Watch!'

'Sir!' Pontius the Pilot leapt forward, placed himself in front of the Commander, and saluted.

'Why is that cadet,' demanded the Commander, pointing at Paul who was lethargically cheesing down a rope by the after capstan, 'not wearing a lanyard?'

'Petty Officer Moody!'

'Sir!' Petty Officer Moody doubled out of the quarterdeck locker, where he too had hoped to remain unnoticed.

'Why is that cadet not wearing a lanyard?'

'Cadet Cleghorn!'

'Yes, P.O.?'

'Why is Cadet Vincent not wearing a lanyard?'

Peter Cleghorn, who was a leading cadet for the week, crossed over to Paul who, now conscious that he was the centre of unwelcome interest, was coiling down the rope with energy and panache. 'Paul, for Christ's sake, where's your lanyard?'

'It says on Daily Orders negative lanyards until eight o'clock,' Paul answered.

'Does it really?'

'Yes.'

Paul's answer was transmitted up the chain of command as far as the Commander. When Paul heard the Commander's voice he knew that it had not been a tactful answer to give the Commander at half past six in the morning.

'Tell Cadet Vincent to go and get his lanyard and report to my cabin at eight o'clock with one lanyard round his waist, one round his neck and two more round his—and now what in the name of God Almighty do you think *you're* doing?'

A junior cadet holding a bucket of dirty water was standing uncertainly on the quarterdeck. The bucket was filled to overflowing and had already spilled on to the quarterdeck, the holy stretch of Borneo white wood valued at nearly £30,000 which *Barsetshire's* Ship's Company treated with a veneration only accorded in previously documented history to the Ark of the Covenant.

The English Language, that splendid instrument of self-expression, forged and shaped through the centuries, had one of its finest exponents in the Commander. The Commander combined the Gunnery Officer's metronome steadiness, the Communications Officer's choice of simile and The Bodger's readiness of resource. He lashed the junior cadet from head to toe, castigated him, scourged him and delivered him almost weeping into despair, while Pontius the Pilot, Petty Officer Moody, Peter Cleghorn and Paul stood by like men on a hillside watching a storm strike a helpless village below.

Later, when the Commander had taken his wrath forward, Paul had fetched his lanyard and the water had been mopped up, Petty Officer Moody said: 'He'll learn. You all have to learn. When you're as green as grass.'

In some obscurely gratifying way Paul was pleased with the remark. It implied that, for the first time, Petty Officer Moody was crediting Paul with more knowledge and common sense than at least one other human being in *Barsetshire*. It was also the first time it had occurred to Paul that, low as he himself was in the scale of living organisms in the Cadet Training Ship, there was now on board a species still lower, namely, the junior cadets. Paul could now see that there might perhaps be compensations in being in *Barsetshire* as a senior cadet. It was true that the advantages were unequivocal; they were similar to those of an old lag returning for another long stretch. Life would still be hard but at least he knew what to expect and everyone knew him. There would be some satisfaction, Paul thought, in being given more responsible duties and in being able to overawe the juniors. Not that they would need much overaweing. Paul had watched them walk wonderingly up the gangway the previous day.

'Pretty scabby-looking lot aren't they?' he said to Michael as he watched them.

'I don't know,' Michael said. 'I expect we looked exactly the same when we joined. It's a hell of a business joining this old gash-barge for the first time.'

'I suppose so. We at least knew what we were coming to this time. They don't. Yet. Better bear the ills we have than fly to others that we know not of.'

'Oh for goodness sake don't start quoting at this stage of the cruise.'

The Bodger had also watched the new arrivals from the quarterdeck.

'Here we go again,' he said to the Communications Officer. 'Here they come, like lambs to the slaughter. Look at them, coming up as though they were stepping into Hades. I wonder what they've been told about this ship?'

'Probably not half of the whole.'

'I shall have to get my notes out again tomorrow and go through my party piece. Do as I say, men, not as I do. Pretty shocking looking lot. *Look* at that character in uniform and *brown* shoes.'

'It's an Australian.'

'Oh God, he's kicked Owen Glendower.'

'Shades of Maconochie. Incidentally, was there any kick-back about that?'

'No. Lucky it was a cadet. If it had been anyone else there might have been some tumult and shouting back and forth.'

'They *are* a terrible looking lot.'

'Remember last cruise's lot.'

The Communications Officer remembered.

'Yes,' he said, 'I suppose these aren't all that bad.'

Two days later, when *Barsetshire* was on her way to the West Indies, Paul was given the most dreaded special duty of all. When he saw the button by his name he knew without looking at the legend that he was Commander's Doggie, better known to the cadets as Sorcerer's Apprentice.

The Commander was the most energetic officer in the ship and he directed all his energy towards one single, unshakeable object, which was to become an Admiral, preferably an Admiral of the Fleet. He committed himself to no private or professional action without first submitting it to the test of whether or not it helped him towards flag rank. He looked upon those above him as hand-holds to help him up and those below him as foot-holds to keep him up. He had won the Telescope at Dartmouth, the Sword in the Training Ship, First Class awards in all his courses as a Sub-Lieutenant, the D.S.C. as a Lieutenant, promotion to Commander at the first opportunity as a Lieutenant-Commander, and he confidently awaited early promotion to Captain. He had played rugby football and squash for the Navy and he still held the Navy javelin and discus records. He was a member of the R.N. Sailing Association, the R.N. Cricket Club and the Junior Army and Navy Club. Several articles written by him under the pseudonym of 'Conrad' on such widely separated subjects as 'The Role of the Navy in a War Against the Mongols' and 'An Outline History of the Voice-pipe' had appeared in the *Naval Review.* He bought his uniforms and caps from Gieves, his suits from Johnson Bros. of Savile Row, his hats from Locks, his shoes from Lobbs and his underwear, ready-made, from Harrods, where he had an account. He was unmarried. He was, in short, the Compleat Naval Officer.

The Commander was complete even to his eccentricities. Achilles had a vulnerable heel, Siegfried had a spot between his shoulder-blades where the leaf masked his skin from the dragon's blood, even Baldur could be touched by mistletoe, and Richard Gilpin was preoccupied by the Yellow Peril. At quarterly intervals he rose at the dinner table and addressed the Mess on the subject of the Yellow Peril. With the oratory of an Athenian and the powers of pantomime of a Port Said street arab, he described an effete, rotting western civilisation overwhelmed by a yelling horde of Asiatics, led by a modern Attila, who laid a bloody trail of murder, rape, arson, famine and pestilence from the Danube to the Rio Grande. The Turks had been stopped at Vienna, Attila had been checked at the very gates of Rome, the Moors had penetrated no further than the Pyrenees, but, Richard asked the Mess, who could stop them now?

The Mess President's rhetoric was so masterly, his choice of words so graphic, and his pantomime so vivid, that it was not unusual, on the morning after the Address, to see Mr Piles furtively trying on steel helmets from the Gunner's Store and the Chief Steward restraining two of the most junior stewards, who happened to be twins, from going about their duties back to back. Richard's Address became a Mess institution, on a par with the silver and decanters, and the Navigation Officer, who was Mess Secretary, threw away all calendars sent to the Mess at Christmas, remarking that the Mess did not need them since the members could adequately observe the procession of the seasonal equinoxes by their President's Address on the Yellow Peril. The Wardroom as a whole treated the Address as Frederick the Great's courtiers must have tolerated his playing

159

of the flute, as the harmless idiosyncrasy of a hard-pressed administrator, although The Bodger had a theory that the one thing which really scared Dickie was the thought that the Yellow Peril might come upon them all before he had become an Admiral. The Bodger maintained that Dickie's most recurrent nightmare was one in which he was massacred by little yellow men while still wearing a Commander's uniform. Popular opinion on the Lower Deck, however, which received each Address *verbatim et literatim* from the stewards, held that Dickie's grandmother had been raped during the Boxer Rising.

At the beginning of the cruise the Commander was recovering from a severe bout of influenza (contracted at a party given for the children of his sister, whose husband was a Rear Admiral) and the Ship's Company had hoped that disease had chastened him. But from the moment on the first day of the cruise when they had heard the pipe—'Chief Bosun's Mate, Sailmaker and Captain of the Side report to the Commander's cabin at the rush' and ever since, the Ship's Company had regretfully concluded that their hopes had been unfulfilled and, by the time Paul reported at six o'clock to start his day's duty, the word had run many times around the length and breadth of the ship— 'Richard's himself again!'

As the Commander, followed by Paul, came abreast the midships cross-passage after attending both Watches, a figure carrying a small canvas bag darted up out of the hatch from the Cadets' Messdeck and scuttled away long the upper deck. The Commander started and pointed like a dog at a shoot.

'You there!' he shouted.

The scuttling figure came to a quivering standstill.

'Yes you! Come back here!'

The figure hurried back.

'D-did you mean *me,* sir?' quavered George Dewberry.

'Of course I meant you. What are you doing?'

'I'm Cadet E.M., sir.'

'Cadet what?'

'Cadet Electrician's Mate, sir.'

'And what in hell's name is that?'

160

'Well, sir, I go around with this little bag and mend electric light bulbs. Or something, sir.'

The Commander thrust his face down to within an inch of George Dewberry's.

'What do you mean, *or something?*' he hissed.

'Well, sir . . . I, well what I mean is . . . you see, sir, nobody's really *told* me . . . !'

George Dewberry's hesitation was excusable. A Cadet E.M.'s duties were nebulous. They had never been properly defined and George Dewberry's definition was perhaps as good as any. When George Dewberry reported to the Cadet Office the Chief G.I. had given him an armband and a small canvas bag and told him to get cracking. When George Dewberry had asked what he was to get cracking on, the Chief G.I. had intimated that it was immaterial so long as it took place removed from the Cadet Office. His equipment gave George Dewberry no enlightenment. The armband had faded to anonymity and the small canvas bag contained the stub of a smashed electric light bulb, a piece of copper wire two inches long, and the Chief G.I.'s shoe-cleaning gear.

George Dewberry had therefore become a Cadet E.M. with an exhilarating sense of pioneering, of having the world before him to do with as he wished. But he had been arrested by the Commander before he had even time to reach the frontier. George Dewberry was unable to account for his movements and Paul was beginning to feel sorry for him when there was a fortunate distraction. The Commander caught a movement out of the corner of his eye and turned his head.

'Mr Badger!' he barked.

The Commander and The Bodger disliked each other. They were natural opposites. The Bodger wished that the Commander would pay more attention to the Ship's Company and leave him to run the cadets as he liked, while the Commander considered that The Bodger's appointment as Cadet Training Officer was a terrible mistake in Admiralty policy, tantamount to training the next generation of naval officers as bookies' runners.

The Bodger saluted politely. 'Yes, sir?'

'Mr Badger, this cadet is skulking. *What* he's supposed to be doing, I don't know, and *he* doesn't know. I'll leave you to deal with him.'

'Aye aye, sir.'

The Commander stalked off. The Bodger beetled his eyebrows at George Dewberry.

'What have you been up to, Dewberry?'

'Nothing sir, really. I'm Cadet E.M. for today, sir, and the Commander asked me what I was doing so I said I was changing electric light bulbs, sir. Or something, sir.'

'Let me give you a piece of advice, Dewberry. This is a golden rule in the Navy. Even if you don't *know* what you're doing, always *look* as though you do. Ninety-nine times out of a hundred nobody will ever know the difference. Now cut along and mend electric light bulbs, or something.'

'Aye aye, sir! Thank you, sir!'

The Bodger watched George Dewberry double happily away.

'Ah well,' he said to himself. 'Little things please little minds, little pants fit little behinds. Let that be today's beautiful thought'.

The Bodger pursed his lips, clasped his hands behind his back, and wandered enigmatically off to shave and change before breakfast.

Meanwhile, the Commander continued along the upper deck. As he walked the decks emptied in front of him and refilled again behind; he seemed to carry an uneasy bow-wave before him which slipped aside to let him pass and filled in again in an uncomfortable wake behind.

Paul, following miserably, began to feel like a leper's dog. This character, Paul thought, could not have been born in the normal manner. He must have been from his mother's womb untimely ripped, and given sour grapes to suck for milk. He must hate everybody, including himself. Poor old George, obviously doing his best in spite of the fact that he had not the vaguest idea of what he was supposed to be doing, torn up for—

Paul looked up. Cadets were still scrubbing decks. Petty Officers were watching them. The sea still heaved and scraped

162

at the ship's side. The horizon was still visible and level, with the sun still normal in the east. Everything was as it was every morning at scrub decks, except the most important item for Paul. The Commander had vanished.

Paul broke into a run. He passed Michael and Tom Bowles who were going through the motions of scrubbing a piece of deck. They had been bored with it since they started it. They welcomed Paul as a distraction.

'What's up Paul?' asked Michael. 'This your morning constitutional?'

'Have you seen the Commander, Mike?'

Michael and Tom paused. This was better than they had hoped for.

'Have you lost him?'

'Yes. He was here a moment ago and now he's just bloody well vanished.'

'Coo-er,' said Tom Bowles. He looked at Paul sympathetically. A doggie who had lost his master was a pathetic sight at any time. A doggie who had lost this particular master was in a perilous state.

'Tell you what! Pipe for him to report to you on the quarter-deck!'

'Don't try and be funny, Tom,' said Paul desperately. 'It doesn't suit you.'

'Have you tried the cable deck?' Michael suggested. 'He sometimes goes up there to nauseate the foc'sle men.'

'Thanks, Mike.'

Paul looked on the cable deck and all along the upper deck and in the likely places, the bridge, the wardroom, and the Commander's cabin. Then he looked in the less likely places, the cable locker, the sailmaker's store, the saluting gun deck, the ship's police office, and the shipwright's shop. Finally, he tried the most fantastic parts of the ship he could think of, the awning store, the cells, the engineroom, the electrical maintenance workshop and the band instrument store. But the Commander had vanished completely.

Breakfast time came and went and just as Paul had given up

the search and was sitting down to a late breakfast, the loud-speaker on the Cadets' Messdeck came to life.

'*Cadet Vincent, report to the Commander's cabin at the double!*'

The Commander was waiting in his cabin.

'Where in Hades have you been, you little worm?'

'I'm afraid I've been looking for you, sir.'

'*Looking* for me? Great heavens boy, you're supposed to be my *doggie* so help me! What's the use of having a doggie who spends his time *looking* for me? You follow me about for two minutes, yawning and stretching like something that's just crawled out of the double bottoms and when I want you you've disappeared!'

'I'm very sorry, sir.'

'Fat lot of good that is. Now stand at the door and call out the names of anyone who wants to see me and what he wants to see me about.'

'Aye aye, sir.'

Paul took up a position near the door.

'Outside! How the devil can you see anybody from there?'

'Sorry, sir.'

Paul stood outside the cabin door. Within a minute he was back again.

'Mate of the Upper Deck, sir. Paint for paint ship, sir.'

The Mate of the Upper Deck went in and came out again. Paul went in.

'Captain of Royal Marines, sir. Boot money for the postman, sir.'

With a wink at Paul, the Captain of Royal Marines went in and came out again. Paul went in.

'Communications Officer, sir. Times of watchkeepers' cinema show, sir.'

'Sorry I didn't bring my card, James,' said the Communications Officer to Paul, grinning.

'Chief Petty Officer Marks, sir. Dartboard for Chief and Petty Officers' Recreation Space, sir.'

'Shipwright Officer, sir. New counter for Ship's Company Bookstall, sir.'

164

'Senior Engineer, sir. Compassionate case, sir.'

'Instructor Lieutenant Evans, sir. Ship's rugby in Jamaica, sir.'

'M.S.O. Messenger, sir. Signals, sir.'

The stream of callers was continuous. There was always another waiting when Paul came out and as they came and went Paul began to have an inkling of the amount of work the Commander did in a day; he also began to understand the Commander's early morning tetchiness.

'Master at Arms, sir. Requestmen and Defaulters, sir.'

Paul stood in an inconspicuous position in a corner of the Keyboard Flat for Requestmen and Defaulters and watched his master begin the daily process of answering requests and administering justice. He noticed the differences in the Commander's manner when dealing with Requestmen and when dealing with Defaulters.

With Requestmen, the Commander was charming. He kept his most genial manner for them, whether their request was for compassionate leave or to discontinue shaving. He beamed, he prompted, occasionally he laughed out loud. His good humour was such that other officers attending the table had sometimes wondered whether Dickie had had unexpectedly good news, perhaps even an answer to the Yellow Peril. But with Defaulters the Commander's manner changed, as though a steel shutter had dropped over his good humour. His eyes were bleak and cold and his voice clipped. His attitude was so menacing that the officers standing round the table were forced to conclude that they had been mistaken about the Yellow Peril. It had clearly gained the upper hand again. The Commander studied each charge sheet as though it were an ultimatum from Genghis Khan himself.

Paul's stomach began to bother him. Deprived of its customary breakfast it made an audible protest.

After Requestmen and Defaulters, the Commander went back to his cabin, sat down at his desk, and took out a trayful of papers. Paul assumed his old position outside the door but the procession of callers had stopped. The Commander was no longer at home.

Paul shifted from one foot to the other. He counted the rivets in the bulkhead and carefully studied a notice describing the proper use and maintenance of a nearby fire extinguisher. He traced all the pipes in sight across the deckhead until they disappeared. He examined a crack in the paint work which closely resembled, from a certain angle, a profile of Pontius the Pilot.

'Vincent!'

'Yes, sir.'

'We shall be streaming paravanes next week. How much do you know about paravanes?'

Paul hesitated.

'Obviously nothing. Get out the Seamanship Manual and read it up.'

'Aye aye, sir.'

The Commander's bookshelf was typical of the man himself. There was the Seamanship Manual, all three volumes, three life histories of Nelson, four or five books on naval history, a copy of Brasseys, the R.N. and R.M. Sports Handbook, Jane's Fighting Ships, the Navy List, several back numbers of the Naval Review, and a miscellaneous bunch of files, standing orders and signal logs. There were no novels, no poetry, no books indicating any pastimes or interests outside the Navy. The books depressed Paul. The man was invulnerable.

Paul took down the Seamanship Manual and found the section on the streaming and recovery of paravanes. He had not expected to find it interesting reading and, after the first sentence, he saw that he was not mistaken.

The cabin was peaceful. The sea made a regular hushing beneath the open scuttle and the Commander's pen scraped methodically over a page. Paul was thankful for the peace and hoped it would last until dinner time.

Paul's stomach then began its revolutionary debate of protest. The argument was subdued at first, led by an obscure backbencher, and it sounded like the preliminary rumblings of an approaching summer storm.

The Commander looked up.

'Vincent,' he said, 'I can't stand this. Self-control is one of the foremost requirements of a naval officer. If there's one thing that gets under my skin, it's a doggie sitting in my cabin *bubbling* and *rumbling* like a blasted hookah! Take this signal log outside and find me a signal about a Stoker Foster whose wife is supposed to be having a baby prematurely. Don't come back until you've found it.'

Paul took the signal log, leant it against the Keyboard Sentry's desk and began to read.

The signal log was a mine of detailed information. Paul was amazed at the number and variety of signals in it. There were signals about ship's movements and intentions; ratings taken to hospital, qualified for advancement, or absent over leave; R.P.C.s from one wardroom to another for drinks at lunch time and from one captain to another for dinner; demands for spare parts, fuel, water, and stores; information on officers' and ratings' rigs for sporting and social functions; and weather reports, reports on accidents and reports on examinations. The Signal Log was the complete daily conversation of ship, flotilla, squadron, fleet, depot and command, neatly recorded for months past, each signal with its date and time, addressee and priority, and it contained every kind of signal except one relating to the premature baby of the wife of Stoker Foster.

Paul laid down the Signal Log with a new sense of wonder and of humility that there had been so much happening, so much organisation, of which he had known nothing. He looked at his watch and saw that he had been reading signals, entranced, for over half an hour. He hurried back to tell the Commander that he could not find the signal.

But the Commander was not so easily satisfied.

'I *know* that signal is on board somewhere. Look in the M.S.O. and Captain's Office Logs. There must be a copy somewhere. Don't come back until you've found it.'

The signal was not in the Captain's Office nor in the M.S.O. and Paul asked the Yeoman of the Watch if he had any back numbers. The Yeoman brought down a pile of old files and logs.

'There you are, sir,' he said. 'That's all the signals we've got. If it's not in there we haven't sent it and we haven't received it.'

Paul delved further and further back. He read signals relating to political crises long since resolved and forgotten, to machinery declared obsolete and removed, even to ships which had been broken up or sunk by the enemy years before. He found signals concerning every refit, recommissioning and full power trial the ship had ever had. Finally he came to a signal in which *Barsetshire's* first Captain proudly informed the Admiralty that he had, on that day, commissioned the ship for the first time. Dinner time came, the Yeoman of the forenoon watch was relieved, and still Paul could not find the signal.

'What you looking for?' asked the Yeoman of the afternoon watch.

Paul told him.

'Well, it's no good looking in *that* lot. Any premature sprog in there'll be on pension by now. Try the P.T. and Welfare Office. They've got a special log there for compassionate cases.'

The P.T. and Welfare Office was empty when Paul arrived but a large file lay on the desk.

Feeling as though he were approaching one of the books of the Sybil, Paul opened the file and straightaway plunged into one of the most appalling catalogues of human disasters ever collected under one cover. The Welfare File was a tale of catastrophes unsurpassed by any of Dante's in the Inferno or of Poe's in the realm of the supernatural.

He read of ratings whose families had vanished without trace, ratings who arrived on leave to find their families in the street, and of ratings who had discovered their houses infested with rats, cockroaches, mice and ants. Some had swarms of bees in the back room, others had lorries crashed into the front room. There were mothers electrocuted in the bath, grandmothers scalded by Lancashire hotpot, uncles who died of a surfeit of winkles, babies choked by rattles, fathers who fell into the coalcellar and grandfathers who dropped dead whilst clearing snow off the front step.

Just as Paul was becoming absorbed in the Welfare File and was lighting his second cigarette, the P.T. and Welfare Officer himself came into the office.

168

'Hello,' he said, 'reading my "Tales of Mystery and Imagination"? What can I do for you?'

'I was looking for a signal about a Stoker Foster, sir,' Paul said. 'His wife is having a premature baby.'

'Oh, that one. It's not in there. I sent the whole pack down to the Commander's cabin before lunch.'

The loudspeaker outside the cabin door suddenly blared.

'Cadet Vincent, report to the Commander's cabin at the double!'

The Commander was waiting.

'Where in Hades have you been, you little worm?'

'I'm afraid I've still been looking for that signal, sir.'

'You mean to tell me that you've been three hours looking for a signal?'

Paul's stomach had long since given up its struggle for its constitutional rights and had lain in uneasy, mutinous but nevertheless silent quiescence. Now, however, in close proximity to the Commander once more, it began to stir itself for a fresh attempt. The Commander glared at Paul.

'I will not tolerate a doggie who cannot control his digestive processes. Go away, go *right* away, and don't come back until Evening Quarters. And in the meantime for pity's sake get something to eat!'

In the days of sail, Evening Quarters had two functions, to exercise the Ship's Company and to check their numbers for absentees. In *Barsetshire* only the first object was applicable, since the loss of a cadet overboard was hardly considered a sufficiently grave reason for stopping the ship and inconveniencing the entire Ship's Company, and it was achieved by sending the seaboats away to pick up danbuoys, while the cadets who were not in the crews doubled round the upper deck to the music of the band until the boats came back.

When Paul followed the Commander up on to the quarter-deck, the divisions had already fallen in and the boat's crews had been detailed. The day's exercise was meant as a demonstration for the junior cadets and the boat's crews were entirely composed of senior cadets. Looking over his own division's boat,

169

Paul saw that Tom Bowles was the coxswain and Michael was also in the crew as stroke and looking, Paul thought, scared.

Michael was scared. When he heard the seaboats piped away and saw the sea that was running, Michael had assumed that the pipe had been made by an inexperienced junior bosun's mate only because he had seen it written on the routine. But when Michael noticed that the ship was slowing down and Tom Bowles told him he was in the crew Michael looked over the side, where massive waves were flinging their crests up at the waiting keels of the boats and sliding aside to leave dark abysses far below, and felt again that fear which had gripped him on the day Maconochie was drowned.

Watching Michael sitting in his lifejacket, bearing the boat off the ship's side with the butt end of his oar, Paul sensed his fear and knew they were both thinking of Maconochie.

Tom Bowles checked the oars, the disengaging gear and the tiller. He caught Michael's eye.

'Going to be a bit dicey today, Mike,' he said.

'You can say that again. Tom, will you shout out the time all the way? With this kind of sea it's murder trying to keep the stroke. It makes it much easier if you sing out all the time.'

'Roger. Let's hope old Pontius drops us *on* the wave this time. Last time it felt as if we fell about twenty feet.'

They felt the jarring of the falls as the ropes passed through the blocks and the ship's side rose up beside them. Just before they passed under the level of the deck Michael saw Paul and grimaced. Then the boat sank slowly, until it was poised over the sea.

Pontius the Pilot bent over the guard-rails and studied the sea. He was glad he was not in the boat as he watched the waves sweeping past. He waited for a large wave on which to drop the boat.

'Ready in the boat?'

'Ready in the boat, sir.'

'Out pins.'

170

'Pins out in the boat, sir.'

The wave came.

'*Slip!*'

With the jangle of the dislocated chains and the thud as the boat hit the water, Tom Bowles slashed the twine securing the tiller to the inboard gunwhale and took the tiller in his hand. The first crash and spatter of spray drifted over the bows as the boat forged ahead on the boat-rope.

'Slip the boat-rope!' Tom shouted.

The rope flicked over the side.

'Hold water port, give way starboard!'

The boat wheeled away from the ship, rolling and plunging across the line of the waves. When the boat had turned, the waves seized it and forced it downwind. A larger wave cradled the boat on its slope and Michael could see its bubbling crest above Tom's head. He shut his eyes momentarily and concentrated on nothing but Tom's voice calling out the time.

From the quarterdeck Paul watched the boats go downwind to the red and yellow specks of the danbuoys. As it reached a buoy, the leading boat rolled until Paul could see its pale belly and the oars sticking up into the air. The crew had disappeared on the lee side and Paul was sure the boat was capsizing until it rolled back and he could see the coxwain holding the danbuoy in his arms, the crew already pulling to position the boat for its return.

On the way back the boats disappeared into the hollows of the waves and soared up again, their oars spreadeagled between sea and sky. The nearest boat was close enough for Paul to recognise Tom Bowles leaning forward to urge his crew.

'*One* . . . out, *two* . . . out, *three* . . . out, quicker, Mike, quicker, quicker.'

Michael was unable to reply and kept his venomous eyes on his oar. He caught a glimpse of *Barsetshire's* stern out of the corner of his eye. Several more pulls brought it plainly in view. Tom moved the tiller sharply to the side and back again. The boat slid in under the falls and the crew ducked to avoid the swinging blocks.

171

On deck, lines of cadets stood holding the falls, waiting to hoist the boat. The Commander started a stopwatch.

'All hooked on in the boat, sir!'

'Hoist away the forrard fall.'

Leading cadets and petty officers stood at intervals to relay the orders along to the end of the line.

'High enough. Marry the falls.'

The lines of cadets moved together, each cadet grasping both falls.

'Hoist away!'

The lines of cadets ran backwards until they reached the end of the line when they threw down the falls and doubled forward again, keeping the pot boiling like schoolchildren on a slide. The boat came swaying up out of the water, the crew looking hunch-backed and exhausted in their lifejackets.

'High enough!'

The cadets on the falls leaned back and took the weight while the crew rigged lifelines between the blocks and the davit-heads

'Ease to the lifelines.'

The falls slackened as the weight of the boat came on the lifelines. The crew set up the disengaging gear again.

'Lie to. Carry on, hands on deck.'

The falls were thrown down and gathered in. The blocks through which the falls had been led were unrigged. The boat was triced to the boom by grapnels and the crew climbed over the jumping net and down to the upper deck. The Commander stopped the watch.

'Not good,' he said. 'Four minutes, twenty-one seconds. You'll have to do better than that, du Pont.'

'Aye aye, sir.'

The Commander remembered Paul.

'All right, Vincent. You can carry on.'

'Thank you, sir.'

Drinking tea in the Wardroom with The Bodger, Pontius the Pilot said: 'I do think Dickie might have been a bit more pleasant. For the first time in the cruise I thought today's effort was damned good.'

172

'What was Bowles like?' The Bodger asked.

'Couldn't have been better. Came in like a bird and stopped the boat dead under the falls. It almost hooked itself on.'

'I'm glad of that. I was afraid last term's little episode might have shaken him.'

'Not it. It takes more than that to shake Bowles. He's almost a genius in boats.'

'He's almost a genius in everything. A natural.'

Back in the gunroom, Paul was greeted with sympathetic interest.

'You had a pretty sticky time today with Dickie didn't you?' said George Dewberry. 'He shaved off at *me* this morning before I'd even had a chance to get a grip on things. How the hell should *I* know what a Cadet E.M. does?'

'What did The Bodger say to you?'

'Oh, just gave me a Bodgerism to remember and sent me on my way rejoicing. Always look as though you know what you're doing, even when you don't.'

'Typical Bodger.'

'Dickie seemed to be piping for you a lot, Paul,' said Raymond Ball. 'Were you avoiding him or something? Was it the end of a beautiful friendship?'

'No, he just didn't like my stomach.'

'Good God! How come?'

'Hell, I hadn't had anything to eat all day for one reason or another, mostly reasons to do with Dickie, and my poor old tum began to complain a bit. Dickie objected so we agreed to differ, or rather he differed and I agreed.'

The whole gunroom burst into laughter, even Spink, who had just seen on the Cadets' Notice Board that he was the next Commander's Doggie.

'I've heard of senior officers not liking someone's face,' Michael said, 'but that's the first time I ever heard of one not liking someone's stomach!'

Later that night, just before they turned into their hammocks, Michael said: 'Were you thinking of old Ted today, Paul?'

173

'Yes. Were you?'

'I thought we were going to have a repeat performance with me as Ted's stand-in.'

'You looked a bit scared.'

'I was petrified. There was a time when I really thought we were going over. Did you see it?'

'I saw it but I wasn't sure it was you. How did Tom react?'

'He was superb. Really good. He didn't look at all scared, or worried, or concerned, or anything. He just went on and did about the finest recovery and approach to the ship I've ever seen in weather like that.'

'I'm glad. That business last cruise might easily have shaken his nerve. If someone had been drowned today, on a bloody silly exercise which they could easily have cancelled if they'd felt like it, I would have resigned, I think.'

'Why, you sorry you joined?'

'No,' said Paul doubtfully. 'I just hae me doots.'

Barsetshire settled imperceptibly into the routine of a long ocean passage. Each day brought warmer weather. The sea took on a deeper, richer blue and the trade wind blew steadily day after day carrying the funnel haze ahead of the ship. Flying fish appeared at the bows, skating away from the approaching ship in silver swarms. The water over which *Barsetshire* steamed was not now a landlocked sea but the heart of the Atlantic itself, the home of the whale and the dolphin and the playground of the trade winds where huge waves, generated by the wind over thousands of miles of untrammelled ocean, had time and space to reach their full stature. Uncurbed by any land upon which to dash their power, undisputed in their strength, the mighty hillsides of water gathered behind *Barsetshire* and lifted her on her way to Trinidad.

A week after Paul's day as Commander's Doggie the Ship's Company changed into tropical whites and Tom Bowles was Captain's Doggie. His duties began with breakfast with the Captain.

The Captain was a thickset, barrel-chested man with a brick-red complexion. Dressed in any clothes he would still have been taken for a sea captain. In private life he was an enthusiastic, almost fanatical breeder of red setters and he lived for little else, and certainly not for his service career, in a gigantic house built by an ancestor who had won a packet off the Prince Regent. Apart from its convenience as a base for breeding setters the house had nothing to recommend it, but the Captain continued to live alone in it because he was unable to find a purchaser or have it taken over by the National Trust. The Captain had not seen his wife for over fifteen years, having separated from her soon after the birth of a son whom the Captain visited once a year at Eton. Apart from his annual visit (and one consultation of a Harley Street eye specialist to satisfy himself that his son's eyes were good enough for the Navy) the Captain ignored his paternal responsibilities. His wife meanwhile devoted her energies to running a women's magazine and to preventing her son joining the Royal Navy. Having renounced his family, the Captain's two pleasures were his red setters and the satisfaction of seeing the remaining members of his term at Dartmouth being passed over and, one by one, retiring.

The Captain was already eating breakfast and reading a bunch of signals when Tom Bowles was shown in by the Captain's steward.

Tom Bowles waited for a few moments but the Captain showed no sign of having noticed, or wishing to acknowledge, his presence, so Tom Bowles quietly sat down.

Silently, the steward served him with bacon and eggs. Tom Bowles began to eat silently and without relish.

'Tea or coffee, sir?' the steward whispered.

'Tea, please,' whispered Tom Bowles.

The steward brought the tea and Tom Bowles drank it quietly, without tasting it. The cabin was so quiet that he felt as though he were drinking tea in an empty library.

Suddenly the atmosphere changed. There was a subdued hum of merriment, a gentle, mirthful murmuring. The Captain was laughing.

The signal he had just reached in the log was affording the

Captain enormous amusement. His shoulders shook. He looked up and noticed Tom Bowles. He grinned. Tom Bowles awkwardly grinned back.

'Old Fruity Manchester has run *Vertigo* aground in the Skagerrak, I see,' the Captain said, pointing at the signal. He shook his head jovially. 'That's him finished. Never laugh that one off.'

The Captain took up his cup and drank it off.

'Knowles!' he shouted.

The silent steward appeared at the door.

'Sir?'

'Bottle, Knowles.'

Almost without disappearing, Knowles reappeared with a bottle of gin and glass on a silver tray which he placed in front of the Captain.

'I won't ask you to join me,' the Captain said to Tom Bowles. 'This is a celebration. Private one, you know. Sorry about Old Fruity really. Damn bad luck.'

The Captain swallowed and said: 'Well? We ready?'

'Yes, sir,' Tom Bowles said.

Outside, the Captain paused. He searched his pockets and found a piece of paper which he read closely, turning it over several times. Then, putting it back in a pocket, he said: 'Ah, yes, Bowles. Stuffy's boy. Bowles, I'm going to have my Morning George now. Report to me again at nine o'clock.'

At ten past nine, the Captain came back, the rite of the Morning George completed. When he saw Tom Bowles, he searched for and found the piece of paper again.

'Ah, yes, Bowles. Stuffy's boy. Bowles, always have your George in the *morning*. Your father used to have his during the First Watch and while he was away his clot of an Officer of the Watch ran into a merchantman. They asked your father at the court martial where he was at the time and what could he say?'

The Captain proceeded to the bridge followed, in column of route, by Tom Bowles and the red setter Owen Glendower. Officers and ratings coming in the opposite direction stood at

176

attention, flattened against the bulkheads, to let the Captain pass. They remained flattened for Tom Bowles and Owen Glendower; it was a rash man who came between the Captain and his Doggie or his dog. Tom Bowles felt himself borne along on a wave of reflected glory, like a member of a successful matador's cuadrilla. Owen Glendower, on the other hand, was used to the deference paid him and carried himself like one born to greatness.

A deputation waited for the Captain on the bridge. It consisted of the Navigating Officer with the morning's star sights and the ship's dead reckoning run for the day; the Communications Officer with a fresh batch of signals; the Gunnery Officer, who was Officer of the Watch, with a nervous smile; and Raymond Ball, who was Cadet of the Watch, wearing a look of deep depression, having been on watch with the Gunnery Officer for an hour and a half.

'Anything special there?' the Captain asked the Communications Officer.

'No, sir.'

'I shall be in my sea-cabin if anyone wants me then.'

'Aye aye, sir.'

In his sea-cabin, which was a spartan apartment containing a bed, two chairs, a small bookcase and a writing desk, the Captain picked up a book and began to read. After a time he remembered Tom Bowles, who was still standing uncertainly by the door.

'Read much?'

'Not a lot, sir, but . . . '

'See if you can find anything to interest you there.'

The Captain waved Tom Bowles towards the bookcase as though he were offering him the entire resources of the Reading Room at the British Museum.

There were four books on the shelf. They were: 'The Care and Breeding of Setters and Spaniels,' 'The Hound of the Baskervilles,' 'Distemper, Rabies and Miscellaneous Canine Diseases,' and 'Every Boy's Book of Dogs.' There was also a small pamphlet issued by the National Trust.

Tom Bowles chose 'Distemper, Rabies and Miscellaneous Canine Diseases,' opened it at random, and began to read.

'Whenever a dog pays particular attention to his anus,' Tom read, 'impaction of the anal glands may be suspected. This is *not* always attributable to worms . . . '

'Captain, sir?'

The Captain looked up, keeping his finger in his page. The Senior Instructor Officer, who was the ship's meteorological officer, stood in the doorway holding a chart.

'Ah, Schoolie!' cried the Captain. 'What's the trouble?'

'The weather, sir.'

'What's the matter with it?'

'Nothing's the matter, sir. No change on the chart.'

'Splendid! Let me know the minute you see a typhoon, Schoolie.'

'Yes, sir.'

The Senior Instructor Officer retired. The Captain turned to Tom Bowles.

'When you're a Captain, Bowles,' he said, 'never take any notice of what the Met. boys say. The trouble with the Met. branch is they *will* not look out of the bloody scuttle and see what the weather's actually *doing*. Barney Liverpool once altered course to avoid a typhoon the Met. chaps told him about and hit a reef instead.'

The Captain's eyes sparkled at the memory.

'. . . *not* always attributable to worms, but may be caused by the animal rubbing himself along the . . . '

'Captain, sir?'

'Yes? Ah, yes, come in, Scratch.'

The Captain's Secretary came in carrying a briefcase. The Captain took his Secretary's pen, shook it vigorously over his Secretary's white shoes, and prepared to sign papers.

'You can carry on, Bowles. Come back here again after stand-easy.'

At half past ten, the Captain came out of his sea-cabin and said to the Gunnery Officer: 'I'm going for a mooch round.'

Again in column of route, the Captain, Tom Bowles and Owen Glendower prowled along the upper deck. All about them the normal routine of a hot forenoon in *Barsetshire* was taking place. Cadets were putting paint on bulkheads and scraping paint off the deck, scrubbing out boats, polishing brasswork and wire-scrubbing chains and shackles. The voices of lecturers floated out through the open scuttles of the gunrooms.

'The Admiralty Light List, this blue tome here,' said the voice of Pontius the Pilot, 'tells you all you want to know about lights, always supposing you *want* to know anything about lights . . .'

The Captain stopped and crouched outside the scuttle. He looked round at Tom Bowles with his finger to his lips.

' . . . it tells you what colour the light is, whether it's flashing or occulting, how many flashes or *occults,* per minute, the intervals of flashes or *occults,* the height of the flashes or *occults* above sea-level, what colour polka-dot bow tie the lighthouse keeper wears and so on.'

Pontius the Pilot paused. Immediately the Captain popped his head in through the scuttle.

'What's the difference between flashing and occulting? You?' he demanded of a cadet in the back row.

The class swung round and gaped at the silhouette of the Captain, framed in the round scuttle. The cadet whom the Captain had addressed was so startled that he could only open and close his mouth silently; no words came to him. Paul, in the front row, was the first to recover.

'Flashing means that the dark is shorter than the light and occulting means that the light is shorter than the dark, sir,' he said.

'*Wrong!*' said the Captain. 'Other way round. *Nincompoop!*'

The Captain vanished from the class's sight. He resumed his stroll, chuckling. Tom Bowles and Owen Glendower fell in behind.

The next scuttle was The Bodger's. The well-known voice carried stridently and confidently with the cadences of an experienced speaker.

179

'. . . most books provided by a benevolent and all-seeing Admiralty are B.R.'s, B.R. as no doubt you will readily grasp, standing for Book of Reference. There are B.R.'s for every subject under the sun. There's even a B.R., Guide to Heaven. All B.R.'s have a number, for the use of civil servants. If you ask a civil servant for a Ship's Fire Fighting Manual he won't know what the hell you're talking about, but if you ask him for a B.R.1257 he'll give you one in triplicate. B.R.1066, the Advancement Regulations, is another example. B.R.1066 gives you the regulations for the advancement of every type of rating except the one you're interested in. You'll find all the others. You can read how to go from Leading Airman to Chief Blacksmith without taking the Naval Storekeeping Course, and how to get from Ordinary Sick Berth Attendant to Admiral of the Fleet without marrying money, but you'll never find anything in it about anyone in your own division. So I'll give you a little bit of advice. Whenever you're consulting B.R.1066, always pretend you're looking for a different sort of rating than the one you want. If you're looking for the regulations for asdic operators, pick up the book and say aloud : "Now, I wonder how I would become a parachute packer in the R.N.Z.N.?" and sure as fate asdic operators will be on the first page you look at.'

The Bodger paused, but this time the Captain did not interrupt. He merely leaned against the bulkhead and listened. The Captain knew better than to interrupt an artist in the middle of a performance.

'The next category of book is the C.B., C.B. as your quick and agile minds will again interpret, meaning Confidential Book. B.R.'s are normally classified as Restricted, which means that you can't show them to the Press or to your old uncle who's interested in the Navy, but C.B.'s have to be kept locked up and mustered page by page by an officer. Every ship has a C.B. Officer. In this ship the C.B.'s are mustered by the Chaplain's Doggie, as no doubt you know. Anything confidential, as its name implies, will be found in a C.B. Such things as publications on signal codes, some types of machinery handbooks, things like that. Incidentally, what the Admiralty normally do about machinery handbooks is to pinch the manufacturers' handbook word for word and make it a C.B. Then when the manufacturers find out and start beefing about copyrights the Admiralty merely say : "This book is a C.B. How did you get to hear about it?" and have one or all of the firm's directors up under the Official Secrets Act. It's just another case of what I'm always telling you blokes about. There's always a simple way of doing things which puts the other feller in the wrong if you only take the trouble to sit down and think about it.'

The Captain shook his head and passed on to the next gun-room where the Communications Officer was lecturing.

'. . . the normal methods of passing visual signals in the service are by flashing, using the Morse Code, or by flags, using Sema-phore. We do not shoot arrows in the air, nor do we use smoke signals, carrier pigeons, Nigerian runners with cleft sticks, nor telepathy, though I have no doubt that we shall use television. Now, if you look at the sheets of flag hoist examples which I have provided and of which you should all by now have a copy, I will show you another method of passing signals visually. The examples are designed to be read from left to right and from top to bottom in the normal manner, negative Chinese. Will any cadet who has been accustomed to another convention please prove? No? Well then, when I direct your attentions to example one you should all by now be looking at the top left-hand diagram which consists of two flags and carries a message fraught with meaning to any sailor. This is a signal which a parsimonious country permits to be flown only on occasions of great national rejoicing. It is not "England Expects" nor is it Gentlemen will please adjust their dress before leaving." It is "Splice the Main-brace." Do not trouble to memorise it. The instances when it is flown are few and the knowledge that it will be flown will have been common for some months previously. The next hoist con-sists of one flag and it carries a cry from the heart. It is the ensign of the Ancient Mariner, the house flag of Alcoholics Anonymous. It is the Turn Pendant and flown singly in harbour it means "Waterboat Required." This is one worth memorising.

181

In H.M. Ships it usually goes up as the anchor goes down. Now Rorari, moderating your voice to a dull roar, try to tell me what the third hoist means . . .'

Again the Captain made no comment, recognising once more the voice of a master. Tom Bowles had the shameful thought that perhaps the Captain was reluctant to burst in on either The Bodger or the Communications Officer because he was afraid he might get the worst of the encounter. But the next lecturer sounded more promising.

It was Chief Electrician Pocock, conducting a class with heavy tread and scrupulous attention to detail through the intricacies of lighting circuits. The Chief Electrician had been bequeathed a comprehensive set of notes by his predecessor and he never departed from them if he could avoid it. They were his rod and staff through a swamp of technicalities. Once Chief Electrician Pocock had been drawn from his notes he floundered like a heavily armoured legionary enticed off the Roman road down into oozing marshes.

'Electrical Lecture Number Seven,' intoned the Chief Electrician. 'The Seventh Electrical Lecture. Lighting Circuits. The basis of all lighting circuits is Ohm's Law. Ohm's Law states that the current through a circuit is proportional to the voltage or, expressed another way, the voltage is equal to the current times a constant. This constant is the same for any given circuit and is termed the Resistance. I'll give you a for instance . . .'

'Excuse me, Chief, but did you say *Ohm's* Law?'

The Chief Electrician consulted his notes.

'I did.'

'But, Chief, in Electrical Lecture Number Six last week you said it was Faraday.'

The Chief Electrician thumbed back several pages in his notes.

'I did say nothing of the sort . . .'

'Don't believe a word he says, Chief. *We* all know it was Watt, don't we, fellows?'

Several voices answered at once.

'What what?'

'It was Ohm sweet Ohm.'

'It was Jan Faraday.'

'Old Uncle Tom Oersted and all . . .'

'Ah well, they also serve who only stand and watt.'

'*Who* said that?'

'John Milton, Chief.'

'Come out the front of the class, Milton.'

The Captain strode in through the doorway.

'*Class!*' roared the Chief Electrician.

The class struggled to their feet, sheepishly trying to assume the position of attention in the limited leg space between bench and table. Some of them looked resentfully at Tom Bowles, as though they felt it was his fault.

'Don't mind me, Chief,' the Captain said mildly. '*You!*' The Captain turned suddenly on Spink, in the front row. 'What's the difference between a watt, a faraday and an oersted? Eh?'

'I-I don't know, sir,' Spink stammered.

'Well, listen to the Chief Electrician in future when he's trying to teach you something!'

The last lecture was one on the causes of funnel smoke, by Ginger Piggant. The Captain was not interested in the causes of funnel smoke, only in the means of its swift removal from the funnel whenever he complained about it. The Captain snorted and passed on.

His peregrinations had brought the Captain back to the quarterdeck. He looked at his watch.

'I usually have a small glass of something about this time, Bowles,' he said. 'I won't ask you to join me because I'm sure the Cadet Training Officer would be most displeased. You can carry on, and thank you for your assistance, Bowles.'

'Thank you, sir.'

Tom Bowles saluted and doubled away. It was just after eleven-thirty in the forenoon and the rest of the day was his own. On his way forward he met Paul.

'How did you get on?'

'Fair enough. He's not as dumb as he likes to appear. He's much sharper than anyone would think.'

'I imagine so, or he wouldn't be a Captain.'

Barsetshire called for an afternoon at Point à Pierre, Trinidad, to refuel, during which Paul visited the refinery and George Dewberry discovered rum. *Barsetshire* then sailed for Grenada.

11

WHEN *Barsetshire* visited a Mediterranean port, the local people were interested in her, undoubtedly they were interested in her, but then there had been a ship last week and most assuredly there would be another ship next week. One more ship was nothing to get excited about. But in the West Indies *Barsetshire's* visit was a yearly event much looked forward to and enjoyed to the full while it lasted. The residents competed to invite parties of cadets to their houses. The girls packed their regular boy-friends off to the hills for the week or ten days while *Barsetshire* was in. And the distillers of rum and the weavers of straw hats rubbed their hands with glee and promised themselves a harvest of profit unequalled since the visits of Nelson's fleets in search of those of the ruffianly Bonaparte.

On board, feelings were mixed. Those of the Ship's Company who had not visited the West Indies before could not wait to go ashore and sample the legendary hospitality of West Indian women; they could not understand the caution which old hands to the station displayed before getting out of the boat. They could not know that this caution was well-founded. Old hands on the station, like the Chief G.I. and the Master at Arms, had no wish to repeat last year's experience when they had each been greeted, on stepping ashore, with the joyous hail of 'Daddy!' bubbling from innocent piccaninny lips.

Feelings were also mixed in the Wardroom. The Communications Officer wondered whether that little octaroon girl was still there. Ginger Piggant was afraid that the little octaroon girl would still recognise him. The Commander (S) wondered whether he would have to pay more for grapefruit. While the P.M.O. retired to his cabin to read up his handbook on venereal disease.

The Captain's calls on the dignitaries of the island were returned immediately. The Governor travelled from shore in a bright blue barge. The Colonel commanding the island garrison came off in a dull black barge. A large black gentleman in a bright red barge named *Lullaby of Broadway* followed to arrange for the sale of grapefruit and soft drinks on board and he himself was succeeded by his brother in a bright yellow barge named *Red Hot Lips Baby* to arrange for the removal of the rubbish and waste the ship would discard during her stay.

By lunch time the Cadets' Notice Board was covered in invitations. They were all of a pattern. They were for 'Swimming, Cocktails and Tennis—six cadets'; 'Visit to a Nutmeg Plantation and Tennis—two cadets'; 'Tour of a Rum Distillery and Tennis—eight cadets'; 'Deep Sea Fishing Expedition and Tennis—two cadets'; and 'Midnight Barbecue and Tennis—ten cadets.'

Every invitation, without exception, had this curious insistence on tennis. It seemed that whatever else a man might do in the island, he had at least to play tennis. The invitations gave the impression that the business administration of the island was done by people who broke off several times in the course of a working day to practise their backhand smashes and who formed a society which occupied itself, not in taking in each other's washing, but in umpiring each other's tennis matches.

There were more invitations than there were cadets prepared to accept them, but those cadets who did not wish to play tennis, or who hated tennis, or who had never learned how to play tennis, discovered that the word 'invitation' was meaningless. When The Bodger found several invitations not filled, his policy was quite definite. The Bodger had entertained the Governor's Aide-de-Camp at lunch time and had disliked him on sight.

'If the bastards want ten cadets to look round a straw hat

factory and play tennis, they're bloody well going to *get* ten cadets to look round a straw hat factory and play tennis. Mr Piles, detail off the watch ashore until those invitations are all filled. If that isn't enough, detail off the non-duty part of the watch on board. If *that* isn't enough, then go on detailing off cadets until every invitation is filled. Nobody's going to tell me my cadets are not being sociable. They can all play tennis until their eyeballs drop out. If they don't know how to play tennis, they'd better learn between now and going ashore.'

Mr Piles, the Chief G.I. and the Chief P.T.I. organised a witch-hunt. They scoured the cadets' quarters and rounded up every cadet, duty or not duty, sick or well. Cadets who had not intended to go ashore, cadets who had intended to go ashore later, and cadets who were under stoppage of leave and not allowed to go ashore, were routed out of the hiding places about the ship where they had hoped to read, sleep or write letters. They were herded together and ordered ashore to play tennis.

Tennis racquets were at premium. The ship's sports store was quickly exhausted and the supply of private racquets ran out soon after and it looked for a time as though The Bodger's plans to launch his cadets in society were to be defeated for lack of tennis racquets. But The Bodger was indefatigable.

'It doesn't have to be a *tennis* racquet, godammit! *Any* racquet will do. All cadets proceeding ashore must have a sporting implement of some kind.'

The later boatloads of cadets were armed with tennis racquets which had strings broken, handles split and splices missing. The very latest departures carried badminton and squash racquets, cricket bats, hockey sticks and billiard cues. One cadet merely wore a fives glove.

The cadets were mustered by the Chief G.I. on the upper deck and detailed off in parties.

' . . . from 'ere to the left—Museum and Tennis Party. Party, left turn, quick march, carry on to the museum. From 'ere to the left, you as well—Botanical Gardens and Tennis Party. Party, left turn, quick march, carry on to the botanical gardens. From 'ere to the left—Visit to Sugar Cane Plantation and Tennis Party. Got your sporting implement? Let's see it. Right. Party, left turn, quick march, carry on to the sugar cane plantation. From 'ere to the left—Scottish Country Dancing and Tennis Party. . . .'

George Dewberry was ordered ashore to visit a rum distillery, taking with him a croquet mallet, one of a set of six owned by the Navigating Officer. Tom Bowles found himself in a massed party who were going to visit a straw hat factory; they had two tennis racquets, a putter and one old football boot between ten of them. Raymond Ball, with The Bodger's No. 7 Iron, and a strange cadet whom Raymond had never seen before, with a fencing foil, were allocated to a visit to a nutmeg plantation.

Michael took his own racquet and Cartwright a superb Slazenger's championship racquet to the botanical gardens. Paul was Cadet of the Watch and glad of it.

George Dewberry's party were met by one of the distillery's lorries, redolent with rich spirit and promising well of the visit to come. Tom Bowles was met by an orange bus and Michael by a young negro clergyman leading a crocodile of small black children. A gigantic black chauffeur in a gigantic black Ford waited for Raymond Ball.

The chauffeur introduced himself by backing the Ford into a melon-stall. Amidst the rolling water-melons, the screams of the stall-keeper, George Dewberry's raucous shouts from the top of the rum lorry and Michael's puzzled face on greeting the clergyman, Raymond Ball and the strange cadet drove off.

'The Chief Stoker won't half be worried,' said the strange cadet with the fencing foil, as they drove through the crowded streets of the town.

'Why?' asked Raymond Ball.

'I was supposed to be dipping the tanks for the readings, see, and I was just on me way through the Cadets' Messdeck when the Cadet Gunner give me this and told me to hop down into the boat sharp. So I did. But the Chief Stoker won't half be worried.'

'You mean you're not a cadet?'

'Cadet? I'm the Fresh Water Tanky!'

'Good God! Hey, driver! Stop a minute, there's been a mistake!'

The driver turned round. A huge grin split his face from cheek-bone to cheek-bone. The car swerved towards the side of the road.

'No stop, sir,' said the driver. 'Stop when we get there, sir.'

A black face swam nearer Raymond Ball's eyes. The car squealed as the driver wrenched it away from a wall and headed it down the middle of the street.

'Oh, well,' Raymond said. 'It's too late now. We're on our way to a nutmeg plantation, by the way.'

'That's O.K. by me, sir. I could just do with a little bit of black ham.'

The Fresh Water Tanky put his fencing foil on the floor of the car and sat back to enjoy the ride.

A mile out of St George the tarmac stopped and the track began. The track was loose gravel and sand and it plunged up and down hills shaded on each side by trees and cane. The sun struck vivid patches of brightness across the car's path between the intervals of the trees. The openings gave glimpses of more green hills and vegetation in the distance. In villages chickens and children ran across the road almost under the wheels of the car. Sometimes the car passed a bus crammed with cheerful black faces and startlingly coloured cotton dresses. Through the open car window came the smell of the West Indies, the compounded aroma of sugar, ripe fruit already decaying, and rich fertility.

When the nutmeg planter, a fat, olive-skinned man in a crumpled palm beach suit, greeted his guests, he seemed puzzled by the golf club and the fencing foil.

'You must be very fond of sport,' he said. 'I am afraid that we have few facilities here. We haven't even a tennis court. Did somebody tell you . . . ?'

The planter broke off in perplexity. Raymond Ball and the Fresh Water Tanky hid their sporting implements behind their backs. A mistake had been made. (Later, The Bodger discovered that the residents had sent their invitations to the Governor's office and some of them had genuinely been for tennis but a clerk in the office, thinking that all Englishmen played tennis and would be disappointed if not invited to do so in Grenada, had added '& Tennis' to every invitation regardless of the host's original intentions.)

'Never mind,' the planter said. 'Now you would like to see the nutmegs.'

But it was a hot afternoon and they went no farther than the first shed where the nutmegs were laid out to dry, being occasionally raked over by a bored negro. After that, they sat in deck chairs on the verandah and drank iced lime and lemon. The planter did not seem anxious to entertain them further and Raymond Ball and the Fresh Water Tanky were happy to sit in the shade and do nothing; that in itself was a sufficient change from *Barsetshire*. They were in the position of people sitting at ease in the house of a stranger who was not anxious to make polite conversation or bother them in any way. It was more than likely that they would leave without even introducing themselves.

In the evening the planter introduced his wife who was fat, placid, gold-toothed and as incurious as her husband. She made supper of iced coconut milk and grated nutmeg, fried fish and fruit. The planter brought out his whisky and they sat down and drank it as calmly and as unhurriedly and in the same companionable silence as they had drunk lime and lemon.

After dark they went inside and the planter and his wife set up a mahjongg board. Then the planter clapped his hands and at this signal two octaroon girls came in through the open french windows from the garden and sat down by the guests. They were both young and had the peach-down freshness of skin and the large sloe eyes of their race.

The planter and his wife yawned, shook hands with their guests and went out of the room. The inference was plain. They had done all they could to make their party a success. They had

190

provided liquor, entertainment, and young women. It was now up to the young men.

The young men were not at first disposed to take advantage of the facilities offered to them. Drugged by the sun and by successive unaccustomed whiskies, they sat drowsily in their chairs, like the victims of Circe. There was magic in a house which could produce two beautiful young girls at the clap of a hand; it smacked of witchcraft, of a genie's palace where strange wonders could be wrought from the darkness at the rubbing of a ring.

The octaroon girls sat at the feet of the chairs seemingly content to wait until some form of activity was suggested to them. Even Raymond Ball, who was normally stimulated by the presence of women, found it difficult to broach the conversation, having so little upon which to start.

'Would you like to play mahjongg?' he asked at last.

They played mahjongg. The girls won easily. After the game the girls resumed their positions at the feet of the chairs.

'Would you like to see the nutmeg trees?' asked the girl nearest Raymond Ball, suddenly.

'Eh? O.K., if you want to. I suppose that's what we came for, after all.'

Outside, the evening had grown cool. The house stood on the northern slope of a valley which led to the sea. As Raymond and the octaroon girl stood on the verandah, a fresh wind rustled up the valley from the sea and shivered the tops of the palms. Behind the trees on the crest of the hill on the other side, the moon climbed slowly, its silver circle glowing in the night sky like a jewel. Small clouds sailed high and powdery in an indigo sky. The fronds of the trees in the valley bent together and dappled as the wind touched them; the whole of the opposite hillside rippled like a smooth ocean breaking into tiny waves, spreading out and fading back into stillness again. Faint sounds came up out of the darkness, the tinkling of an instrument like a triangle, the throb as of drums, and calling voices, but up on the hillside it was quiet.

191

Raymond Ball felt the girl close to him. He stood looking down the valley, conscious of her closeness.

Suddenly she turned and put her arms round his neck, and lightly kissed him on the lips. Her lips were firm and warm and caressed him as they left him.

'I know what you want,' she whispered.

'Do you? What?'

'It looks out of your eyes.'

He put his hands on her hips and felt their suppleness. 'All right,' he said firmly, '*show* me these bloody nutmeg trees.'

When Raymond Ball arrived back on board *Barsetshire,* George Dewberry was giving trouble. The tour of the rum distillery had been a roaring success. Dewberry had been helped back from it, paralysed with rum. Raymond Ball helped to undress George Dewberry, pack him in his hammock and lash him down.

'I don't know how he gets like that,' he said to Michael, as they stood panting after their exertions. 'Just show him anything remotely connected with the alcohol family and he gets paralytic!'

Raymond Ball began to undress.

'Where've you been today, Ray?' Michael asked.

'Oh, visiting a nutmeg plantation.'

'What have you been doing to them, cutting them down or something? You look positively *grey*. And, my God, look at your back! It's all scratched to hell! Looks as though you've been *wallowing* in nutmeg trees.'

'They're very interesting things. I don't think I've ever enjoyed looking at a tree more in my life.'

The novelty of being Cadet of the Watch had long worn off for Paul. He had helped the Gunnery Officer supervise the unloading of three boat-loads of cheering, rum-stricken sailors and he could hear a fourth boat approaching the ship.

The fourth boat brought Paul's reward. It contained Able Seaman Froggins. Just before he went off watch Paul was privileged to see Able Seaman Froggins, armed with a palm-chopping machete, chasing the Gunnery Officer round the quarterdeck.

12

AT Georgetown, Barbados, *Barsetshire* gave an official cocktail party, as she had done at every port she visited. The
invitations for the party were distributed before *Barsetshire*
arrived, and although it might have been a matter of concern to
the British residents whether or not they were invited, the cadets
worried not at all.

The quarterdeck decorations in *Barsetshire* were identical at
every cocktail party and were indeed standard for all cocktail
parties in all H.M. Ships. They depended for their effect, not
on any especial artistic merit, but upon their novelty for the
guests, most of whom only rarely visited a warship. 'We could
cover the ship with fishhooks and barbed wire,' The Bodger said,
'and they'd still be thrilled to bits.'

The quarterdeck was scrubbed and every piece of visible brass
was polished. The vulgar and utilitarian wooden cages which
concealed the bollards and the after capstan were covered with
white cloths and vases of flowers. The quarterdeck guard-rails
were bound with canvas screens and flags were hung from the
quarterdeck awning. Burnished shell cases were placed at
intervals as ashtrays. One bar ran down one side of the quarterdeck and a second bar ran down the other. A third bar was
placed across the after end at right angles to the other two. The
guests were thus confined in a small arena surrounded on three
sides by a barricade of drinks and glasses; a guest who struck out

in three out of four directions would find something to drink and in the fourth he would find the toilet.

While the duty watch of cadets were rigging the quarterdeck, Mr Sammidge, the Commissioned Catering Officer, and a working party of stewards were preparing innumerable canapes, cocktail sausages, potato crisps and tiny sandwiches. Mr Sammidge watched the preparations with a careful eye. He had been in the Navy long enough to know his way about and, as this was his last commission, he hoped to make enough out of it to add to what he had made out of other commissions and set up in a small hotel of his own when he left the service.

'Come out from among them flowers,' he said to a steward whom he could see lurking behind a thick zareba of tropical flowers which he and the ship's postman had brought on board that morning.

'Here,' he shouted at another steward who was letting his appetite for the canapes get the better of him. 'Keep your hands off them c'naipes. Them c'naipes is for the tables. You two start taking them plates up. Crisps at the far end for the cadets and the c'naipes in the middle. Keep the keviar this end for the Governor. Not too many now. Take some up now and some later. Them olives has got to *last*. They don't grow on trees, you know.'

Next door in the Wardroom Wine Store, the Captain's Steward, Knowles, and one of the Wardroom barmen, Marine Stubble, were mixing the drinks under the supervision of the Gunnery Officer, who was the Wardroom Wine Caterer.

'White Lady! Cointreau, one bottle!' The Gunnery Officer read out the recipes as though he were giving the detail for loading and firing a gun.

Knowles lifted the Cointreau bottle and gravely allowed its contents to gurgle into the silver soup tureen in which the drinks were being made. He let the bottle drip until it was empty and solemnly replaced it on the table with the dispassionate composure of a priest of Rome pouring a libation to Jove on the Capitoline Hill amongst the swirling incense, the fluttering pigeons and the chanting choirs.

195

'Gin, Gordon's! Six bottles!'

Knowles took the bottles as Marine Stubble handed them to him and repeated the lugubrious sacrificial procedure.

'Ice!'

Marine Stubble carried up a bucket and let slide a glittering avalanche.

'Lemon. Cherries.'

Knowles and Marine Stubble took turns to bring up the ingredients in obedience to the whiplash tones of the Gunnery Officer.

'What's that other bottle there?'

'Sherry, sir,' said Marine Stubble.

'Put that in as well.'

Impassively, Marine Stubble poured the bottle of sherry into the tureen. No expression crossed his face. Marine Stubble was a teetotaller.

'Now, then. Next. Planter's Punch . . .'

Several decks down and some way forward of the Wardroom Wine Store, the Double Bottom Chief Stoker was also preparing for the party. His was a vital part.

Past cocktail parties had shown that the normal trim of the ship left a gap between the decks of the motorboats and the bottom step of the gangway; lady guests had been forced to draw up their skirts to an unconscionable extent, under the licentious eyes of the boats' crews and the gangway staff. Whenever *Barsetshire* gave a party the D.B. Chief Stoker lowered the stern of the ship by transferring oil fuel. It was a proceeding which never failed to arouse comment amongst his stokers but the Chief Stoker had not served twenty years in the Navy without learning how to quell junior ratings.

'Stop nattering and get on with it. You're being butchered to make a wardroom holiday, that's what.'

Ten minutes before the start of the party Mr Sammidge came up on to the quarterdeck to check the distribution of canapes, the Gunnery Officer surveyed the disposition of glasses and drinks, and the D.B. Chief Stoker measured the distance from the gangway to the water line by eye. The preparations were completed and everything now depended upon the conversational powers of the hosts.

The hosts stood in groups on the quarterdeck, dressed in white uniforms, sampling the work of the Gunnery Officer and his staff; none of *Barsetshire's* officers would have contemplated the idea of entertaining a quarterdeck full of complete strangers while sober. No man can be sociable, neither can he dance, in cold blood.

The Bodger had briefed the cadets in the art of broaching a stranger. 'Offer him a cigarette,' The Bodger said, 'and a drink, ask him if this is his first time on board, and tell him what wonderful weather he has in the West Indies. All quite simple. Remember he's not the vaguest bit interested in you and he knows everybody else at the party and you don't. He's probably only come because it's the right thing to do and shows that he moves in the right circles and he's just waiting to get away from you and talk business to someone. A good many of the people you'll meet will be either social or professional climbers and that holds good all over the world. Whatever you do, let *him* talk if he wants to. They all speak English here, which is an advantage you won't always have. Everybody has got some particular subject which will keep him happy for hours. All you've got to do is find it and then say "How interesting" and "You don't say" and "Well, I never knew that" and so on and he'll think what a wonderful conversationalist you are and invite you to dinner and introduce his daughter and then you're all set. Then it's your turn. You can bore the daughter as much as her father bored you.'

Michael approached a negro clergyman. He was very tall, with a dead black complexion and startlingly white hair. He wore a white linen suit, black surplice and white dog-collar. The man's whole appearance was an ensemble of black and white.

'Would you like a cigarette?' Michael asked.

'No,' said the Black and White Padre. 'I do not smoke.'

'Would you like a drink?'

'No. I do not drink.'

'Oh well. . . . Is this your first visit on board this ship?'

'Yes.'

'What do you think of it?'

'I have been on board only five minutes.'

'Oh I see. What lovely weather you have in the West Indies. Much nicer than England.'

'Except for the hurricane last month.'

'That must have been terrible.'

'It was good.'

'Dear me, a hurricane good?'

'Never has my church been so full as after that.'

'How do you mean?'

'People wished to give thanks for their lives.'

'I see. It's an ill wind which blows no one any good. Hurricane, I mean.'

'My church is still full.'

'That must be very encouraging for you, sir.'

'Another hurricane is expected next month.'

'Oh.'

Michael and the Black and White Padre gazed helplessly at each other. They both spoke English but that was all they had in common.

Near by, Colin Stacforth was entertaining a stout woman in a flowered print dress. Her eyebrows were severely plucked, her eyes were haloed in mascara and her lipstick exceeded the natural line of her lips by an eighth of an inch. Two bright red spots of rouge stood out on her cheekbones and she wore long dangling earrings which were miniature goldfish bowls. She had a low growling voice and Colin Stacforth, who was the acknowledged cadet expert at cocktail parties, mentally dubbed her the Scarlet Woman.

'Would you like a drink?'

'Would I,' growled the Scarlet Woman.

'What would you like?'

'What've you got?'

'White Lady, Rum Punch or . . .'

'Got any Scotch and soda?'

'I expect so.'

198

'Not too much soda.'

'By all means.'

'Before you go, have you got a cigarette?'

'Certainly. Virginia this end, Turkish the far end.' Colin Stacforth held out his cigarette-case. The Scarlet Woman was impressed.

'You're pretty smooth,' she growled. 'What you doing tonight?'

'I'll get you something to drink.'

The noise level rose as the party gathered momentum. At first scattered and subdued, like the earliest arrivals of a symphony orchestra tentatively tuning their instruments, the sounds of the party merged and swelled as though more and more instruments had arrived, found the right key and taken up the strain in sympathy, until they achieved that final sustained roar, that unmistakable babble of a large number of people contained in a group and obeying that same instinct which once caused their ancestors to assemble by companies in the treetops to gibber and howl at the rising moon.

Raymond Ball was shouting with an elderly man and his very pretty daughter. Raymond Ball was persevering with the elderly man in the hope of being introduced to his daughter. As The Bodger had predicted, Raymond was not having any difficulty in making conversation with the old boy. His problem now was to stop him.

'You know!' bawled the elderly man. 'It's a damned good show this ship coming out here like this! Reminds us all out here that we've got a Navy! Yes! You should come out here more often! Why don't you come out here more often?'

'Well . . .'

'I'll tell you! Dollars! The Almighty Dollar! We can't afford it! And why can't we afford it?'

'It's . . .'

'I'll tell you! We can't afford it because we're spending so much on rearmament! That's what it is! Rearmament!'

'But, Daddy, if we spent less on rearmament we'd be even less likely to have a ship out here.'

'Be quiet, Louise, you're as bad as your mother used to be! By the way, my boy, you haven't met my daughter! This is my daughter Louise! I didn't catch your name, my boy?'

'Raymond Ball, sir.'

'Good, I must leave you for a moment! I see an old friend of mine over there and I must catch him before he goes. You look after this young fellow, Louise!'

'This is a lovely party,' Louise said. 'Oh, do look, there's a boy on the floor. I hope he hasn't hurt himself?'

'No, he hasn't hurt himself. He's used to it. Can I get you another drink?'

'No, thank you, this one is quite enough. They're terribly strong, aren't they?'

'Yes. You have to be careful otherwise you'll get terribly drunk on them.'

'That boy on the floor looks drunk already.'

'Oh, no, I expect he's just tired.'

'Shouldn't he go to bed then?'

'I expect someone will take him soon. Now tell me . . .'

'Are you playing in the cricket match tomorrow?'

'No, I'm not actually playing but I expect I'll go and watch.'

'I love cricket! If you watch them playing it here, they look *really* happy. Have you got a good team?'

'We have one or two good players. You see that tall dark chap over there talking to the girl in the red dress? He's very good. I expect he'll play for the Navy one day.'

'Will he?'

The elderly man came back as Louise was beginning to look at Paul with interest and Raymond Ball was wishing he had never mentioned him.

'There you are! Louise, the Governor has been kind enough to invite me to dinner tonight so you'll have to take this young man home and give him something to eat. Take the car, old Pertwee will give me a lift home. Does that suit you, young man?'

'I'd be delighted, sir!'

'You must look at our bamboos,' Louise said.

200

Raymond Ball looked up sharply. Now what does she mean by that, he asked himself. He looked at Louise again. She really was a most delicious specimen.

'Are they like nutmeg trees?' he asked.

'No. Why?'

'Nothing.'

The hard work put in by Knowles and Marine Stubble began to show itself. Strangers bumped into one another, apologised, and fell to talking as though they had been at school together. The Governor's party, who had started by standing remotely at one end sipping White Ladies, now circulated through the crowd. The Governor himself was exchanging stories with the P.M.O. while his Aide-de-Camp was trying, unsuccessfully, to break into a group where The Bodger was entertaining his fiancée; the Governor's Aide-de-Camp had lost two fiancées at cocktail parties in H.M. Ships and he knew the danger signals. Michael and Isaiah Nine Smith were picking George Dewberry up off the deck and getting him to bed.

The Corporal of the Gangway, who was a Plymouth Brother, stood by the quartermaster's lobby and looked scornfully aft.

'Anointing their throats with hell fire, that's what they're doing,' he said to the Marine Bugler, with relish.

'I could do with a drop of that meself,' said the Marine Bugler wistfully. 'They doan't half seem to be enjoying themselves.'

'They'll go the way of the rest,' the Corporal of the Gangway said firmly. 'Slipping down the broad high road to damnation, the lot of 'em.'

'Oh, I doan't know. A bit of a shindig does no one any harm.' The Marine Bugler was a Wesleyan.

'Ah. You wait till it's time to go. Till some of them women try to get down the gangway. Then you'll see what I mean, lad.'

The Corporal of the Gangway was a man of experience. When the time came for the guests to go, the scene was indeed diverting.

Ooooh *Bodger!*' squealed one girl, who had been drinking rum punches faster than The Bodger could provide them. 'Those *steps!* You'll have to carry me! No, I can't, you'll have to carry me. No, I can't face them and I daren't even look at them or I'll be sick. You'll have to—don't prod me, Jane, you cat! I think I'll just give this little boy a kiss before I go. Come here,' she said to the Cadet of the Watch. 'But I'm sure he *needs* someone to kiss him. He looks lonely. I'm sure you're beastly to him, Bodger. No, you'll have to carry me. . . . *No!*'

The Gunnery Officer and the Communications Officer were trying to stop another girl going up a ladder into the after gun-room where Michael and Isaiah Nine Smith, whose blasphemy could just be heard, were slinging George Dewberry's hammock and putting him into it.

'But Guns, *please,* don't be such a prude. Oh, what lovely language! I'm not going to stay long, I just want to see how they do it. I've always wondered. Can't I just peep? Just a teeny . . . weeny . . . peep—hup! Whoops! Pardon my French!'

The Commander, who disliked cocktail parties personally but attended each one because all successful naval officers attended them, strode around the quarterdeck tapping officers on the shoulder with his telescope and muttering to them to get their guests ashore. The band played the National Anthem to inti-mate that the entertainment was now over and they wanted to get to their supper. The stewards were clearing up the tables by emptying the contents of glasses down their throats. The D.B. Chief Stoker appeared at the forward end of the quarterdeck and summed up the situation. The party was over.

But it took time before the last of the guests was escorted and, in the case of one excited young lady, carried kicking by the Corporal of the Gangway down to the boats. At last it was done. The Bodger and his mates stepped back and wiped their brows.

'My God!' The Bodger said. 'What does Guns do to that stuff! It must start off as normal liquor but after he and that satellite of his Knowles have had a go at it we might just as well be drinking neat dynamite. One sip of that rum punch nearly blew the top of my head off.'

'Still,' said the Communications Officer, 'I can die at rest now. Did you hear what that woman in the earrings told Dickie to do with his telescope?'

The cricket match at Barbados was an annual fixture and it was played under special rules. Every member of the fielding side except the wicket-keeper was called upon to bowl two overs; each innings therefore lasted a maximum of twenty overs. A batsman retired when he had made thirty runs, and a boundary, a wicket, or indeed an incident of any kind was the signal for planter's punch to be brought out on trays from the pavilion. The rig for the teams was white shorts and shirts but hats were optional and according to personal preference; the rules stated that a player's hat could be anything but a cricket cap. *Barsetshire* had never within the memory of anyone on board won a match, and when the ship's team arrived at the ground they understood why; they saw that they would have to play not only against the opposing side but also against the ground, the crowd, and the calypso steel band.

The ground sloped towards the sea and was enclosed by a low cliff which dropped down to the beach, a row of tall palms, a deep ditch and the road on the fourth side. The wicket was concrete covered with matting and provided as good a batting surface as any in the world but the outfield was tough, slippery grass broken up by pot-holes, ridges and heaps of stones. The pavilion was a structure of four poles supporting a roof of thatched palm leaves and it was placed on the far side of the ditch so that an incoming batsman descended into the ditch, scrambled up the other side and picked his way between stones and pot-holes to the wicket. A scoreboard was nailed to one of the four posts, but it was only kept up to date when the home team were batting. The feet of the spectators marked the boundaries but four runs were only automatically granted when the ball actually hit a spectator. During the home side's innings the boundary contracted and the younger members of the crowd risked life and limb to impede the ball; when the visiting team were batting, the boundary expanded and the crowd opened to provide a passage for the ball and the fielder.

Except for a loyal group of British residents in deck chairs by the pavilion, the crowd were entirely West Indian. They made a brilliant border round the ground of red, yellow and blue shirts and dresses, black faces, yellow straw hats and white teeth. They laughed, cheered, joked and shouted to each other across the pitch. They had come prepared to cheer their team home; if will power and cheering could make an opposing team drop catches and lose wickets, the home side were already on the way to winning the game.

But the most formidable opposition a visiting team had to face was the calypso steel band. They squatted in a circle near the pavilion and their only instruments were petrol and kerosene tins with the bottoms heated and peined in parts to give out different notes when struck. The steel band were playing when the visiting team arrived and they played throughout the match, being led by a man in a suit of flame-red pyjamas known as 'Firedrake Fred' who sang a running calypso commentary on the play.

The Bodger, who was umpiring, in a long white coat and a grey bowler, went out to the pitch with the other umpire while the captains tossed. The steel band played 'With Catlike Tread They Creep Upon Their Prey' in time to the umpire's footsteps.

Cartwright, *Barsetshire's* captain, won the toss. He was wearing a deerstalker decorated with fishing flies. He chose to bat.

> 'The Englishmen, they have won the toss,
> In this fair land of Barba*dos* . . .'

sang Firedrake Fred.

> 'They are going to bat, all can see,
> We must bowl them out with alacri*tee*.'

The fielding side came out to the 'Entry of the Gladiators' and were followed by Paul and Pontius the Pilot, *Barsetshire's* opening pair (in straw boater and flight deck beret) to the 'Entry of the Queen of Sheba.'

Paul's first ball was a slow full toss on the leg side. He caught it in the middle of the bat and struck it hard and head high towards square leg. The Bodger and square leg threw themselves flat on the ground. The ball hummed over the heads of the crowd, cannoned off a palm tree, and rebounded back into the field to midwicket who hurled himself sideways to catch the ball before it touched the ground. The crowd leapt and hugged themselves. The steel band played 'Let's Have Another One.' The first round of planter's punch came out from the pavilion.

'Well held, sir,' said the elderly man whom Raymond Ball had met at the party, who was sitting with his daughter Louise and Raymond Ball by the pavilion.

'The first man he go to a very good catch,
Just nine more and we win the match . . .'

sang Firedrake Fred.

Paul's place was taken by the Fresh Water Tanky in a sombrero who drove his first ball straight at the bowler. The bowler took the catch with a triumphant yell, back somersaulted and stood up holding the ball and grinning. The crowd howled. The steel band doubled the tempo. The planter's punch returned.

'Never mind,' said the elderly man in the deck chair, 'at least they're *playing* the ball. The ball hasn't beaten the bat yet.'

'Another man go down down down
And give the happy bowler great ren*own* . . .'

The next batsman was Cartwright. He made a leisurely crossing of the ditch, walked slowly to the wicket, took guard, calmly surveyed the placing of the field, settled his deerstalker more firmly on his head, and blocked or ignored the rest of the over. The crowd began slow clapping. The steel band played 'So Tired.' The ice melted in the planter's punch.

'That's more like it,' said the elderly man.

Cartwright scored steadily in ones and twos but he was given little support. Pontius the Pilot was bowled by a slow ball which hit the wicket on its fourth bounce. Mr Piles was given out l.b.w. when a rising ball removed the mortar-board from his head, and

Able Seaman Froggins, wearing a knotted handkerchief, hit one six over the palm trees and was caught next ball by an old lady in the crowd who accepted the ball on her lap. The rest of *Barsetshire's* batsmen were disconcerted by the small boys who capered and gesticulated behind the bowler's arm, by the steel band's drum roll and crescendo as the bowler ran up to the wicket, by the concerted jump and yell of the fielders as the ball left the bowler's hand, and by the wicket-keeper who crouched over the stumps muttering 'You going to get a duck' not as a question but as statement of fact as the batsmen attempted his stroke. The *Barsetshire* innings closed for fifty-five runs, of which thirty-five runs had been contributed by Cartwright who reached a total of twenty-nine and retired with a six on to the beach.

During the planter's punch interval, the steel band gave a recital conducted by Firedrake Fred. The *Barsetshire* team were astonished at the quality of the music the steel band could make from old petrol drums. They played minuets and marches, carols and calypsos, serenades and sambas, and romances and ragtime. They put fragments of tunes together to build up an intricate melodic structure which Firedrake Fred allowed to reach its height and then demolished with a gesture. The parts were properly orchestrated with counterpoint and contrast. Soloists made their entries faultlessly. Sometimes they sounded like the drums of a military band and sometimes like the percussion section of a large orchestra; they could imitate the pizzicato of a violin, the throbbing of a bassoon, and the strumming of a guitar. The band enjoyed playing and the crowd enjoyed listening to them and they made the liveliest, most genuine music the *Barsetshire* team had ever heard.

Cartwright opened the bowling for *Barsetshire*. He normally opened the bowling for *Barsetshire's* official cricket team, and he stood head and shoulders like a colossus over the other bowlers in the match. He was allowed twelve balls in the match and, bowling downhill and down wind, he determined to make every ball count.

His first pitched short, sailed over the skiing cap of Chief

Electrician Pocock, who was keeping wicket, eluded the Chief G.I.'s outstretched topee on the boundary at fine leg, and landed first bounce on the beach near the sea. The Bodger signalled six byes reluctantly and held up play for the arrival of the planter's punch. Cartwright tightened his jaw, swung his arm rapidly in a windmill motion, and prepared himself for his second ball.

Cartwright had been the first visiting batsman ever to have retired voluntarily on that pitch and he was now the first bowler ever to have bowled six byes. The crowd warmed to him and cheered his every move. The steel band paid him the supreme compliment of a drum roll as he ran up to the wicket.

This encouragement was a gross tactical error. It gave Cartwright the spur he needed. His second ball scattered stumps, bails, ball and bat in a wide spray. The crowd were dumbfounded. The British residents applauded. The steel band played a few disconsolate chords in a minor key. The Bodger called for planter's punch.

'Well *bowled*, sir!' called Louise's father. His eyes sparkled. It was the first piece of real cricket he had seen that afternoon. It reminded him of cricket as he had played it long ago at home with his brothers, in a setting of parasols, strawberries and cream, horses under the chestnut trees, and Victoria on the throne. Cartwright's easy, powerful action recalled other bowlers he had seen, Maurice Tate at Hove, and Larwood and Voce at Trent Bridge. The old man was roused by the gasp which followed after Cartwright's second wicket, which was a duplicate of the first.

During Cartwright's two overs, while Paul bowled from the other end, the home side lost five wickets for ten runs. Four were bowled by Cartwright and the fifth was run out by the Captain's steward, Knowles, who unexpectedly trapped the ball in his glengarry at cover point and threw the wicket down. Paul did not take a wicket but gave away only four runs.

'Tragedee, tragedee, gentlemen this is trage*dee*,' sang Firedrake Fred.

Cartwright had no bowlers to replace himself or Paul once

their two overs had been expended and the new batsmen settled in and began to score. The *Barsetshire* team were tired by the sun, by the shouting and music, and by the planter's punch, but they persevered in the field. Pontius the Pilot awoke in the slips to see a ball speeding at his head and, putting out his hands to protect himself, held the catch. Fresh Water Tanky hurdled over the legs of the crowd to save boundaries at midwicket. Meanwhile, Cartwright and Paul ran and gathered, the Chief G.I. ran and scooped, Knowles ran and trapped, and Chief Electrician Pocock ran and stopped with his foot. When the last man came in to bat, the West Indians still needed five runs to win with four overs in which to score them, the overs to be bowled by Mr Sammidge and Petty Officer Moody.

Petty Officer Moody handed his tam o' shanter to the umpire and bowled three balls on the off side. They were not far enough to be termed wides but too far for the batsman to reach them. Cartwright crossed from mid off and advised Petty Officer Moody to bowl on the wicket. Petty Officer Moody's next ball was straight and was clouted over his head for four runs. Cartwright held his peace. The last two balls of Petty Officer Moody's over were on the off side, not far enough for wides, but too far for the batsman to reach them.

The crowd who had recovered from their shocked silence while Cartwright was bowling, stood up to encourage their last batsman. The sound they now made dwarfed any they had made during the afternoon. The cheers rolled around the ground and deafened the fielders.

'Show him de blade, man !' bellowed Firedrake Fred.

Mr Sammidge retained his fez while he paced out a long run, longer even than Cartwright's. The batsman, who had visions of another whirlwind bowler, tightened his grip on the bat.

Mr Sammidge placed his fez on the ground to mark the end of his run and started back towards the wicket. Accelerating like a runaway juggernaut, Mr Sammidge bore down on the wicket. The batsman braced himself. At the moment before release, Mr Sammidge shifted the ball to his left hand and bowled slowly underarm.

208

Bat upraised, the batsman searched the air for the ball. Then, seeing his opponent low down, he leapt forward and flailed his bat. When the ball passed under the bat it had long lost all momentum for bouncing. The batsman landed on one knee and turned to see the ball rolling towards the wicket. It hit a stump. The bail quivered, as though to some light summer breeze, and fell.

'A tie, by God,' breathed Louise's father.

13

'Brownskin girl, stay home and mind babee!' sang The Bodger under the shower. He soaped and rubbed himself vigorously and sang up into the streaming water. The noise of the water distorted his voice so that weird liquid echoes reverberated round the bathroom. 'Ah'm goin' away *in* a sailing boat an' if I don' come back stay home and mind babee!'

'Oh dear, what can the matter be?' sang the Navigating Officer under the next shower, 'Three old ladies locked in the lavatory. They were *there* from Monday to Saturday, nobody knew they were there.'

'Looking forward to our little trip, Pilot?'

'Wassat Bodger?'

'I said looking forward to our little trip?'

The Navigating Officer turned off his shower and scowled. 'No, I most certainly am not! If I'd wanted to live like a bloody Bedouin I'd have joined the bloody Boy Scouts.'

'Don't be that way, Pilot. Don't you like banyans?'

'I *loathe* banyans.'

At least once a cruise *Barsetshire* anchored in a remote part of the coast where every boat was lowered, filled to the gunwhale with food and drink, manned by everyone who could get away, and sailed as far from the ship as possible. Banyans were popular with the whole Ship's Company except the Navigating Officer and Owen Glendower. The Captain's red setter could protest by being sick on the Captain's carpet and disappearing two minutes before the boat left, and having the duty watch of cadets called out to look for him, but the Navigating Officer had no choice but at attend banyans. He attended banyans for political reasons, because the Commander made himself unpleasant towards any of the ship's officers who did not participate in cadets' activities; the Commander looked upon such officers as Nero looked upon any of his courtiers who did not openly enjoy the efforts of Christians in the arena to escape from the lions.

The Navigating Officer was a man who loved his creature comforts. He contemplated a night spent under a lone star with the same horror as he would have contemplated one spent under a cold shower. Normally the Navigating Officer's life was orderly, comfortable, and as predictable as the course of the stars. He had trained his steward to make his tea, press his suits, and clean his shoes in exactly the manner he preferred. He had a chart pinned to the door of his wardrobe which laid down in detail the combinations of clothes which he customarily wore. Before going to bed at night or going ashore in the evening, the Navigating Officer turned the chart so that a number appeared in a little slot. Number One, for example, was the Navigating Officer's rig for Sunday divisions, weddings and Admiral's inspections and it consisted of his best uniform, best cap, black satin tie, and his sword and medals. Number Five was his double-breasted grey suit, white poplin shirt, Old Carthusian tie, light tan socks and brown brogues; Number Twelve was white tennis shorts, white shirt, naval blazer with the silver crown embroidered upon the pocket (not the Charterhouse 1st XI blazer which was included in Ensemble Number Fifteen), white shoes and socks, and Incogniti silk square. By a system of crosses and secondary numbers, the Navigating Officer had provided in his clothing chart for every sartorial occasion or emergency. He had rigs for funerals, point-to-points, hunt balls, abandoning ship, Highland games, underwater fishing, and for watching drop-forges. The Navigating Officer's Clothing Chart was, in the opinion of his steward, better than a novel. Number Thirteen on the List was marked with a red circle and the Navigating Officer's steward had learned to dread it. It was the Navigating Officer's Banyan Rig.

His bitterness was made overflowing because he was normally called upon to choose the ship's anchorage for banyans.

'Have a look at the map, Pilot,' the Captain said when the ship left Barbados, 'and see if you can't find us a spot in the Virgins where we can all get away from civilisation for a bit.'

Looking like a man condemned by the Inquisition to choose a spot for his own *auto da fe,* the Navigating Officer directed the ship through an intricate and dazzlingly beautiful necklace of tiny islands, like drops of golden sand scattered upon the blue sea. They had names which conjured up memories of the glorious days of the Spanish Main; Dead Man's Chest and Fallen Jerusalem and Virgin Gorda. The Navigating Officer anchored the ship in gleaming blue water in the midst of a small group of islands which were green with palms and bordered with blindingly white sand, looking as though they had never been visited since Blackbeard himself called there to maroon mutineers.

The Ship's Company looked about them, sniffed the air, and agreed that the Navigating Officer had done a good job.

The Captain clapped him on the shoulder.

'Well done, Pilot!' he said.

'Thank you, sir,' said the Navigating Officer. He went and sat down in the Charthouse, looking like a man congratulated by Torquemada upon his choice of faggots.

The Bodger, on the other hand, loved banyans. It was a stroke of luck for him that Pontius the Pilot was on duty over the week-end and asked The Bodger to take his place in charge of his division's banyan. The Bodger superintended every stage of the banyan's preparation and execution. It was The Bodger who ordered the drinks and the food, selected the boat, detailed the crew, and took the tiller.

The boat was loaded with three crates of beer, some rum, potatoes, eggs, bacon, lettuce, tomatoes, loaves of bread, a kettle, a saucepan, several pots, a barricoe of water, tins of soup, some hammocks, fifteen cadets, Ginger, Evans the Slide Rule, the Navigating Officer, and The Bodger.

The Navigating Officer sat in the stern sheets. He wore light-weight fawn slacks, a pale yellow silk shirt with a tea-rose embroidered on the pocket, straw espadrilles, and on his head a tiny black skullcap with a design of pine trees and the word 'St Moritz' worked on it in green silk. In his right hand he carried a portable radio and in his left his private First Aid Box; carefully placed by his feet were his custom-made sleeping bag and his picnic hamper from Fortnum and Mason's. It was the Navigating Officer's Banyan Rig.

The rest of the crew wore football shirts and shorts, except The Bodger, who wore blue and white checked jeans, a red shirt and a Paisley scarf.

There was a delay at the gangway while the Navigating Officer sent up for the yellow cushion, filled with Merino flock, which lay on his desk-chair, not, the Navigating Officer emphasised, the blue cushion embroidered with the Rape of Lucrece which was on the stool by the door. The Bodger grew impatient.

'Come on, Pilot,' he said. 'There won't be any photographers there.'

'I know,' the Navigating Officer said gloomily, 'but there will be stones. And insects.'

The Bodger could wait no longer.

'Let go, bear off. Let go aft. Let's get out of this, men.'

The boat sheered easily away from the ship, caught the wind, and bobbed under nicely filled sails towards the shore.

'Feeling better now, Pilot?'

The Navigating Officer said nothing. He was mentally estimating the hours which must elapse before he returned to the ship, a hot bath, and his creature comforts. If they ran out of food and liquor, the Navigating Officer calculated, they might just be back in time for dinner. That made twenty-nine hours.

The cadets stretched out on the thwarts. Some of them tended the sheets for The Bodger, but most of them looked back at a sight of which they never tired, *Barsetshire* receding into the distance.

A wind off the sea took the boat in through the surf towards the beach. Fifty yards from the line of the sand, The Bodger swung the boat around in a wide reach.

'Let go the anchor! Down foresail, brail up. Take that kedge ashore!'

The boat hung stern on to the shore by its anchor. Two cadets, already naked, leapt into the water with the kedge anchor and carried it up the beach where they embedded it in the sand. The boat was suspended between two anchors, bows on to wind and sea, twenty yards off the beach, in five feet of water. Tom Bowles was impressed. The Bodger had shown once again that he was much more competent at the mechanics of seamanship than he made out.

'Well done, Bodger,' said Ginger. 'Captain Bligh himself couldn't have done better.'

'All out, men,' said The Bodger. 'I expect the bar to be open by the time I get ashore.'

The cadets ferried the equipment on their shoulders to the beach. The Navigating Officer watched closely; he had not forgotten last year's banyan, when an Indian cadet had wantonly dropped his portable gramophone into the sea.

The Bodger took a last look round the boat and waded ashore, where Paul was waiting with a bottle of beer.

The Bodger took the bottle and poured a drop on to the sand.

'First let us pour a libation to the gods,' he said. 'We're now in the home of voodoo and it wouldn't do to neglect the local witchdoctors. You may think that funny, Vincent, but a chum of mine was out here as Number One of a frigate some time ago. He told an old man on a beach to make himself scarce, dived into the water and broke his neck on a rock. And nobody could find that rock afterwards. So always drink the local wine and respect the local gods and you can't go wrong.'

The Bodger finished his beer and looked about him.

'Vincent and Hobbes, you can be in charge of the bar. Put all that liquor in the sea to keep it cool. Bowles, Dewberry, Ball and Cartwright start collecting firewood. Cleghorn, start a fire. Stacforth and Smith give Instructor-Lieutenant Evans a hand with the cooking. Spink, climb that tree and get some coconuts.'

Half an hour later, the cadets gathered round the fire for soup, eggs and bacon, buttered bread, tinned peaches, and a bottle of beer each. Just as they were about to drink, in the silence which fell as steaming mugs were raised to lips, a coconut fell into the fire and scattered sparks and half-burnt pieces of wood in a circle. They looked up.

A pale face peered down at them from the top of a palm-tree.

'Good grief!' said The Bodger. 'It's Spink!'

Spink had climbed the tree and got a coconut. While the bottles were being submerged in the sea, while a pile of driftwood enough to keep a beacon alight for a week was being gathered, while the food and hammocks were being laid out, and while Evans the Slide Rule and his assistants were cooking the meal, Spink had removed his shoes, edged upwards inch by inch along the smooth, shiny bark and, wrestling all the time on the brink of vertigo, he had grasped a coconut. Success had made him tremble and the coconut had fallen. He began to climb down.

'Chuck down a few more while you're up there Spink, there's a good chap,' called The Bodger.

Spink shook the tree. A coconut landed in the sand a foot away from the Navigating Officer. The Navigating Officer recoiled and another coconut thumped down where he had been sitting. More coconuts rained down, in and around the fire.

'All right, all right, Spink, old boy! That's enough. Come down now.'

The party gazed up at Spink's legs appearing beneath the clump of leaves at the top of the tree.

'You can come down now Spink!'

'I know, sir,' a faint voice answered from the leaves, 'but that's the trouble. I can't.'

The Bodger stood at the foot of the tree.

'Just clasp the trunk with your legs and . . .'

Spink landed on top of The Bodger in a halo of leaves and a flurry of sand.

After lunch, the cadets sunbathed on the beach and swam.

Tom Bowles lay down near George Dewberry.

'Very peaceful sound the sea makes, doesn't it?' said George Dewberry drowsily. 'No wonder people write music about it.'

'George, you shouldn't get drunk so much.'

'God, talk about changing the subject! What's got into you, Tom?'

'It's a miracle how Pontius or The Bodger haven't caught you yet. They've only got to catch you once coming off shore like that and you'll be measured for a bowler hat before you can turn round.'

'So what. It's my hobby. I enjoy it. Let's face it, there's not much else to do ashore, is there? Unless you can get all excited over museums and things, like Paul. We lead such a cramped and bloody awful existence. Let's face it, there's only one word for it. Bloody awful. It's O.K. for characters like you, you enjoy it and you're good at it, but for me it's sheer hell. Always being chased about the place, made to do bloody silly things at bloody silly times of the day, not even any decent music to listen to . . .'

'There's the Gramophone Club . . .'

'The *Gramophone* Club!'

'Well, the Padre does his best.'

'I know, Beethoven's odd-numbered symphonies, not including the Ninth, Grieg's piano concerto, Rossini's overtures, music from "Swan Lake" and the Hallelujah Chorus, that's about all that man's ever heard of. No Brahms because he's too heavy, no Mozart because he's too *superficial,* no Schumann because he went round the bend, no Prokofiev because he's a Russian, no Gershwin because he's too modern. What that man wants is some nice Germanic composer, born in wedlock, happily married, sane, who died just after Beethoven and composed nice sedate music with no discords or sudden changes of key, light enough so that you can hear it on the bandstand at Folkestone on Sunday afternoon but deep enough so that you can talk knowledgeably about its deeper meanings.'

Tom Bowles was startled by George Dewberry's vehemence; it was the first time he had heard George Dewberry talk knowledgeably and enthusiastically about anything.

'I'd no idea you felt so strongly about it George,' he said. 'Although I do feel you're exaggerating a little.'

'I don't feel all that strongly about it and I am exaggerating, but I'm just saying it to show you that there are more things in heaven and earth than are considered in the Cadet Training Ship.'

Tom Bowles laughed. 'I knew *that,* for heaven's sake. But seriously, George, you want to watch these runs ashore of yours. You'll soon be the youngest alcoholic in the Navy.'

'Well, I suppose that's fame in a way. Better to be notorious than unknown.'

'That sounds like The Bodger speaking.'

'It is.'

'And anyway, when you had the chance to listen to some decent music you were asleep! You slept right through "Pagliacci." '

'I wasn't asleep. I'd rather listen than look at an opera, and besides, I don't like looking at Italians. That tenor was awful. It needs a really big tenor to sing Canio. It was Caruso's great part. That chap had the notes all right but he just didn't look the man for the part. He didn't *look* annoyed because somebody was playing about with his wife. He just looked mildly hurt as though someone was pinching his bottom. I'll give you one thing, it was at least in Italian. I can never understand why people listen to operas in English. You never understand what's going on anyway, so why not *not* understand what's going on in the original Italian instead of not understanding what's going on in some bastard English translation? Come on, let's get some sleep. It's the only reason I came on this trip.'

Tom Bowles turned over and lay face down on the sand. He had discovered, as the Interview Board had discovered before him, that there was more to George Dewberry than met the eye.

Banyans were an excellent opportunity for The Bodger to talk to cadets whom he rarely saw on board and who would in any case never have come near him while he was vested in the trappings and regalia of his authority. He was talking to Isaiah Nine Smith, a quiet serious boy who attacked everything set before him in the Training Cruiser with a zeal which The Bodger had rarely seen so early in any officer. He was perhaps so zealous that it struck The Bodger as unhealthy.

'Where do you live, Smith?' he asked.

'Winchester, sir.'

'Winchester? That's a nice little town. I used to know one or two very good pubs there. The police are very considerate too, I remember. What are you going to do with yourself in the service, Smith? What are you going to specialise in?'

'I thought of being a pilot, sir.'

'Why?'

'Oh, it's what I'd like to do, sir. My family are all against it, of course.'

'Why do you say "of course"?'

'They're Plymouth Brethren, sir. They're not really very happy about me being a naval officer at all. They believe in peace or something. They think I'm bound to get killed.'

'You mustn't believe all you hear about pilots, Smith, in fact you mustn't believe all *I* say about them. A chum of mine is married, has three children and not a drop of insurance. He daren't get insured now. He's superstitious. Perhaps that doesn't quite illustrate what I meant to say, but he's training pilots at the moment and he told me that when a new course comes in he can tell in a few days which are those that are going to be good pilots. He says he can tell which are going to kill themselves too, by their attitude. I think you'll make a very good pilot, Smith. As long as you don't take life too seriously.'

'I don't think I do that, sir, really?'

'Perhaps not. The people I've known in the Navy who seem to have enjoyed life most and who have been promoted have all seemed to treat the Navy as a huge joke.'

'It's rather hard to split your sides in *Barsetshire,* sir.'

'Don't I know it! You wait until you're a Cadet Training Officer, Smith, and you'll wish you had as much to laugh at as a cadet. You'll find that your real struggle will come when you've finished your training, believe me.'

*　　　*　　　*

218

In the evening Michael and Paul put on jerseys and walked along the beach. They walked barefooted close to the sea on the smooth wet sand where an occasional further wave washed inwards. Ahead of them the red ball of the sun was setting in layers of orange and yellow cloud. The sky showed clear between the clouds in pure blue. The clouds mounted overhead and thinned in their path, from piled masses to trails of vapour. When the sun dropped through the clouds to the sea it lit the sky in a last burst of green incandescence. The sand changed swiftly from white to yellow and through the spectrum to blue. The shadows of the palm trees crept out and swallowed up the last of the light. There was no twilight, but a withdrawal of the sun's light over the horizon and darkness.

Michael and Paul walked to the end of the beach where a group of rocks jutted into the sea, and turned back. The solitude of the beach and the majesty of the sunset which they had both witnessed in silence had given them a sense of companionship.

'I suppose the rest of the Navy's not going to be like this, is it Mike?' Paul said. 'Because if it is, then it's me for the shore by the first boat. I'm only putting up with this in the hope of something better to come.'

'It's bound to be. They can't keep this pace up all the time.'

'I'll bet they have a good try.'

'No, this is just the start. The breaking-in process.'

'All right, I'm broken in. Now where do we go?'

As they came near the camp, they heard The Bodger's voice.

'Ginger, if I've told you once, I've told you a hundred times rum punch must be *hot*. We must prepare a draught for the gods, not mouthwash for spavined mules!'

When The Bodger's punch was ready, the cadets sat huddled in blankets round the fire, which had been built up into a roaring pyramid, with their mugs ready. Looking round him, Michael was oddly reminded of many Boy Scout camp-fires except that here there was an element of unexpectedness, almost of preposterousness; Boy Scouts were expected to gather round camp-fires, naval officers were not. There was a touch of fantasy but also a kind of remote logic in the sight of The Bodger, Ginger, Evans the Slide Rule, the Navigating Officer and the cadets, all in banyan rig.

After The Bodger's toast, to the next banyan, they sang songs. The Bodger sang the verses, Evans the Slide Rule sang the harmonies, and the cadets sang the choruses. The Bodger had an extensive repertoire which ranged from the traditional to the profane and included 'The Harlot of Jerusalem' which they sang in memory of Mr Froud.

The fire was allowed to die out. Those cadets who had brought their hammocks slung them between palm trees and the rest laid out their blankets on the sand. As he lay and looked up at the stars shining through the leaves where Spink had shaken down the coconuts, Michael thought that he had never been so happy in the whole of his time in the Training Cruiser.

An hour later, when even the last had settled his blankets and snuggled in between them, the camp was still and quiet except for the faint sound of an engine far away along the beach.

The beat of the engine grew louder and nearer. It was an inappropriate sound, as out of place on that beach as the sound of a pneumatic drill in the high Himalayas. Some of the cadets turned over and tried to shut it out of their ears. When the noise was almost opposite the camp it was amplified by voices calling. A light shone over the sea. The Bodger got up and walked down to the water's edge. He stared out over the sea.

'Ahoy there!' he shouted. 'Who's there?'

The Navigating Officer left his sleeping bag and joined The Bodger.

'What's going on, Bodger?'

'I don't know. There's someone out there in a motor-boat. Sounds as though he's looking for someone.'

'I wonder if he's looking for us?' A sudden joy entered the Navigating Officer's voice.

'I don't think so. What would they want us for at this time of night?'

'Ahoy there!' the Navigating Officer called. 'What are you looking for?'

A beam of light stabbed out from the boat, searched the beach and rested on The Bodger and the Navigating Officer.

'Is that Lieutenant Commander Badger?' asked a voice from the darkness.

'They *are* looking for us!' cried the Navigating Officer exultantly.

The Bodger cupped his hands. 'Lieutenant Commander Badger speaking. What's the trouble?'

'From the Captain, sir, you are to return to the ship at once. There's been a revolution in Central America, sir, and the ship has been ordered to proceed there at once. If you'll man your boat, sir, I'll give you a tow.'

Every word fell like blessed manna upon the Navigating Officer's ears. But The Bodger shook his fist.

'Name of a name! Why can't these bloody wogs have their revolutions at a civilised hour like everybody else? They can't have a revolution *now!* It's the middle of the night!'

'*Saved!*' breathed the Navigating Officer. 'Saved at the eleventh hour, by George! Who'd have thought it? Saved by a lot of bloody wogs! Bless you, fuzzy-wuzzies, every one!'

Some of the cadets by the fire sat up and stared at The Bodger.

'What are The Bodger and Pilot carrying on about?'

'Something about a revolution in Central America.'

'Why on earth do they come and tell *us* about it?'

'Specially at this time of night.'

'Pilot looks as pleased as punch about something. He's jumping up and down like a mad thing.'

'Perhaps he wants to wear a tin helmet. Anyway, let's for Christ's sake get some sleep. That's what we came for, remember?'

'Will you hurry please, sir?' said the voice from the boat. 'I've got two other banyans to pick up. I'm going round to the other side of the island to pick up the Foretop and I'll be back in about twenty minutes.'

'Very good,' The Bodger said. 'Blast all wogs!' he said under

221

his breath. He walked back to the fire and looked at the sleeping figures.

'All right, everybody, time to get up. I'm sorry but there's been a revolution somewhere and the ship is sailing. We've got twenty minutes so chop chop. Wakey, wakey, everybody.'

The banyan parties returned to the ship. The ship had already raised steam, the Chief G.I. had detailed the sea watches, and the cranes were ready to hoist the boats. At midnight, by the glare of flood light, with officers and cadets still in banyan rig, *Barsetshire* sailed to quell a revolution in Central America.

14

As soon as the banyan parties had returned, the Captain rang down revolutions for thirty knots. But, as Commander (E) remarked to the Senior Engineer, it was one thing to ring down for thirty knots and quite another to achieve them. In her day *Barsetshire* had been one of the fastest ships in the Navy. Like all her class, she was comfortable, economical, and capable of thirty knots. A quarter of a century later, her spirit was willing but her engines were old.

George Dewberry was understudying the Engineer Officer of the Watch when *Barsetshire* put to sea. The Engineer Officer of the Watch was Mr Pilgrim, a withered Branch Officer who had been steaming ships since the days of coal and triple-expansion steam engines. He had the engineer's mistrust of anything new. He had remarked bitterly on the coming of the steam turbine, prophesying that the Admiralty had overstepped themselves this time. He had seen diesels as a short-lived experiment. The possibility of a ship powered by a gas turbine had made him bombinate on the crass stupidity of the Admiralty, who tried to run before they could walk. The conception of a ship driven by an atomic pile Mr Pilgrim placed on the level of science fiction, all very well for schoolboys to read about, but unworthy of the consideration of practical men. This was the man in charge of *Barsetshire's* main engines when the Captain rang down for all the speed he could get.

Mr Pilgrim watched the revolution counters ring on and on,

demanding speeds at which *Barsetshire* only attempted to travel in grave emergency, and past them into the realms of fantasy where the counters moved stiffly through infrequent use, to a final unbelievable speed where the counters jammed. They could go no further. Their appealing immobility suggested that, had they been able, they would have continued, past the world water speed record, through the sound barrier, and out into interstellar velocities greater than human being had ever before achieved.

'Well,' Mr Pilgrim said, glaring at the jammed counters, 'they can ring them on all right. But can we give them them? Eh? What do you say, eh, you boy?' He prodded George Dewberry. 'Eh Boy?'

'We can try, sir,' said George Dewberry. It was the first time he had ever been down into *Barsetshire's* engine room and he had no idea whether *Barsetshire* could achieve the revolutions or not.

Mr Pilgrim grunted and went across the plates to stand behind the E.R.A. on the throttle. The E.R.A. was slowly opening his throttle. Steam screamed through the pipes. The red pointer on the revolutions dial circled faster and faster, and the numbers in the small cage flicked past each other as fast as the eye could read them. Temperature gauges crept up with the revolutions. The engine room grew perceptibly hotter. The Chief E.R.A. in charge of the engine room walked round to inspect his thermometers. George Dewberry could see him appearing and disappearing behind pipes and down ladders, his expression becoming more anxious as he went round.

A harsh crackling voice came over the broadcast. The words were unintelligible to George Dewberry but Mr Pilgrim heard them and looked significantly at the Chief E.R.A. Mr Pilgrim leaned over and shouted.

'That was the chief stoker in the boiler room! Says he's got all his sprayers on all boilers! Can't put any more on! He'll have to start burning his socks now!'

George Dewberry nodded. Mr Pilgrim gestured contemptuously at the revolution counters.

'They can stuff those! They won't get any more!'

The Senior Engineer came down the ladder into the engine room. He conferred with Mr Pilgrim. George Dewberry could see Mr Pilgrim pointing to gauges and shouting in the Senior's ear. The Senior inclined his head and looked grave. George Dewberry felt alarmed.

The broadcast crackled again but this time with an urgent, clamouring note. George Dewberry clutched the hand rail in front of him and an icy wave of panic shuddered down his spine. It's happened after all, he thought, something terrible has happened. The Chief Stoker's voice could just be heard above the devouring roar of the boiler room fans, sounding like the voice of a doomed man shouting that the boiler was about to burst. He had obviously put too many sprayers on. George Dewberry shut his eyes and waited dumbly for the explosion.

The moments passed and nothing happened. George Dewberry opened his eyes again.

'What was that?' he asked Mr Pilgrim.

'Chief wanted to know what's happened to the limers issue! Should have been sent across half an hour ago!'

While the ship raced westwards through the starlit Caribbean night, the officers and Ship's Company made their preparations for quelling a revolution. The Gunnery Officer, Mr Piles and the Gunner's party laid out rifles, lanchester carbines, sten guns, pistols, steel helmets and webbing equipment. The Communications Branch tested portable radio transmitters and signalling lamps and made up sets of signalling flags. The ship's bakery worked all night baking loaves. The P.M.O. and the Sick Bay staff filled haversacks with bandages, splints and morphia tablets. By breakfast time the ship was ready and it was only then that a thought struck The Bodger.

'Where the hell are we going, incidentally?' he asked.

The Gunnery Officer looked up from his grapefruit.

'Place called SanGuana Annuncion. It was on the news last night.'

'Where's that?'

'Next door to British Honduras. I looked it up on the map. It's a Crown Protectorate.'

'Then what are they rebelling for?'

'God knows, it's the season for it, I suppose. It's the national sport in this neck of the woods. The Captain's going to tell us all about it at nine o'clock.'

The Captain spoke to the ship over the ship's broadcasting system. The Captain abhorred public speaking and avoided it if he could; it was one of his favourite sayings that a Captain should address his Ship's Company on commissioning and on going to war and at no other time.

'As you must all know by now,' he said, 'we are on our way to sort out a bit of unpleasantness in a place called SanGuana Annuncion. I've never heard of it myself but I'm told on good authority that it's important. It's a Protectorate of the Crown, which means that to a certain extent we're responsible for what goes on. This place has only a short history. It was virgin jungle until after the first World War when they found oil and minerals and all sorts of valuable things there. The capital, a place called Cajalcocamara, where we're going now, is something of an international city, something like Tangier. They're always having revolutions in these parts so I don't suppose this one will be up to much. I expect we'll find the whole thing settled and they're all asleep when we get there. If that's so we can all go away and get on with our cruise. That's all.'

Afterwards, the Captain addressed all officers in the wardroom.

'For your benefit, gentlemen, I'm going to amplify a little of what I told the sailors. This country we're going to has been almost completely developed and opened up by people from outside. The Americans have a strong interest in the oil, the Swiss have got several banks there, several mining firms and fruit shippers have factories and property in the country, and there's a thriving brothel area. They're moderately civilised now, in fact. I'm told that Gieves have got a branch in Cajalcocamara. Foreigners have put a lot of money into the place and they more or less say what goes on. The hereditary ruler, a man called Dominquin Monterruez, is not much more than a picturesque figurehead. Dominquin claims to be descended from the Sun God, but from what the Foreign Office say he seems to be little more than a Red Indian, but he did send his son, Aquila, to England for his education. And that's the cause of the trouble. Aquila seems to have got in with a very bad set at Oxford and he now knows something about democracy and, according to the Foreign Office handout, he can play the guitar. When he got back to SanGuana a year ago, Aquila immediately started to pester the old man to let San-Guanos have more say in the government of the place. I suppose that's reasonable, but it put the British Consul there in an embarrassing position because it was he who suggested sending Aquila to England. Yesterday afternoon, during the siesta, Aquila and his party took over Radio SanGuana, blockaded all roads from the capital, picketed the railway station and closed the harbour. They also locked Dominquin and the British Consul up in the Consulate. This sounds very amusing to us but H.M. Government take a very serious view of it because, here I'm quoting, "Any continued instability in the political situation in SanGuana Annuncion will further the ends of undesirable elements in Central and South America." What that means exactly I can't tell you, gentlemen, but there it is. Commander, I suggest that you get the ship's company together this forenoon and explain the details a bit more fully about landing parties and so on. That's all I have to say, gentlemen.'

Barsetshire expected to arrive off Cajalcocamara in the late afternoon. In the forenoon, the Ship's Company mustered by divisions for the issue of small arms, webbing equipment, rations, and instructions on the technique of dealing with street riots. After the issue, the Ship's Company closed aft for an address by the Commander.

The Commander stood up on the after screen where everybody could see him. He was conscious of a repressed excitement in the mass of faces below him.

'I've called you aft,' he began, 'to give you an idea of our organisation for this afternoon and to let you get some picture of the problems you're likely to have to face when or if, you get ashore. I say "if" because these sort of affairs look a lot more exciting than they actually turn out to be. They're often very disappointing, like following a woman up the street and then seeing her turn round. Remember that it is possible that some of you will be separated from the main body and may be surrounded by unfriendly, if not hostile, crowds. You will have to act on your own initiative and the ship will be judged by the actions of small groups just as much as large ones. You can have just as much effect on the situation, one way or the other, with a few of you as with a big platoon. So all listen carefully to what I have to say. You will all be in platoons by departments, using the same sub-divisions as for the regatta, that is to say the Communications Branch, if they are required, will land with the Band, and so on. The Royal Marine Detachment will provide the first landing party under the command of the Captain of Royal Marines. They will be supported by a special riot squad provided by the engine room and supply and secretariat branches. They will carry tear gas, and lanchester carbines, and will be under the command of the Gunnery Officer. That should be enough, but the remainder of the Ship's Company will follow as required. The cadet platoons will provide reinforcements, under the command of Lieutenant Commander Badger. So much for the outline of the organisation. The Gunnery Officer will give you the details after I've finished. Now for the purpose of this landing, if we make a landing. The reason why we are going ashore.'

The Commander paused. The Ship's Company braced themselves.

'Our aim is not to take an active part in this affair,' said the Commander. 'Our job is to act as an aid to the civil power. Remember that, we are here as an *aid* to the Consul if he wants us. The ship is not in any way responsible for the administration of this place, we're just here to give help if we're needed. We hope, and the authorities ashore hope, that our mere presence here will help to stabilise the situation a bit. So when you go ashore don't look for trouble or I can assure you you'll find it. We want to keep everything as quiet as we can. These Latin countries can be very hot-tempered. That's all I want to say. Special sea dutymen will be piped at thirteen-thirty, hands will fall in by landing parties when we anchor at fourteen hundred. I recommend you all to eat a hearty dinner. You don't know when you'll be eating a hot meal again.'

'If ever,' said a funereal voice from the stokers' division, amongst hollow laughter.

'Keep silence!' roared the R.P.O.s standing around.

The ship anchored off Cajalcocamara in the afternoon. Some of the more excitable of the Ship's Company expected an immediate answering rattle of machine-gun fire and a fusillade of bombs from the shore but they were disappointed. It was the afternoon siesta and SanGuana slept. Revolutions were for the evenings when the blood quickened and the mind was clearest. Not even the thundering of *Barsetshire's* anchor cable roused the town. The shoreline lay still and peaceful, shimmering in the midday heat.

On board, the quietness was regarded as ominous. The Captain had expected the Consul to come on board as soon as he was able, to inform the ship of the latest situation and to state his requirements for assistance in the way of arms, hospital facilities and food. If the Consul did not appear, then it might mean that for some sinister reason he was prevented from coming.

After an hour's wait there was still no sign of activity on shore. The Ship's Company mustered in the waists grew restless.

'Eerie, ain't it?'

'Wonder if they've all been murdered?'

'I always thought wogs was a noisy lot. I reckon this revolution must be about the quietest in history.'

'Keep silence!'

On the quarterdeck, the Captain was also concerned by the lack of contact with the shore.

'This is bloody stupid,' he said to the Commander. 'I don't know what's going on in there but we'll look a lot of Charlies if they're up to no good while we stick here doing nothing.'

'I agree, sir. Shall we send the first landing party in, sir?'

'Damned if I know what to do. This is the queerest set up I've ever come across. All right, Commander, send the Marines and the Gunnery Officer's party in shore to find out what's going on.'

'Aye aye, sir!'

A ripple of movement spread along the upper deck as the Royal Marines and the Gunnery Officer's riot squad prepared to embark in the boats. The Chief G.I. was on deck and ready, as always, with the *mot juste*.

'Now remember,' he said, 'keep your thumbs over your bayonets when the boat touches. You don't want to stick it up the man in front's arse before the battle even starts, *do* you?'

The Royal Marine Detachment headed for one end of the harbour and the Gunnery Officer and his party headed for the other. It had long been one of the Gunnery Officer's ambitions to lead a landing party ashore. He looked with pride at his force, sitting in the pinnace with their thumbs over their bayonets. The Gunnery Officer's heart filled with the remembrance of other landing forces: Gallipoli, Salerno, Anzio, Guadalcanal, Normandy. The Gunnery Officer was proud that he and his motley band of stokers, cooks, stewards, writers and stores assistants were the latest in a great and illustrious tradition.

They were not opposed on the beach head and the Gunnery Officer formed his party up in three ranks, dressed them, and marched them into the town.

At the other end of the harbour, the Royal Marines were exciting as little attention. When the Captain of Royal Marines landed on the jetty there was no one in sight at all. The Captain of Royal Marines looked bewilderedly about him. There was a sense of anticlimax, of abandoned desolation in the appearance of the deserted roadway, the motionless railway trucks, the silent cranes and the shuttered windows.

'Hoy!' shouted the Captain of Royal Marines. His cry echoed down the waterfront and lost itself in whispers in the dust and the tattered scraps of paper.

A head belonging to a man who looked like a waterfront policeman or customs official appeared at a window.

'Where's the revolution, mate?' asked the Sergeant-Major.

'What revolution?'

'*The* revolution! El Revolutionario!'

'Oh that! See that road up there? Up there a bit, first on the left.'

'Thanks, mate.'

The head disappeared.

The Captain of Royal Marines, remembering his lecture notes on street fighting, formed his men into two single files and led them along the street, keeping one file on each side of the road. The Royal Marines kept in the shadows as far as possible and carefully negotiated each corner before they crossed into the sunlight. They were watched with interest by several sleepy San-Guanos from their first floor windows.

The first turning on the left led into a square. The Marines silently infiltrated into it and stood waiting for the Captain of Royal Marines to give them a lead. The Captain of Royal Marines surveyed the square.

A clump of palm trees in the centre of the square shaded a small brick building which had the words 'Urinario Revolutionario' white-washed in large straggling letters on one wall. In smaller letters were the subsidiary words 'Hombres' and 'Senoras.' By the small brick building were the Gunnery Officer and his landing party.

The Gunnery Officer and the Captain of Royal Marines met in the road.

'Now what?'

'Now we consolidate our position, of course,' said the Gunnery Officer. 'This looks like the main square of the town, so we might as well take charge of it. I'll do that with my party, while you press on and see if you can find the British Consulate. There must be someone alive in this town.'

'It's all a bit too quiet for me. Don't you think we'd better hang on a bit before we start consolidating and all that?'

'This is just the siesta, when they wake up there'll be all hell let loose again. We want to be well trenched in and ready for them before that happens.'

'I suppose you're right.' The Marines formed up in single file once more and infiltrated out of the square as silently as they had come in.

The Gunnery Officer called his party together.

'Chief,' he said to the Regulating Chief Stoker, 'take your stokers over to that side of the square and occupy a house. Be tactful about it and try and not disturb people too much. Set up a position on the first floor where you can command the square. Chief Steward, you do the same with your party on this side.'

'Aye aye, sir,' said the Regulating Chief Stoker and the Chief Steward.

The platoon of stokers doubled across the square and vanished into a house. The platoon of cooks and stewards did the same on the other side of the square.

There was silence for a few moments and then, as though a fuse had been lit and run its course, the square exploded into life. Both platoons erupted back into the roadway, each pursued by a huge old woman, who waved her fists threateningly. The Gunnery Officer could hear the shouts from where he stood.

'Seex o'clog! Go way! My girls mus' have sleep somptimes! Gom bag at seex o'clog! My girls waits for you!'

The sailors stood uncertainly in the sunshine, perplexed by the uproar.

'Try the next one!' bellowed the Gunnery Officer. 'That's a bloody flop-house you've got there!'

'Aye aye, sir.'

The sailors rallied and charged into the next house.

Again the house was filled with clamorous squealings and shriekings and again the stokers, and the cooks and stewards, were driven back out into the square by further angry old women who pursued the sailors and chased them with a torrent of language which made them blink and gasp as though under a cold shower.

'Bordello!' shouted the Gunnery Officer.

232

'But, sir . . .' wailed the Chief Steward.

'Don't answer me back, man! Try the next one! They can't *all* be bag-shanties!'

'But, sir . . .'

'Go *on,* man!'

'Aye *aye,* sir.'

A third time a wave of sailors swept into a house and a third time they were swept out again by infuriated women. By now the square was wide awake. Women hung out of every window, three-quarters of them having neglected to dress. A few made their way purposefully towards the Gunnery Officer; any man who had the temerity to disturb them during the afternoon siesta must be particularly in need of their services. The shouting increased as one house passed the news of the outrage on to the next and all joined in pouring maledictions upon the Gunnery Officer's head.

The Captain of Royal Marines hurried back to the square, having heard the tumult. He was afraid that he had unknowingly left the Gunnery Officer in a hornet's nest of rebels and he hastened back to help before it was too late. When he reached the square the Captain of Royal Marines stopped, scarcely believing his eyes.

The peaceful square which he had left only a few minutes before deserted except for the Gunnery Officer and his landing party was now seething with women in dressing gowns. More women leaned out of the windows displaying their charms. The Gunnery Officer himself was surrounded by upraised fists and buffeted by furious voices.

The Captain of Royal Marines forced his way through to the Gunnery Officer.

'Guns, have you gone stark staring mad? If there wasn't a revolution before there will be now! You know how sensitive these people are about their brothels!'

'But every house seems to be a brothel!'

'Well look at the name of the square, man!'

The Gunnery Officer looked up through the fists and saw a sign on the side of a house. It read 'Plaza del Concubinas.'

The noise in the Plaza del Concubinas had awoken more than the women who lived in it. A group of young men carrying banners pushed through the crowd. They were led by a young man in a blue poplin suit. He was olive-skinned, with dark wavy hair brushed back over his head, and he was flashing a smile. He advanced to meet the Gunnery Officer, hand outstretched.

'My dear chap!' cried the young man. 'I don't think we've met. I am Aquila Monterruez, of whom you've heard perhaps? I must say I'm delighted to see you. But how hot and bothered you look! And no wonder, when I see what company you're in. Let me first get rid of the lacrosse team.'

Aquila waved the women away. They fell back respectfully, but reluctantly.

'And now, where was I? I must say it astonishes me how you naval types always seem to gravitate to this part of the town. Is it some extra sixth sense they teach at Dartmouth? Give a naval type half an hour in a strange town and he'll find the red light quarter as sure as . . .'

'Allow me to introduce myself,' the Gunnery Officer said stiffly. 'My name is Lieutenant Commander Blake and this is Captain Gumshott, Royal Marines.'

'My dear chap how do you *do*?'

'How do you do?' said the Captain of Royal Marines.

'*Well* now. What *shall* we flee at next? A drink, I think. You must come to my house or no, better still, we'll go to the British Consulate and you can meet my old man.'

Bemused, the Gunnery Officer and the Captain of Royal Marines fell in behind Aquila, who led the way chatting gaily. The landing parties tore themselves away from the attentions of the ladies of the square (who were beginning to regret having repulsed the advances of these lovely sailors so vigorously) and marched behind Aquila's young men.

On board, The Bodger had heard the roaring from the Plaza del Concubinas and he had listened during the silence which followed it. His first thought was for his brother officers, the Gunnery Officer and the Captain of Royal Marines.

'*Name* of a *name!*' cried The Bodger as the shouting died away on the wind, 'they're massacring Guns and Boots! Quartermaster, call away cadets landing parties!'

He caught the Commander's eye.

'Carry on, please, sir?'

The Commander nodded and shook The Bodger's hand as though it was likely that they would not meet again.

'When you get ashore, set up a shore signal station to let us know what's going on,' the Commander said. 'We've heard nothing from shore yet. Good luck, Bodger.'

'Thank you, sir.'

In ten minutes the cadets were on their way. The Bodger sat in the leading boat, smelling the battle from far off, and snorting.

The cadets were not met with the same indifference as their predecessors. On the contrary, the SanGuanos were now used to landing parties and The Bodger was met by a large and enthusiastic crowd who pointed out the way the other landing parties had gone.

SanGuanos lined the route to the Plaza del Concubinas, cheering and waving flags. Although it went past their understanding why the Englishmen should choose to come ashore with guns and steel helmets, it seemed to them entirely natural that the English should want to visit the Plaza del Concubinas first. They were anxious that no Englishman should mistake the way.

The Bodger and his cadets entered the square at a smart trot and ran straight into the arms of the waiting women. It was now past six o'clock and the Plaza was open for business. The girls were delighted and not a little flattered that their square should hold such importance in the eyes of the English. 'Nombre de Dios,' they whispered excitedly amongst themselves, 'but these Englishmen *ran* here all the way from the boat!'

The Bodger hesitated, looking wildly about him, and was engulfed in a happy, struggling mass of women. The cadets could see his head now and then, tossed hither and thither, now submerging, now appearing, as The Bodger was carried towards the largest of the houses in the square. The name of the house was 'The Sign of Maria of the Seven Breasts' and in the doorway stood an enormous old woman in a dressing gown, Maria herself by the look of her, beaming a welcome. Simultaneously, the cadets were themselves hustled towards 'The Sign of the Donkey's Buttocks' and 'The Sign of the Satisfied Monkey' where in the doorways stood other huge women, also beaming welcomes.

The cadets often speculated afterwards on their fate had there not been an interruption. A thunderous shout cut through the clamouring of the women. The Bodger was released on the threshold of the house.

'Let go of that man!'

A tall man wearing a sun-helmet, a white linen suit and a flower in his button-hole was standing on the edge of the square. He was accompanied by another, smaller man who appeared to The Bodger to be wearing only a blanket and by a squad of men in uniform whom The Bodger assumed were the SanGuana equivalent of the Carabinieri. The square cleared. The women vanished into their houses and it seemed to The Bodger that they vanished, not because of the man in the linen suit but because of the small man in the blanket, who had swarthy Indian features and a look of cynical disillusionment.

The Bodger replaced his cap, brushed down his uniform and stepped forward.

'I am the British Consul for SanGuana Annuncion,' said the tall man. 'This is Dominquin Monterruez, the rightful ruler of SanGuana.'

The Bodger bowed and the man in the blanket nodded.

'How do you do, sir,' The Bodger said. 'My name is Lieutenant Commander Badger, Royal Navy, of H.M.S. *Barsetshire*.'

'Just what were your intentions in this square, Mr Badger?'

'To support our two advance landing parties, sir. They landed three hours ago and as we hadn't heard from them we thought on board that they might have run into trouble, sir.'

The Consul frowned. 'There's been no *trouble* that I've heard of. In any case, this is not the place to discuss the matter. I'll show you to the British Consulate.'

The British Consulate was a large white building facing the town hall. It had been built of the local stone brought by mule from the hills inland under the orders of the Consul's predecessor. The building was in the shape of a hollow oblong with a small garden in the centre. A wide verandah ran round the garden, its roof supported by high stone pillars. There was a fountain in the garden, some grass, and a few tiny orange trees. It was a pleasant place in which to sit with a drink and there Aquila had taken the Gunnery Officer and the Captain of Royal Marines.

The landing parties had stacked their rifles, carbines, steel helmets, tear-gas bombs and haversacks in the hall and were drinking beer brewed locally, under the supervision of an expert from Milwaukee, which was renowned through South and Central America for its strength and flavour. The bottles carried labels representing a panther urinating into a remarkably accurate facsimile of a grecian urn and the beer was marketed, and enjoyed a wide sale, under the name of 'Panther's Water.'

'I'm glad you fellows have come,' Aquila was saying to his guests. 'We don't often get visitors here and those we do get are mostly down-and-outs, or queers. The people inland don't like them. We had a chap a few months ago, called himself a painter. Public-school type, too. So he said, anyway. We've got some of his stuff hanging in the lavatories. He gave us it for saving him from being eaten. I must say when I looked more closely at it I began to feel we'd made a mistake. We should have let them eat him. We're still very conservative here, you know, in spite of all that's happened in the last twenty or thirty years. Especially the people who live in the remoter parts. They don't even like modern buildings or cars. It's hardly surprising that they don't like modern painting.'

Aquila glanced at the armoury of weapons piled in the hall.

'Nice of you to come all togged up in your bow-tie and all that,' he remarked. 'But you really needn't have bothered. The old man and I have more or less come to an agreement. That's why there was no one down there to meet you this afternoon. We were still talking when you arrived and by the time we'd decided that I should go and do the honours, you'd already landed. The old man's going to retire to the hills and keep bees while I run the show here. I let him out this afternoon. I wonder you didn't run into him? You didn't happen to see him while you were passing through the town, did you? He's about the place somewhere with that ridiculous old Consul.'

'I'm afraid we must have missed him,' said the Gunnery Officer.

'Not to worry. He'll be along soon, I expect. Extraordinary chap, my old man. Goes about the place looking like Geronimo. The people love him. He represents the old way. I represent the new. That's what all the argument's about, as a matter of fact. But I suppose you knew about that?'

'We were given an inkling of the situation,' replied the Gunnery Officer.

'However, that's all settled now. I wonder what can be keeping the old man? He's supposed to be here to meet you chaps. Ah, talk of the devil, the Consul I mean, here he is!'

The Gunnery Officer and the Captain of Royal Marines turned to see the British Consul, Dominquin and The Bodger stride into the hall and stop in stupefaction.

'*Guns!*' cried The Bodger. 'Do you realise you're *drinking* with the rebels?'

'Your protest would carry more weight if you cleaned your collar first, old chap,' said Aquila amiably. 'That lipstick's ferocious stuff, I happen to know. But let's not squabble over peccadilloes. I think we can consider the revolution, such as it was, officially over, can we not? Now I don't think all you people have met. . . .'

The news that the revolution was officially over was greeted with wild excitement amongst the citizens of Cajalcocamara, none the less wild because most of the town were unaware that the Englishmen had arrived to quell the revolution. The town gave itself over to celebration. The landing parties returned to the Plaza del Concubinas, not as aggressors, but as heroes.

238

'Panther's Water' flowed like rain water in the gutters. The Bodger made a speech from the balcony of the British Consulate. The signals from the shore signal station became more and more incoherent.

At nine o'clock the Commander stormed into the M.S.O. waving the latest signal.

'*Yeoman!*'

'Sir!'

'What's the meaning of this gibberish? R.P.C. Plates of Concubines? Have you all gone mad?'

'That's the signal from shore, sir. We asked them to repeat it and they made R.P.C. Concubines, sir. Request the Pleasure of your Company signed Concubines, sir. The last time we called they just made R.P.C., sir.'

'Ring the quarterdeck and tell them I'm going ashore.'

'Aye aye, sir.'

As the Commander stepped up on to the jetty a figure darted forward. It was a small man wearing soiled shorts and shirt, sandals, and a growth of stubble on his chin. He held out a notebook.

'I'm from the *Daily* . . .'

'Stand *back!*'

The Commander thrust out his arm. The figure in shorts tottered back on his heels to the edge of the jetty and dropped into the water. The Commander strode on into the town.

The revolution ended to everyone's satisfaction. Aquila governed the SanGuanos much as his father had done before him; the only overt effect of his government was in the composition of the programmes broadcast by Radio SanGuana which showed a preponderance of music by Granados and Castelnuovo-Tedesco played by Andres Segovia. The Captain received a signal of commendation from the Admiralty; the Gunnery Officer received that ultimate accolade for a member of his Branch, a letter of congratulation from the Captain of Whale Island; The Bodger received the Freedom of Cajalcocamara; and Captain Gumshott, Royal Marines, received a knitted balaclava helmet from a Girl Guide Company in Manchester who saw his photograph in the newspapers and liked his face. The Consul was made a K.C.M.G. in the next Honours Lists and promoted to Zagreb, while Maria of the Seven Breasts, to everyone's surprise and delight, was given an M.B.E., for services to the Crown, unspecified.

15

THE SanGuana Revolution was the end of the West Indies cruise. *Barsetshire's* headlong dash across the Caribbean did enough damage to her main engines to make it necessary for her to return a week early to England. She spent a day in Kingston, Jamaica, to refuel, two days in Gibraltar for the traditional buying of presents, and then sailed for home.

The senior cadets' examinations began in the Bay of Biscay. Although *Barsetshire's* examinations were seldom difficult and had little ultimate bearing on a cadet's future, the cadets took them seriously because they were the only means of leaving *Barsetshire* and becoming a midshipman.

When *Barsetshire* had been in the dockyard for several days and the Ship's Company were preparing for leave, an Admiral arrived alongside with his flag flying from his car. The ship was not expecting an Admiral and there was some speculation about the purpose of the call until The Bodger took the Flag-Lieutenant aside. A Prize-Giving was quickly organised.

Tom Bowles won the Sword for the most outstanding cadet of the term. Isaiah Nine Smith won the Seamanship Prize, the Navigation Prize, and the Prize for the highest aggregate of marks in the examinations, while Paul won the set of drawing instruments awarded to the cadet who gained the highest marks in the Engineering Paper.

The cadets were called at five o'clock on their last morning and left *Barsetshire* as they had joined her, in gentle but persistent rain.

Halfway through the leave period, while the cadets were waiting for their appointments as midshipmen, Mrs Vincent gave a party for Paul. Michael was very pleased to receive an invitation. After the excitements and hurly-burly of *Barsetshire*, Michael was already beginning to be a little bored with being at home. Michael was impressed when he saw Paul, standing with his mother waiting to welcome his guests.

Paul's hair was brushed, his face was scrubbed and shining, his dinner jacket had been freshly pressed and his tie had a crisp bow.

'Paul, you look disgustingly smooth,' Michael said enviously.

'Thank you, kind sir, she said,' said Paul. 'Mother, I'd like you to meet a great friend of mine. This is Michael Hobbes. He and I have been through a lot together.'

Mrs Vincent held out her hand. 'How do you do, Michael. Paul has mentioned you in his letters.'

'It's all lies, Mrs Vincent,' Michael muttered.

'Dear boy. Now go straight in and make yourself at home. You'll find lots of people you know.'

'What a nice boy,' Mrs Vincent said to Paul. 'He must look charming in uniform. I *do* wish you'd all worn your uniforms, darling.'

'Mother dear, I'll wear my uniform when I get married. That's a promise.'

Michael hesitated on the threshold. Going into a room full of people was for him a sensation like plunging into cold water. He braced himself and went in. At first he could see no one he knew. Everyone was talking without looking in his direction. Then he saw Raymond Ball talking to a blonde girl in a red dress, and George Dewberry standing by the bar.

'What ho, Mike,' George Dewberry said. 'Nice to see your ugly mug again.'

'Don't keep talking in clichés, George, for God's sake,' Michael said nervously. 'Tell me, do you know anybody here?'

'Not a soul. What're you drinking?'

242

'Nothing yet. What's that?

'Dry Martini. First time I've tried one. Try it. It's good.'

Michael wavered. He was still a novice at drinking. He had made far less use of his opportunities than George Dewberry.

'I think I'll just have some sherry.'

Michael stood sipping his sherry and after a time became conscious that someone was looking at him. He looked round and caught the eye of a young man whom he had never seen before standing with a dark-haired girl in a russet-coloured dress.

'Don't mind us,' said the young man, grinning. 'I was just betting Mary that you were in the Navy.'

'Oh.'

'Am I right? What *do* you do between drinks?'

'Well, actually, I *am* in the Navy.'

'There,' said the young man to the girl triumphantly. 'What did I tell you?'

'Very clever of you, Stephen,' said the girl.

'I shouldn't really have asked you. It stands out a mile.'

'I'm sorry about that,' Michael said.

'You National Service or Regular?'

'Regular.'

'Tough luck. What was the trouble, your old man hard up at the time?'

'No, not exactly, I rather wanted to do it.'

'Well, there's no accounting for taste.'

'No, I suppose not.'

Michael flushed and felt himself growing angry with this supercilious character who talked so airily about the Navy. He was taller than Michael, and fair-haired, with very pale blue eyes. He was wearing a single-breasted dinner jacket which hung open to show a grey brocade cummerbund decorated with a design of chrysanthemums. To someone as fresh as Michael from the dedicated atmosphere of the Cadet Training Cruiser, this conversation tasted of heresy. Michael wondered what The Bodger would make of it.

'By the way, we haven't introduced ourselves. It's an old

custom, you know. My name is Stephen and this is Mary. I don't know your name?'

'Michael Hobbes.'

'Please to meet yer.'

'Where are you stationed at the moment, Michael?' asked Mary. 'Are you with Paul?'

'I was, but I'm not now. We've both just come from the Training Cruiser. I don't know where we'll go now.'

Stephen was interested. 'Not the *Barsetshire?* Were you on board when they had that revolution?'

'Yes. Why?'

'My goodness, that must have been quite a party. We had the most *garbled* stories here. We got cables that sounded as if our man there was drunk. All about blue-jackets committing the most frightful atrocities amongst the local women, and the hereditary ruler of the place being chased about the streets in a nightshirt. . . .'

'Stephen's on the staff of the *Daily Disaster,*' Mary said.

'He said later on in the night that he was assaulted himself by a drink-crazed sailor. It was all meaty stuff. All the more pity we hadn't space to print most of it.'

'Why ever not?' said Michael. 'I thought you printed anything about the Navy which made a good story?'

Mary clapped her hands. 'Oh, well said.'

'Sarcasm will get you nowhere, my good man,' said Stephen. 'Ordinarily we would have pounced on it and played it up but just now with the General Election coming off soon we're giving all our scandal lines to the Government. Can't afford to take the heat off them just yet.'

'Never mind. I expect you'll find plenty of other opportunities.'

'Bitter, isn't he?' Stephen said to Mary.

'I think Michael's quite right.'

The longer Michael talked to Mary, the more he liked her. His feeling for her was indeed more complicated than liking. He was attracted by her voice and her way of dealing with Stephen, but he was repelled by her poise. From her shoes to her hair Mary was smart, even chic, and perfectly balanced; she

244

made Michael feel like a yokel. It galled him to see that she and Stephen knew each other well enough to be able to dispense with polite conversation. With Michael she was polite, with Stephen she was easy and familiar. Michael wondered whether he would ever be able to achieve the same intimacy. It was the first time in his life that he had ever bothered to wonder whether he was interesting a girl in himself or not.

Michael joined Paul. 'I've just met someone who would interest The Bodger,' he said.

'He's coming later on.'

'The Bodger is?'

'Yes. He rang my mother up a few days ago. He's got a pink ticket from his wife for the evening and he's going to a dinner at Whites. He said he'd look in here afterwards. By the way, Mike, will you take Janet Willoughby-Cox into dinner? I'll introduce you.'

Mary and Stephen sat opposite Michael at dinner. On Michael's left was a girl whose name he saw from the place card was Angela, and on his right was Janet Willoughby-Cox.

While they were drinking clear soup, Janet turned to Michael.

'Do you hunt?' she asked.

Michael had anticipated the question on first seeing Janet Willoughby-Cox and he thought that at last it was his turn to be witty.

'As a matter of fact, I don't,' he said. 'I'm inclined to agree with Oscar Wilde, that hunting is the pursuit of the uneatable by the unspeakable.'

The polite smile vanished from Janet's face, as though Michael had slapped her. She turned her shoulder and did not speak to him again.

Soon afterwards, Angela remembered that she had someone on her right.

'Do you play hockey?' she asked Michael.

Michael was caught in the act of putting some smoked salmon in his mouth and in trying to answer he choked and spluttered.

'Well, there's no need to be like that about it,' Angela said.

245

'I was just asking.' She tossed her head and she too turned away to talk to her partner on the other side.

Mrs Vincent did not allow any smoking or dancing during the meal. Michael ate steadily and in silence. In between courses he listened to the conversations around him.

Opposite George Dewberry, Raymond Ball was regarding his blonde hungrily.

'What are you thinking about?'

'Do you really want to know?'

'Yes.'

'Well,' said Raymond Ball, 'I was just considering asking you whether you would like to go to bed with me after this is all over?'

'*What?*'

'Shush, my dear, don't *shout*. This is a personal offer which I don't make to everybody.'

'*Well!* It's the first time anyone has ever asked me.'

'Where have you been all your life? In England, I suppose.' Raymond Ball shook his head sadly. 'That's where these foreigners have the edge on us every time. We just haven't got the word about these things.'

Opposite Michael, Mary and Stephen were giving a faultless exhibition of how to talk to a partner at a party. They were blatantly enjoying themselves. They spoke to no one else but entertained each other. They exchanged gossip and scandal about mutual friends, discussed plays, books and exhibitions, and commented on the latest happenings in London. When they had no subject in particular they filled in with effortless small talk which kept them both laughing. Michael watched them with envy and with growing rage. It was not that Mary was beautiful, or at least not startlingly so, but she had a gaiety and a sincerity which fascinated Michael. He could not bear the sight of her enjoying herself so much with Stephen, especially as he knew Stephen had noticed and was enjoying his discomfort. Michael leaned forward.

'Do you work for a newspaper too, Mary?' he asked.

Mary and Stephen both stopped laughing and stared at him. Stephen's expression made it plain that he was struggling to adjust himself to the phenomenon of this peculiarly gauche young man actually addressing them.

'My dear *chap*,' he said. 'How long have you been in London? Asking a girl a question like that point blank is as good as asking her does she sleep with strangers!'

'What was that?' Raymond Ball asked from down the table.

'Never you mind,' said Stephen.

'I'm a secretary,' Mary said.

'Oh.'

Michael was saved and distracted by the arrival of the coffee.

'You'd better watch out, my dear,' Stephen murmured in Mary's ear. 'You've got an admirer there, unless I'm very much mistaken. If you're not careful, he'll start following you about.'

Mary looked across at Michael, who was despondently sugaring his coffee.

'I think he's rather sweet,' she said.

Michael drank some of his coffee and tried again, this time with Angela. He could think of no subject upon which to start a conversation except the one she had herself suggested.

'As a matter of fact, I'm rather fond of hockey,' he said.

'I *beg* your pardon?'

'Oh never mind.'

Michael finished his coffee miserably. This was not one of his socially successful evenings. There was nothing he could do now except hope it would soon be over and leave as soon as he decently could.

After dinner the band, which had been playing all evening in a desultory manner, began to play in earnest. The drummer preceded and ended each number with a roll and the saxophonist, trombonist and trumpeter periodically stood up to take solos.

The party split up into groups. Cedric, spruce and hospitable like an usher at the best man's party after the wedding, had been watching the progress of the party from his place next to Mrs Vincent. When Mrs Vincent was asked to dance by Stephen, Cedric came over and sat next to Michael.

'Well, I take it you're in the Navy too, eh?'

'Yes, sir.'

'For heaven's sake don't call me "*sir*"! Cedric is my name. If you ever want to lose money on the Stock Exchange, come and see me. I can do it better than most.'

'My name is Michael.'

'Happy to meet you, Michael. I believe I remember seeing you on the platform at Paddington Station, don't I? You didn't look very happy then, and you don't look very happy now, old boy. Let me introduce you to some people . . .'

'Oh that's all right, Cedric. I've met all the people I want to meet already.'

'Then why don't you go and ask her to dance?'

Mary was sitting alone, watching the dancing.

'I *will*,' Michael said. 'Excuse me, please.'

'Certainly, old boy,' said Cedric.

Michael crossed the floor purposefully, conscious that Stephen was watching him.

'May I have this dance, please?'

Mary looked up.

'I'd love to,' she said.

They took the floor. Mrs Vincent whirled past with Stephen. Raymond Ball was dancing cheek to cheek with the blonde in the red dress who was already wearing a blissful, anticipatory expression.

'Why do all naval officers dance so well?' Mary said.

'What a nice thing to say!'

'But they do.'

'Not all of them. Some of them are shocking dancers. They think it beneath them.'

'Do you think it beneath you?'

'Not at all. I'm not terribly keen on it but I think it's one of the things one ought to be able to do. They had lessons at Dartmouth.'

'When were you at Dartmouth?'

'Last summer.'

'Did you like it?'

'Well, I did and I didn't. Everything was very strange and new and quite exciting but I never really caught on to what it was all about. I still haven't but I expect I will eventually. I was jolly zealous though. I dashed about from place to place with the best of them.'

'What sort of dashing about?'

'Oh, up at zero crack zero zero in the morning, scrub decks . . .'

'Do you still do that?'

'They do in the Training Cruiser. I don't know about the rest of the Navy. I expect they do there too. What was good enough for Nelson's good enough for us. For instance—oh drat, they've finished.'

'They're starting again.'

'Do you want to go on?'

'I'd love to. If you want to.'

'Of course I want to. Let's not talk about the Navy. Tell me what you do, between drinks of course.'

'Don't take any notice of Stephen. He's pulling your leg.'

'I know. You said you were a secretary. What sort of secretary?'

'Just a secretary. I take shorthand and make the coffee in the morning and buy the Christmas cards and flowers for the managing directors' wives and keep out undesirable callers and that sort of thing.'

'How interesting. How do you know which is an undesirable caller?'

'They tell me. Either by their tone of voice, or what they've come about, or just the way they look at you.'

'What does your boss do?'

'I've got two. They're partners. Theatrical agents.'

'How interesting. And you stand at the door and prevent disappointed actors from getting at your bosses?'

'I don't actually stand at the door. It's quite a rich firm. They can afford a chair for me.'

'Oh.'

'There are four rooms, not counting the stairs.'

'Where do the stairs figure?'

'If nobody knows you and the waiting room is full you have to wait on the stairs. The first room is where we put all the unknowns and the debt-collectors and the people who serve writs and people like that. It's only a small room and there are only two chairs in it. That's why they have to wait on the stairs. The next room is my room where people wait who are quite well known or people the partners want to see. Then there's the inner office where Sam, the booking agent, sits. He does most of the work and all the very well-known stars sit in Sam's office. The very innermost office is the partners' office. Only the wives go in there.'

'The holy of holies?'

'That's right.'

'Would I be considered an undesirable caller, do you think?'

'Michael, that wasn't very subtle, was it?'

That, Michael thought, just about summed it up. He was not very subtle. He was trying harder to impress Mary than he had tried to impress anyone before but never had he achieved so little. He was easy and comfortable in her company. She accepted every conversational cue he offered and she answered every question he put to her but he knew that she would have done no less for anyone who danced with her. When he tried to make their conversation less general and more personal, she slid adroitly away. He was not subtle enough.

'What a charming person Mrs Vincent is,' said Stephen as Mary and Michael came off the floor. 'I sometimes think that women are not really entertaining until they're at least forty. I find debs crashingly boring but some of the mothers . . . they're more like it! Did you *enjoy* your horn-pipe, my dear?'

'Excuse me,' Michael muttered.

George Dewberry and Paul were sitting by themselves at a table. They had a bottle of whisky in front of them.

'Wotcher, Mike,' said Paul. 'Have some whisky.'

'I think that's just what I need,' Michael said.

'I hope Raymond's not thinking of going to bed with that woman *here*. The maître d'hôtel's a friend of ours.'

'Good luck to him.'

'You don't seem to be doing so badly yourself, Mike,' said George Dewberry.

'Do you think so? I don't. She seems to treat all naval officers, particularly me, as a huge joke.'

'It's fashionable,' said Paul. 'Always has been, since Nelson died. You should hear Cedric. He's always harping on the fact that our pay comes out of his income tax. He seems to think he owns a whole ship by now with all the income tax he's paid. He reckons we never do any work worth speaking of but just travel round the world at his expense having cocktail parties and going to bed with all the women. He feels particularly bitter about it because he was in the R.N.V.R. during the war. . . .'

'Cedric was?'

'Yes, he was. He's got the D.S.C., though you'd never guess it. He says they were the best days of his life and it was a black day when they chucked him out to do some work.'

'To get back to Mary, do you happen to have her telephone number?'

'I don't, but Mother will have it written down in her little black book. She's got all the young females written down in her little black book. My mother's a born match-maker. She says that after a girl's finished her first season she gets too few chances to meet a possible husband and it's up to those who've succeeded and hooked their men to help those who are still trying. Mother says that's half the trouble with the world today. Too many lonely people about the place. You've only got to look at the roaring trade marriage bureaux do these days.'

'Do they do a roaring trade?'

'I should say so. My mother's got shares in one and Cedric regularly tells her she could have a holiday in the south of France on the money she's making from lonely spinsters. There's something callous about Cedric.'

'Is he married?' asked George Dewberry.

'No fear. He'd rather jump over a cliff. He carries on a mild flirtation with my mother. He's been doing it for about twenty years. He maintains that he's got an attractive intelligent woman to take about and he doesn't have to see her in the early morning before she's got her war paint and feathers on. Trust Cedric to arrive at a solution like that.'

'To get back to Mary . . .'

'Of course. She's changed a lot since I saw her last. Is that her dancing cheek to cheek with the smooth player in the cummerbund? I even forget his name now.'

'Stephen.'

'That's him. We used to call him Snakehips at school.'

'I should watch him, if I were you,' said George Dewberry sagely.

'Watch him! I'd like to punch him on the nose. He's been doing nothing but make cracks about the Navy all night. He's going the right way to get thumped.'

'There speaks my little caveman,' said Paul. 'Ah good, here's The Bodger.'

The first person The Bodger saw was Cedric.

'Cedric, you old swindler!' he roared. 'Good to see you, boy!'

Cedric blushed. 'Good to see you, Bodger,' he said. Cedric, too, was one of The Bodger's old friends and drinking partners.

'It was inevitable, I suppose,' said Paul.

The Bodger was introduced to Mrs Vincent and progressed round the room shaking hands with the cadets he had known in *Barsetshire*. His progress was marked by shouts and loud laughter. The party had taken on a Rabelaisian humour from the moment of The Bodger's entrance.

'My God, The Bodger's in cracking form,' said George Dewberry.

When The Bodger reached Stephen, he stopped.

'Don't I know your face?'

'I don't think so.'

'Yes I do. You were doing your National Service when I was Jimmy of *Voluminous*. Ropehead.'

'Well, the name's right anyway.'

'*Ordinary Seaman* Ropehead.'

252

Mary suppressed a giggle. The Bodger looked at her.

'You must have the next dance with me, my dear,' he said. His bloodshot eye regarded the empty floor.

'Cedric, what was that dance we did on our last run in La Linea when we paid off *Tadpole*?'

'La Raspa?'

The Bodger went up and spoke to the band-leader. The band-leader was handsomely paid to pander to the whims of the customers (had he not played the Hokey-Cokey three times the previous night for a Cabinet Minister?). He nodded and turned to the band. The Bodger stepped onto the floor.

'La Raspa!'

Everybody danced La Raspa.

'Change partners!' thundered The Bodger.

They changed partners and danced La Raspa again.

'Change partners! Faster!'

George Dewberry, who was the only person not dancing, raised his whisky glass and said 'Ole!'

'Faster, faster!'

'Ole torero!' shouted George Dewberry.

The last change brought Michael to Mary. After the dance they sat down together. The Bodger sat down next to them with Mrs Vincent.

'Well, young Hobbes,' said The Bodger, 'glad you've left *Barsetshire*?'

'Very glad indeed, sir.'

'You wait. You're going out into the jungle now. We've told you one thing, now the people in charge of you will tell you others. Half the officers you'll meet won't agree with training at *all,* and the other half will think that Dartmouth are doing it all wrong. I sometimes think that half the Navy spends its time training and the other half spends its time criticising training. Still, we do our best. Think of me next term struggling with a new lot, won't you Hobbes?'

'I will, sir.'

The Bodger led Mrs Vincent off to dance, saying, 'Now let me tell you something about Cedric's past, Louise.'

'What a nice man,' said Mary.

'One of the best,' Michael said. 'I was going to ask you, can I take you home tonight?'

'Michael, I'm terribly sorry, but Stephen's taking me home.'

Stephen joined them, as though he had sensed that his position was being, if not menaced, at least approached.

'What a sight it was to see the Navy letting its hair down for once!'

As Michael was leaving, Paul said: 'You might see old George home.'

'Oh for heaven's sake, I spend most of my time in the Navy putting bloody George Dewberry to bed! Where does he live?'

'He's staying at an hotel tonight. He's got the address on a label in his coat pocket.'

'O.K., I'll do my best for him. Well, thanks for a wonderful party, Paul.'

'Glad you enjoyed it. D'you know what your appointment is yet?'

'Not a clue.'

'I expect we'll all meet up again some time.'

'In about fifty years' time.'